BAILEIGH HIGGINS

Trial by Fire

Heroes of the Apocalypse - Book 1

First edition

This book was professionally typeset on Reedsy.
Find out more at reedsy.com

Contents

Your FREE EBook is waiting!

If you'd like to learn more about my books, upcoming projects, new releases, cover reveals, and promotions, simply join my mailing list. Plus, you'll get an exclusive ebook absolutely FREE just for subscribing!

Yes, please. Sign me up!
  https://www.subscribepage.com/i0d7r8

Acknowledgments

Thank you to Alex for the stunning book cover design. You can find him right here on Facebook for more information: 187 Designz.

Dedication

This book is dedicated to Robert Stephenson, a volunteer firefighter. Thank you so much for the work you do, Robert. I hope you enjoy reading this apocalyptic adventure as much as I enjoyed writing it.

And I'd also like to dedicate this story to all the unsung heroes of the world. The men and women who work tirelessly each day to ensure our comfort and safety. Firefighters, paramedics, policemen, doctors, nurses, operators, and more. You are all amazing human beings.

Prologue

Ana hummed under her breath and leaned back into the deep tub filled with bubbles. Candles lit the room with a soft golden glow, and a freshly laundered towel hung on the heated rail. She'd locked up the house and tucked the children into bed. All was at peace.

Luke, her husband, was working late as he often did since he'd hired a new assistant. Red-headed and shaped like an hourglass, she looked like a twenty-year-old Ana, exactly Luke's type. Fresh from college, the girl was eager to please and ambitious. Too ambitious, perhaps.

But for once, these thoughts didn't bother Ana. She pushed aside her nagging doubts about her marriage and allowed herself to relax. The warm water caressed her skin, and the fragrant bubbles tickled her nose. Essential oils soothed away the world's cares, and the fine lines on her face receded.

Vaguely, she registered the front door opening and the heavy tread of feet on the stairs. They paused in front of the bathroom door, and a knock sounded.

Smothering an annoyed sigh, she sat upright. "Luke? Is that you?"

"It's me," he said, his voice strained.

Ana frowned. "Is something wrong?"

"I got attacked on the way home by some drunk asshole," Luke said. "He bit me on the hand."

"Oh? Is it bad?" Ana asked, finding it hard to care.

"It hurts, and it's pretty swollen," Luke said, a whiny note entering his voice.

Ana rolled her eyes. "There are band-aids and disinfectants in the kitchen cupboard. Your supper is in the oven."

"But it hurts, Ana," Luke repeated.

"I'll be right down," Ana said, shaking her head. *So much for peace and quiet.*

"Promise? I might need to go to the hospital," Luke said.

"I swear, I won't be long," Ana said. *Drama queen.*

Luke retreated down the stairs, and she sank back into the warm bath. She had no intention of cutting her alone time short for him, the cheating bastard. *Screw him. His new assistant can kiss his boo-boos for all I care.*

After another thirty minutes spent soaking in the tub, Ana finally dragged herself out with a sigh of regret. She patted her skin dry with the warm towel and pulled on her pajamas, dressing gown, and slippers. Tying her hair in a loose knot, she prepared to face Luke.

As her hand reached for the door, the shrill screams of her children caused her to freeze. Oliver and Paisley sounded like the demons from hell were after them, and a spurt of adrenalin rushed through her veins.

Ana rushed toward the children's bedroom without a thought for her safety. In her haste, she knocked over a candle. It rolled toward the wall and came to a rest an inch below the delicate lace curtains. Before the flame could snuff out, it caught hold of the material. Instantly, fiery flames raced up toward the roof.

Smoke billowed outward, and sparks caught alight on the towels, washcloths, and shower curtain. It was an old house, its walls like tinder, ready for the match. Within minutes, the house was on fire, burning out of control. A neighbor called the emergency services, and a fire truck was dispatched.

It raced toward the scene, its crew unaware of the horror that awaited them at their destination. Caught in the grip of a pandemic, Burlington teetered on the edge of destruction.

Ignorant of these events, Ana rushed to her children's aid. She dashed into their room only to stumble to a stop. Looming over the kids was their father, Luke. They were huddled together in a corner, trapped.

Luke turned when he heard her enter and stared at her with blank eyes. His lips peeled back from his teeth, and he snarled.

"Luke? What are you doing?" Ana cried.

Her eyes fell to his hand, and she noticed the puffy bite mark that stretched the skin. Blood dripped from the wound onto the carpet, and she idly wondered how she'd get the stain out of the fibers.

"Luke? Are you listening? You're scaring the children," she said, desperate to calm him down.

Luke snarled, the picture of insanity, and she wrung her hands in an anguished plea. "Luke, please. Stop this."

He ignored her words and barreled toward her with his arms outstretched. She danced around one of the beds on nimble feet, dodging his reach. He tried to follow, but his movements were awkward and stiff, and he tumbled over the bed.

Ana eyed his every move as he struggled to regain his feet. She had to get her children to safety, but something was off. Smoke drifted into the room, stinging her eyes, and she

3

coughed when it invaded her lungs. *The house! It's on fire!*

"Oliver, Paisley, get out of —" Clawed fingers grabbed hold of her leg, and she screamed with fright. Lashing out, her foot connected with Luke's face and smashed his nose to a pulp. She broke loose and sped across the room, searching for a weapon to fend him off.

But she never made it to the door. Brutal hands whirled her around and slammed her up against the wall. Crazed eyes stared into hers, and she wondered if anything human was left inside her husband. There was nothing but emptiness.

Luke was gone.

Dizzy with fright, she tried to hold him at bay, but he was stronger than her. Inch by inch, his gnashing teeth grew closer until they sank into the tender flesh of her shoulder.

Ana screamed as pure agony raced through her nervous system. Through tear-filled eyes, she spotted the horrified faces of Oliver and Paisley. Summoning the last of her reserves, she shouted, "Oliver. Take your sister and hide in the cupboard. Now!"

Oliver nodded and rushed Paisley away from the scene. With a grunt of fury, Ana shoved Luke away and ran down the stairs. He followed, but his gait was clumsy, and he crashed to the bottom of the landing.

Ana never stopped running, sprinting toward the front door. She yanked it open and tore out into the night. On auto-pilot, she looked back just as Luke regained his feet. He came howling toward her, and her blood turned to ice. Without thinking it through, she slammed the door shut in his face.

Bright, flashing lights caught her attention, and the blare of sirens filled her ears. She clutched her robe to her chest, conscious of her naked body. A paramedic ran toward her and grabbed her by the arm.

"Ma'am, please come with me. It's not safe here."

"No, I have to go back. Please," Ana begged. "My children."

Ignoring her pleas for help, he dragged her toward the waiting ambulance.

Ana fought him every step of the way, her eyes fixed on the upper story. Smoke billowed from an open window, and her heart jumped into her throat. "Wait! My children are still in there."

"It's alright, ma'am. We'll send someone in to rescue them."

"No, you don't understand. Luke will kill them."

"Ma'am, please calm down. You're not making any sense."

"Sense? What sense? My husband bit me," Ana said, baring her wounded flesh to the paramedic's shocked gaze.

"Let me help you," he said. "I need to stop the bleeding."

But Ana refused, screaming like a banshee. The closed front door of the house mocked her, and she cursed herself for shutting it. By doing that, she'd locked her crazed husband inside with the children.

"Oliver, hide! Take Paisley and hide!" she screamed until her voice became hoarse, hoping they could hear her. It was their only chance, trapped inside with a monster.

"Ma'am, please," the paramedic said. "Calm down." A sharp sting in her upper arm followed his words, and Ana sagged as the drug took hold of her muscles. "No, you… you don't understand."

Time slowed, and the world grew hazy around her. Her brain spun in circles, each thought crazier than the last. She imagined her children's soft cries, their fear and pain as real as hers.

Two firefighters ran past, and she caught the nearest by the arm. "You've got to help them. My kids!"

"Ma'am, please. Calm down. I promise we'll do everything we can," the fireman said, pulling free from her grip.

The paramedics grabbed her by the arms and hauled her away. "You don't understand. He's trying to kill them. He tried to kill me."

"He what?" the second firefighter asked with a look of confusion.

"My husband. He's a monster. He bit me," Ana cried.

The first fireman stared at her, his mouth agape. "What the—"

At that moment, someone shouted, "Get in there. Now!"

The firefighters ran toward the house, and Ana sagged with relief. Finally, someone was going after her children. She allowed the paramedics to guide her to their vehicle. There she sat, watching as the firefighters ducked into her house. "Save them. Please, save them."

Her drugged mind was in a daze, but she could feel it even then. Deep inside her brain, it wriggled like a worm on a hook. As the minutes passed, it grew stronger. So strong that it obliterated the effects of the drugs in her system.

Hunger exploded throughout her being, and all rational thought burned away until nothing remained. Ana was no more.

With a guttural growl, she sprang at the nearest paramedic and buried her teeth into his jugular. Warm flesh and blood filled her mouth and pooled in her stomach. For a brief moment, she felt a spark of life, and the hollow void inside her chest faded.

The sensation didn't last.

The hunger returned as it always would.

Never-ending and merciless.
In time, it would devour the world and everything in it.

Chapter 1 - Robert

Robert gripped the seat with both hands as the fire truck took a sharp turn, and the streets of Burlington sped past the windows. The sirens blared, lights flashing through the night as the traffic gave way to the red monster barreling down the freeway.

He sucked in a deep breath to prepare himself for what was to come. Getting called to a scene never failed to stir up a melting pot of emotions—a weird mixture of exhilaration, fear, excitement, and dread. Mason, George, and Susan sat with him, their expressions mirroring his. Lieutenants Briggs and White were in the front with Captain Schmidt.

"Gear up, team. That is a working fire," the captain yelled.

Robert pulled on his full turnout gear and shrugged the air pack onto his back. Next, he secured the mask over his face before reaching for the regulator. As the breathing apparatus settled into place, they swerved to a stop in front of a burning building. He quickly put on the rest of his outfit and checked his equipment one last time—all good.

His boots landed on the sidewalk with a thud, and Robert gazed at the source of the fire. The building turned out to be a suburban home, a two-story mansion with a sweeping lawn and a picket fence—the picture of suburban bliss. Only now, it was a scene from hell.

An ambulance was already on the scene, with two paramedics giving oxygen to a woman on the sidewalk. Her nightgown was smeared with ash, and her eyes glared white from a face blackened by soot.

She was hysterical, fighting the medics every step of the way. Her shrill voice cut through the air, and Robert's heart sank. That likely meant this would be a rescue, probably children. *Man, I hope not.*

The captain hurried over to get a report on the situation while George jumped out and grabbed the hose. He pulled it toward the fire hydrant while the rest of the team got into position.

"Right, listen up," Captain Schmidt said, running back. "This is a rescue. The husband and two kids are still inside. The last report says they're trapped on the top floor. Robert, get ready to go in."

Robert nodded, limbering up as adrenaline flushed through his veins. "Yes, Captain!"

"Mason, you're with Robert. The rest of you, form the line," the captain ordered.

Robert ran toward the house, followed by Mason. They paused a few feet from the front door, waiting for the water to come on. "Ready for this, Mason?"

Mason bobbed his head. "Are you?"

"Always!"

The windows exploded outward as the glass caved under the intense heat, and orange flames flickered to the roof. Smoke billowed into the sky, and ash rained down on the two-person team.

Suddenly, a hand grabbed Robert's elbow. It was the woman.

She tugged at his gear, her expression frantic. "You've got to help them. My kids!"

"Ma'am, please. Calm down. I promise we'll do everything we can," Robert said, pushing her back the way she'd come.

The paramedics grabbed her by the arms and hauled her away, kicking and screaming. "You don't understand. He's trying to kill them. He tried to kill me."

"He what?" Mason asked, standing close to Robert.

"My husband. He's a monster. He bit me," the woman screamed. She flashed a bare shoulder marred by a gaping wound. The flesh was torn to the bone, and blood ran down her arm in a steady stream.

Robert stared at her, his mouth agape. "What the—"

At that moment, the water came on, and the captain shouted, "Get in there. Now!"

Robert turned away from the woman, his mind in turmoil. He eyed the door. *What in hell's name is going on in there?*

"Come on," Mason cried, rushing past Robert.

Robert followed, ducking into the house without further hesitation. Whatever the situation might be, he'd face it head-on. It was what they'd trained for—just part of the job.

Together, Robert and Mason navigated the ground floor. Visibility was poor, and the heat was scorching. Flames climbed up the walls and crawled across the ceiling. The structure groaned as the beams expanded, and he knew they had precious little time left. "Hurry!"

He found the stairs and ran up to the second floor. On the landing, Robert paused for a brief moment. "Hello? Anybody there?" Shrill screams reached his ears, the terrified cries of kids scared to death. It came from a doorway to the left, and he turned to Mason. "In there."

They rushed into the room, searching through the thick haze for the source of the screams. An adult male banged on the wooden closet doors with his fists, ignoring the flames that consumed the room. Vicious growls sawed from his throat, and the flimsy cabinet cracked beneath the force of his blows.

"Hey, you!" Robert cried, running forward.

The man turned, his eyes crazed and his chin covered in blood. He snarled with his teeth bared, and Robert froze to the spot. He barely had time to think before the man tackled him to the ground, hitting him with the force of a freight train. They tumbled across the floor, and the man clawed at Robert's helmet. His teeth snapped at the visor, smearing blood across the clear plastic.

Robert fought to gain the upper hand and kneed the crazed man in the stomach. It didn't work, and the stranger continued his relentless assault. The helmet shifted, baring Robert's throat by an inch. Like a rabid wolf, his attacker went for the opening. Throwing up an arm, Robert barely managed to deflect the bite. Instead, gnawing teeth sank into his forearm. The only thing that saved him was the thick material of his suit.

Pain lanced up Robert's arm, and he screamed, "Mason, help me!"

Suddenly, the crazed man stiffened, his eyes rolling into the back of his head. Blood ran down his face in a trickle, and Robert saw the blade of Mason's fire ax sticking up from his skull.

With a yell, he threw the body aside and scrambled to his feet. "What the fuck was that?"

"I don't know, man. I didn't have a choice," Mason cried. "He went right at you, and he wouldn't stop."

11

Robert forced himself into a semblance of calm. He didn't know what was going on, but they still had a job to do. "Never mind. We'll deal with this later. Let's get out of here."

He yanked open the closet door and found the two kids huddled in the bottom. The nearest, a young boy, gazed at him from a tear-streaked face. "Where's my mom? I want my mom!"

"She's outside, kid. Don't worry. I'll keep you safe," Robert said, scooping the boy into his arms. "Mason, grab the girl."

Mason obeyed, and they exited the room before running downstairs. Chunks of fiery debris rained upon them, and a loud crash sounded as the house collapsed inward. With seconds to spare, they made it outside as a blast of hot air shoved them onto the porch.

Robert stumbled to a halt, heaving for breath while the boy clung to his chest. Mason stopped next to him, still holding the little girl. They exchanged wary looks, and Mason shook his head. "I can't believe I killed him. I killed a man."

"It was self-defense. You and I both know—" Robert was cut off mid-sentence when a news helicopter flew overhead. Or rather, it tumbled through the air with a shrill whine of the rotors.

It crashed into the road three houses down and exploded in a great ball of flame. Robert was nearly thrown off his feet, the vibrations rocketing up his spine. As he straightened up, he noticed something strange: No water sprayed the house, and nobody stood by to lend assistance.

He looked around, ignoring the crashed copter for the moment. "Captain?"

But the captain was down, pinned to the ground by several squirming figures. Two more of his teammates, Briggs and

White, lay sprawled on the tar, the fire hose forgotten. None of them wore helmets, and blood pooled beneath their ripped-out throats. "What the fuck is going on?"

Robert got his answer when he spotted one of the paramedics. The man was pressed up against the side of the ambulance by the woman he'd treated earlier—the children's mother.

She gnawed on his throat, tearing through the flesh like wet tissue. Arterial blood sprayed from the wound, coating the duo in crimson. The other medic was nowhere to be seen, and George and Susan were missing too.

A window crashed further up the street, and screams cut through the air. A woman ran down the road, chased by a group of people. They looked crazed. Insane.

"This can't be happening," Robert muttered, but it was, and standing around wasn't the answer to their problems. He glanced at the boy in his arms before looking at Mason. "We need to get out of here."

"What?" Mason asked, his expression blank.

"Wake up, Mason. We need to get these kids to safety. Now," Robert commanded.

Mason's expression cleared, and he squared his shoulders. "Okay. What do we do?"

Robert placed the boy on the ground and steadied him with one hand. "When I say go, we run. Got it?"

Mason and the boy nodded.

"Don't stop for anything or anyone." Robert pulled the fire ax from his belt with one hand, ready to fight whatever came his way. "Let's go!"

He sprinted across the lawn, followed closely by Mason, still carrying the girl and the young boy. As the first crazy swerved

13

toward him, he cut the man down with a swift blow from his ax. The man collapsed to the ground in a spray of blood and brains.

Another crazy jumped at Robert with a screech, and he reversed his weapon with a backhanded blow. It hacked into the man's neck, and the muscle separated in a red haze. Robert rammed into him with one shoulder, and the crazy spun away on unsteady feet. He looked like a bobble-headed figurine as he went down, his head barely attached to his body.

"What about the captain?" Mason yelled, one hand pointing toward the squirming knot of humanity.

It was too late for the man. Robert knew that in his gut. Even so, he slowed, his gaze drawn to his former mentor and friend. For a brief moment, their eyes met, and his fingers clenched around the handle of the ax. *I can't leave him. I have to try to save him.*

The captain's mouth worked, and crimson blood spilled over his lips. As the mass of biting mouths and tearing hands ripped him apart, he shook his head. "Run."

Robert halted in his tracks, his heart in his throat. The captain was right. He knew it, but he was reluctant to admit that awful fact. "Captain."

"Go," the captain mouthed as he disappeared beneath the crowd of ravenous people.

Robert swerved away and made for the fire truck. Already, his two dead teammates stirred as their broken flesh reanimated. Behind him, the kid's mother abandoned the paramedic and chased after the next-door neighbor.

"Come on, get in," he yelled, waving a frantic hand at Mason and the kids. Together, they bundled the two children into the front seat.

14

"You drive," Robert cried. "I'll close her up."

"What about the hose?" Mason asked, climbing up behind the wheel.

"Forget the damned hose. We need to get out of here," Robert replied grimly.

With his ax gripped in both hands, Robert dashed around the back of the truck. It felt like basic training as he dodged around corpses and barreled through knots of screeching infected.

Moving as fast as possible, he closed all the open hatches and doors before heading toward the front. Halfway there, a crawling woman latched onto his leg and bit into his calf. She chewed at the limb with vicious intent, unable to tear through the thick material. With a roar, Robert shook her off. She flew backward as his heavy boot connected with her face, and broken teeth flew in all directions. *Thank God for turnout gear.*

Three more steps took him to the passenger side, and he reached for the handle. The door swung open before he could touch it, and the boy's terrified face popped into view. "Hurry up, Mister!"

"Thanks," Robert replied with a grunt as he hauled himself into the seat.

"You made it," Mason cried, his face pale.

"Of course I did. Now get us out of here!"

Mason slammed his foot on the gas, and the truck roared up the street. Once they were safely underway, Robert slumped into his seat. Relief coursed through his veins, warring with fear and uncertainty.

"What do we do now?" Mason asked.

"Now, we get our families," Robert replied. "And after that, we head to the station."

"The station?" Mason said. "Why the station?"

"You'll see," Robert replied, reaching for the radio.

In terse terms, he explained the situation to Theresa. She and a couple of the others were operating the station. It took a while, but Theresa was nothing if not practical and intelligent. She quickly caught on.

"Call our families and tell them to pack whatever food, water, medicine, weapons, and other supplies they've got," Robert said. "Mason and I will pick them up in the truck."

"I'm on it," Theresa said, her tone brisk and efficient. "I'll give you the addresses as soon as I get them."

"If they can get to the station on their own, even better," Robert added. "And you'd better fortify the place. Barricade all the doors and windows, make room for everyone, sort out the supplies, and everything else you can think of."

"Yes, yes, I know what to do," Theresa replied.

"And get ready for a fight."

"I'm always ready, Robert," Theresa said, cutting him off.

Robert dropped the mic into his lap, his eyes fixed on the front. There could be no turning back now. He knew what was happening. He'd realized it when he saw that woman chewing on the paramedic's neck like it was a hamburger. A woman who'd been a human being but moments before. A wife and the mother of two young kids.

It was the apocalypse.

The zombie apocalypse.

Chapter 2 - Theresa

After her conversation with Robert, Theresa sat still for several seconds. She gripped the edge of her desk and reviewed the information she'd received in her head. There was no question of panic or disbelief. She could not afford to cry or tear at her hair. In an instant, the world had changed, and if she wanted to survive, she'd have to change with it.

Her mind quickly ran through a series of tasks, starting with the most important one: Secure the station.

Grabbing a clipboard and pen, she left her office and closed the door with a firm click. She made her way down the hall toward the kitchen. There she encountered Timothy, Ellen, and Rick. They were the only staff present, with everyone else off-duty or out on a call.

Without mincing words, Theresa filled them in on the situation. As expected, they had a hard time accepting the situation. After answering the hundredth question, Theresa cut them short. "Listen up. Whether you like it or not, this is happening. More importantly, what we do in the coming hours will determine the fate of this firehouse and everyone in it. Do you understand?"

Rick nodded, his expression stark. "What do you want us to do, Theresa?"

"I need you to secure the station. Close the windows and blinds, switch off unnecessary lights, no television, no music, shut the bay doors, and lock up the reception area. Can you do that?"

"Of course," Rick said, standing up. "Come on, Ellen. Timothy. You heard Theresa."

"Once you have secured the building, report to my office," Theresa said.

"Yes, ma'am," Rick replied, hustling Ellen and Timothy away.

Satisfied, Theresa took her clipboard and made a quick inventory of their supplies. Both in the kitchen and the storage rooms. They had a fair amount of food, cleaning products, bottled water, first-aid kits, medical equipment, blankets, bedding, towels, uniforms, and gear. She believed in buying in bulk and shopping for bargains.

Plus, they had two fire trucks, a response vehicle, a fully equipped garage, a water tank on the roof, solar panels for extra power, a backup generator, and a fuel tank. But they'd need more of everything and had to stock up on other essentials like flashlights, candles, batteries, disinfectants, masks, gloves, light bulbs, toiletries, clothing, tools, and weapons. Especially weapons.

Once she'd made the lists, Theresa returned to her office and pulled up her contacts. She picked up the phone and dialed the emergency services first, followed by the police station, the hospital, the mayor's office, and the town newspaper.

Nobody answered. Either the phone rang non-stop, or she got the busy tone. With a groan of frustration, she gave up. "This is not working. The local networks are flooded. Let's try the cellular networks."

One by one, she reached out to the staff and their families.

It took a long time, and more than once, she lost contact. But in the end, her efforts paid off. When a knock on the door announced Rick, Ellen, and Timothy, she was ready for them. "Is the station secure?"

"Yes, ma'am," Rick said. "She's locked up, and nothing can get in without our permission."

"Excellent. I knew the extra security after last year's burglary would pay off," Theresa said, consulting her notepad.

"Extra security?" Timothy asked. He was new, a raw recruit fresh from the academy.

"Surely you've noticed the bars on the windows, the security gates, and the reinforced locks?" Theresa said, quirking an eyebrow.

"Yes, ma'am," Timothy said with a hasty nod.

"It's thanks to a slew of burglaries last year. We got hit four times in two months, and I decided to beef up our security. We also got cameras at all the exits," Theresa explained.

"That will all come in very handy now," Rick said.

"Indeed, it will," Theresa said, shifting in her chair. "Do any of you have family in town? Someone who might need rescuing right now?"

"No, Ma'am," Rick said, shaking his head.

"Me neither," Ellen said.

"What about you, Timothy?" Theresa asked.

"I got a message from my dad. He's on his way to fetch my gran, and he told me to stay put now," Timothy said.

"Alright. With that settled, we can get down to business," Theresa said. "Rick, I want you and Ellen to take the fire truck and fetch the captain's wife. She's alone, and she needs our help."

"You can count on us," Rick said.

19

"I contacted the families of Briggs and White. They're on their way here. So is Ruby, her husband, and a friend they picked up along the way," Theresa said, referring to one of their off-duty firefighters.

"What about Susan and George?" Ellen asked.

"I haven't heard from them. They're still missing at this stage," Theresa said.

"I hope they're okay," Ellen said.

"Me too. But right now, we need to stay focused," Theresa said.

"Yes, ma'am," Rick said, hurrying away with Ellen in his wake.

"What about me?" Timothy asked.

"I need you to hold down the fort until more of our people return," Theresa said. "We have to be ready to receive them and any other survivors. This is a safe haven, Timothy, and we are their only hope."

"I understand," Timothy said.

"Gear up and meet me in the bay," Theresa said. "We have to set up a decontamination room."

Once Timothy was gone, Theresa shifted in her seat with a grimace. A stabbing pain shot up her spine, and a cold sweat broke out on her forehead. With reluctance, she popped two painkillers. She usually avoided them but needed to be on top of her game.

It was an old injury that killed her career as a qualified Emergency Medical Technician or EMT for short. Instead, she became a pen-pusher and handled all the administration. Still, she didn't complain. While she couldn't go out into the field anymore, she was still part of the team.

While she waited for the worst pain to subside, she contacted

Robert via radio and informed him of her progress, the captain's wife, Briggs' and White's families. Sadly, she hadn't been able to contact Robert's wife or Mason's sister, but she resolved to try again later. The day was far from over, after all. It had just begun.

Chapter 3 - George

George ran as fast as he could, his gear dragging at his limbs. His breath sawed in and out of his lungs, and a hot poker stabbed him in the ribs. He pressed one hand to his side and forced his booted feet to keep moving. One step, two steps, three…

Guilt tugged at his conscience and left a sour tang in his mouth. He'd left his teammates behind to die. The captain… oh, God, the captain. Despite fighting like a lion, those crazy people took Captain Schmidt down like a pack of hyenas. What about Stephenson and Mason? Did they make it out of the house? And Susan? She ran, same as him, and he hoped she was still alive.

These thoughts and many more swirled through George's mind. It was impossible to comprehend what had happened and was still happening. One minute he was holding the hose, and the next, he stood frozen when the housewife went nuts. Numbed by shock, he'd watched her make a meal of the paramedics.

At first, he'd thought she was insane. Maybe she had schizophrenia, or she was hopped up on drugs. Perhaps she was the one that set the house on fire, leaving her family to die.

Then, a bunch of other people attacked his team, ripping into them with ghoulish abandon. None of his teammates were prepared for the onslaught. Some didn't even have their helmets strapped on yet. Though how anyone could be prepared for cannibals, he didn't know.

As ashamed as he was to admit it, he'd run, and he could only hope the others made it out alive. Hell, he hoped he'd make it out alive!

George chanced a glance over his shoulder, and his heart stuttered. Those things were gaining on him. *Come on. Faster, faster!*

An ear-splitting screech caused him to stumble. A shadowy blur caught his eye before something hit him with a glancing blow. George spun wildly, flailing his arms to keep his balance. The thing that attacked him whirled about with its teeth bared. Long strands of dark hair hung across its face, and smears of red lipstick and blood marred its skin—a woman.

No, not anymore.

A thing.

A monster.

She swiped at him with her hands, her fingers arched like claws. Long crimson nails tipped each finger, eager to tear through flesh. George jumped back, and her nails raked across his stomach.

The others were gaining, closing the distance while he dawdled about like an idiot. Within seconds, he regained his footing and launched himself at the witch in his path. He rammed her with his shoulder, and she flew across the tar with a shriek.

George didn't hang around but pelted down the street with a fresh burst of speed. Adrenaline pumped through his veins, and the pervasive terror faded, replaced by a sense of calm. He needed to get off the street. Out here, he was too exposed, and those things were fast. Despite being in peak condition, he couldn't keep going indefinitely.

But everywhere he looked, locked doors and shuttered windows met his gaze. Not a single opportunity presented itself. He wasn't in the suburbs anymore but in the business district. The shops and offices on either side were closed, their signage illuminated by the bright glow of street lamps.

With growing desperation, George cast around for a solution. The crazies were now so close; he almost felt their teeth cutting into his flesh. Not for the first time, he wondered what had possessed him to move to this place. Fresh from the academy, he'd jumped at the chance to move across the country—anything to get away.

A year later, he was still a stranger to Burlington city. A loner, he made no friends and never went out. He knew no one and didn't recognize the area. It was all a blur. One long, messy blur. *Shit, shit, shit.*

A car drove past, its wheels screeching as it sped around the corner. George glanced at the street signs. He wasn't far from the main highway. If he could get there, he could flag down a vehicle and catch a ride. Maybe.

It was worth a shot, and he changed direction, cutting across the curb and taking a sharp turn. The woman followed with several more crazies tagging along for fun. The things were relentless, and once more, fear churned in his stomach. *Faster, faster!*

A few more cars raced past, headed for the highway. Strange faces stared at him from behind the glass windows, their eyes wide with fright. One sedan was piled high with baggage, and he spotted a birdcage strapped to the roof.

A hysterical laugh bubbled up his throat, and he wondered if he was going nuts. Whatever was happening, it could be airborne. Maybe a group of terrorists had released a bioweapon into the air or water. If that was the case, they were all screwed.

George shook his head. He dared not think like that. He had to keep going, keep hoping. *Come on, Georgie Boy! Push, push, push!*

The voice in his head sounded like his drill instructor. How he'd hated the man, but now he was grateful for the months of intense training. It was the only thing that kept him ahead of the pack baying for his blood.

Two more blocks passed before he spotted an off-ramp to the highway. With newfound determination, George headed up the incline. His legs burned with the effort, but he reached the top. There he slowed, his eyes growing wide. "Holy shit!"

The highway was clogged with cars standing bumper to bumper. Horns blared, people screamed, and fights broke out among frustrated drivers. Whole families were crammed into the tiny metal boxes on wheels, their belongings stuffed into every nook and cranny.

Familiar howls from behind sounded, and George glanced back. The group of crazies had grown in number until they jostled for space on the off-ramp. He paled as the realization of his actions hit him. Unknowingly, he'd led the bloodthirsty monsters straight to hundreds of stranded people. People who were sitting ducks. *What have I done?*

But there was nothing he could do to take it back. The deed was done, and George had no other option but to continue. He weaved through the static traffic, ducking around the cars, sedans, trucks, and lorries alike. He slid across hoods and dodged open doors with remarkable agility. It was amazing what fear could make one do.

As he ran, he waved at the people standing around in the open. "Get into your cars! Lock the doors! Close the windows!"

A few obeyed, spurred on by his fireman's uniform. Others ignored him, intent on whatever they were doing. Some waved their fists at him, their mouths screaming expletives at anything and anyone in their path.

George spotted a woman standing in the open door of her car with an infant on her hip. He shot toward her and shoved her back into her seat. "Get inside! They're coming!"

She stared at him with her mouth open, too shocked to offer resistance as he slammed the door shut. Without pause, he continued onward, trying to save as many as possible. But it was a hopeless cause.

Screams rose all around him, filled with panic and fear. The crazies dispersed among the cars, driven by their instincts to hunt. Hunt and feed.

Panicked civilians abandoned their cars and attempted to escape on foot. Within minutes, the highway had become a maze of death. People trampled one another in their haste, a tidal wave of humanity desperate for safety.

A few hid in their cars, but even that turned out to be a mistake. Glass shattered, and grinning mouths slithered through the openings. Blood splattered the windows, and entire families were wiped out within seconds.

The dead didn't stay dead for long. They stirred where they lay, limbs twitching and jaws snapping at the air like piranhas. They rose to follow their brethren, their pack, and as one, they joined the hunt.

George stumbled to a stop and turned around. Horror froze him to the spot, and he watched as hundreds succumbed to the hands and teeth that tore them to shreds. The smell of blood filled his nostrils, and hopelessness flooded his mind. *I did this. This is my fault.*

With growing resignation, George waited for the monsters to reach his position. He didn't want to run anymore. Didn't want to live with the guilt of what he'd done, knowingly or not. It would be better if he died and joined the ranks of the other victims. It was a fitting punishment for his crimes.

George tilted his head back and looked up at the stars. The sky was clear, and the stars shone like diamonds against the velvety black background. With his hands hanging by his sides, he waited, ready to accept his fate.

The howls and snarls grew closer, and he braced himself. It would hurt; he knew that, but he deserved no less. Not when so many others had suffered because of him. Women, children, babies…

Suddenly, fingers grabbed him by the wrist, and he was wrenched around to face a dark-eyed woman. Her eyes fixed on his, and she cried, "What the fuck are you doing? Run, you dumb ass."

"But…" George sputtered, caught utterly off guard.

"Run!" the woman insisted, dragging him along behind her without giving him a chance to resist. "We need to get to that truck over there."

Too stunned to fight back, George found himself in a headlong rush toward a semi-truck with a trailer. The door yawned open, and the driver was nowhere to be seen. It looked like the vehicle had been abandoned.

Once they reached it, the woman shoved George inside. She brooked no resistance, waving away his feeble protests with a stern command. "Get into the truck. Now!"

"Can you even drive this thing?" he asked, sliding over to the passenger side.

"Yes, I can," she said, slamming the door shut. With a determined grunt, she started the engine and shifted it into gear.

George stared at the road ahead. "What about—"

The woman ignored him, and the truck lurched forward. It crashed into the nearest car, shoving the hapless SUV into the next lane. The following vehicle fared just as poorly as the next and the next. Like a row of cascading dominoes, the traffic gave way to them, and they crunched their way down the side of the highway.

George clung to his seat, wincing at every bump and screech of broken metal and glass. "What the hell are you doing?"

The woman shot him a cold glare. "I'm getting us the fuck out of here. That's what I'm doing."

"But all those people!" he protested.

"They're dead already, but we're not. Not yet, anyway," the woman replied. She steered the truck toward an off-ramp and shoved two cars out of the way. The angry drivers shouted at them, their faces a shapeless blur in the passing.

"You're crazy!" George shouted as they roared off the highway and swerved into an adjoining street.

"I saved your ass, didn't I?" the woman countered.

"Why did you?" George asked.

"I spotted your uniform. You're a fireman, right?" she added.

"I am."

"Then you have a station," she said, throwing him a questioning look.

"I do," George said, his brow furrowed. "What exactly are you getting at?"

"The whole city is going to shit, and I need a safe place to ride it out," the woman said. "Your station would be as good a place as any."

"So, you saved me because you want to hole up at my station?" George said, aghast. "You stranded all those people back there just to save your own skin?"

"They were stranded already," the woman said, slamming her hands on the wheel. "What was I supposed to do? Ferry them to safety in my magical cart pulled by fairies and unicorns?"

"No, I... I don't know!" George burst out, angry despite the logic in her argument.

"You're feeling guilty. I get that, but we can't look back. We can't hesitate unless we want to become one of those things, too," the woman said after a few seconds of silence.

George sighed. "So what now?"

"Now, we go to your station and figure things out from there. That's all I've got," the woman offered.

"Alright," George said, though he dreaded returning without his captain and team. What would he say? How would he explain everything? But he didn't have a choice. Going home was not an option. "Do you know the way?"

The woman nodded. "I'm Bobbi, by the way. Bobbi Todd."

"George Shaw," George replied, settling back into his seat.

"Hold on, George," Bobbi said, swerving around a crashed vehicle smoking in the street. "This is going to be a bumpy ride."

Chapter 4 - Robert

Robert held the radio to his lips. He'd removed his helmet, and his hair was plastered to his scalp with sweat. "Theresa, are you there? Over."

Static crackled over the line.

"Theresa? Over."

"I'm here. Over," she replied.

"Any news? Over,"

"So far, I've managed to locate the captain's wife. She's at home, scared but safe for the moment. Over."

"Any kids? Over." Robert asked.

"No, the son lives and works in Dubai with his family. It was just the captain and his wife, the poor woman. Over," Theresa said.

"What about Briggs and White? Over," Robert asked, referring to the two dead firefighters they'd left behind.

"Their families are on their way here," Theresa said. "They should arrive soon. Over."

"What about the other truck? Over."

"I sent Ellen and Rick out with it to collect the captain's wife. Hopefully, they'll make it back in one piece. Over."

"And my sister, Clare? Over," Mason asked.

"I haven't been able to contact her, sorry," Theresa said. "The same goes for your wife, Robert. The phone lines are jammed. Over."

"Have you heard from George or Susan?" Robert asked. "I didn't see them at the scene, and I hope they got away. Over."

"Nothing yet. Over."

"Well, keep me posted. Over," Robert said.

"Will do, and be careful. It's death out there. Over," Theresa said.

"I know. Out."

"One more thing. Don't get bitten. The infection spreads via saliva. I heard it on the television. Over," Theresa said.

"I figured as much. Out," Robert said before signing off. He replaced the radio, his heart heavy. So many people were either dead or missing. It was enough to make anyone go nuts. He glanced at Mason. "How are you doing?"

"Still trying to wrap my head around everything," Mason replied, his fingers clenched around the steering wheel.

"Me too," Robert admitted. He stared out the window, shocked at the scenes of violence and chaos that met his eyes. Despite realizing early on what was happening, it was still hard to believe. *People eating people. This is a nightmare.*

"Where to first?" Mason asked.

"My house is the closest," Robert said, secretly glad for that fact.

"Do you think Amelia will be home?" Mason asked.

"No reason why she shouldn't be," Robert answered, glancing at his watch. It was after seven, and his wife should've finished at the office around five. That left her plenty of time to make it back home. Still, he was worried. *I hope she didn't have to work late.*

"Try calling her," Mason suggested.

"I already did, but I couldn't get through, same as Theresa," Robert said.

"With everything that's going on, the networks must be overloaded," Mason said.

"Please hurry," Robert said, his stomach tied into a ball of knots. "I need to know she's okay."

"I'll try my best," Mason said, his mouth set in a determined line. He steered the firetruck through the congested streets with as much finesse as the bulky vehicle allowed. They swerved around other cars, cut across corners, and ran several red lights along the way.

"Thanks," Robert said, turning toward the kids huddled in the seat beside him. They'd been quiet so far. Too quiet. "Are you two okay?"

The boy nodded, but the girl refused to look at him, and he tried again. "Are you hungry? Or thirsty? I've got food in my bag. If I can find it, that is."

"It's over there," Mason said, pointing to Robert's feet.

"Thanks," Robert muttered, scooping up his go-to bag. He suffered from low blood sugar and had learned the hard way to carry a few supplies. "Here you go."

The boy accepted the apple juice and peanuts without hesitation, but the girl shook her head. "I want my mommy."

"I'm sorry, sweetie, but you can't see your mommy right now," Robert said.

"Why not?"

"Because she's very sick and could hurt you without meaning to."

"Like Daddy?" the girl asked, her wide eyes giving her an owlish look.

"Yes, like your daddy," Robert said, pushing the juice and

nuts into her lap.

"I don't want it," she cried, bursting into tears. "I want Mommy!"

Robert stared at her, at a loss for words. He wasn't very good with children. Neither he nor Amelia had any kids, and they'd never planned on having a family. Amelia was a cost accountant for a big firm and focused on her career. It wasn't an issue for him either.

"Err, there, there. Don't cry," he said, patting the girl on the head. She shook him off, and he cast a despairing look at Mason.

"Don't look at me," Mason said, yanking the wheel to the right. The truck screeched around a corner, the sirens blaring. "I've got enough on my plate right now."

Robert and the kids went flying, and he scrambled to buckle them into their seats. With a click, he secured them each in place and turned to the boy. "What's your name, son?"

"Oliver," the boy replied, his expression solemn.

"Could you help me with your sister, please? I know she's scared, but I promise nothing will happen to you while I'm around," Robert said.

"What about our parents?" Oliver asked.

"There's nothing I can do for them now," Robert said. "They're very sick, and it's not safe for you to be with them."

"So, we're staying with you?"

"For now, yes. Mason and I will take good care of you."

"Okay," Oliver replied, attending to his sister. After a while, she calmed down and stopped crying.

"What's your name, sweetie?" Robert asked, wiping the tears from her cheeks.

"P... Paisley," she hiccuped.

"Paisley? That's a pretty name," Robert said.

"Th... thank you," she said with a shiver.

"Are you cold?"

"A little," she answered.

Robert cast around for a solution and spotted a discarded jacket on the seat behind him. He grabbed it and tucked the thick material around the children's legs. "There you go. Is that better?"

Paisley nodded and leaned against her brother. Oliver placed his arm around her shoulder. "We'll be okay, Mister. I'll look after her."

"Thanks, Oliver. You're a real trooper," Robert said, and he meant it. The boy was a blessing, enabling him to focus on the task at hand.

The radio crackled, and he reached for it. "Theresa? Over."

"I just spoke to Amelia. Over," Theresa said.

"Where is she? Is she at home? Over," Robert asked.

"No, she's trapped at the office. I managed to get through to her cell, but I've lost contact with her since. Over,"

The office?" Robert said, his hopes dashed. "Oh, God. Is she okay? Over,"

"Last I heard, yes, but she can't leave. The ground floor is overrun with infected people. She and a couple of colleagues are stranded on the third floor. Over," Theresa explained.

"Alright, we're on our way. Over," Robert said.

"Robert, no. Over."

"What do you mean no? Over," Robert asked, shocked at her reply.

"There's nothing you can do for her right now. Over," Theresa said.

"Don't be ridiculous. I have to save her. She's my wife. Over,"

Robert said, an edge creeping into his voice.

"Think about it, Robert. The ground floor is flooded with dozens of infected. You and Mason aren't equipped to deal with that many, especially unarmed. Over," Theresa said.

"I have to do something. Over," Robert insisted with a shake of his head. "Mason, head to—"

"What about the kids?" Theresa interrupted. "If something happens to you or Mason, they're doomed. Over."

Robert ground his teeth together. "Nothing will happen to us, but I can't abandon Amelia. Over."

"Robert, listen to me. She's safe for now, and other people need your help more. Over," Theresa insisted.

"I don't care about other people," Robert burst out. "This is my wife you're talking about. Over."

"What about Mason's sister, Clare?" Theresa added. "And our teammates, George and Susan? They're still out there somewhere. Over."

"I… I know, but this is Amelia," Robert said, his shoulders sagging. "My Amelia. Over."

"I promise you can rescue her later, but you've got work to do right now," Theresa said. "You're a firefighter, Robert. Act like one. Over."

Her words were final. The sentiment one that he could not deny, no matter how much he wanted to.

Robert closed his eyes for a moment. It was almost too much to bear. His wife was stuck on the third floor of an office block, and he had no way to reach her. Theresa was right. He'd need help if he wanted to save her: A plan, weapons, or even a distraction.

"Where to, Robert?" Mason asked, glancing at him with a worried frown.

Robert squeezed the radio between his fingers until the flimsy plastic creaked. "Promise me she's safe, Theresa. Swear it on your life. Over."

"I swear it," Theresa said. "They're locked inside, they've got water, electricity, and some food. They'll be fine, I promise. Over."

"I'm trusting you. Over," Robert said with a warning note.

"I know, and I won't let you down. Over," Theresa said.

"Okay. Who's first on the list? Over."

"Clare, Mason's sister," Theresa said. "The last I heard, she was on her way home from work. I don't know if she made it or not. Over."

"Okay, we'll check it out. Over."

"Thanks. Stay in touch. Out."

"You heard the lady, Mason. Let's find your sister," Robert said, his stomach churning with worry.

Mason nodded. "Hold on. We're in for a rough time."

Chapter 5 - Clare

Clare wiped down the bar counter for the last time that day. It was almost five in the afternoon, and her shift was over. The place was quiet for a Saturday, with only a couple of regulars lounging about in their chairs. Grunge rock played in the background, complemented by the dim lighting and worn band posters on the walls. The atmosphere reeked of smoke and leather, an aroma that permeated all her clothes no matter what she tried.

"Can I get you another drink before I head out, Henry?" she asked, reaching for his glass.

Henry nodded. "Got any big plans tonight?"

"No partying for me, I'm afraid. I'm hitting the books," Clare replied.

"Got a big exam coming up?"

"That's right. With any luck, I can start my practical training next year."

"And become a nurse?" he said with a raised eyebrow.

"Yes, a nurse. What's wrong with that?" she said, placing one hand on her hip.

"Nothing, but it's not something I'd expect from you," Henry said.

"Why not?"

"Don't get me wrong. You're one intelligent lady and a good listener, but… well…."

"Well, what?"

"Are you gonna nurse patients like that?" he asked, gesturing at her clothes.

"Of course not, you dumb ass. This is just a look. One side of my personality," Clare said, rolling her eyes. "You shouldn't judge a book by its cover."

"Alright, I get it," Henry said, throwing up his hands in surrender. "You're a complex being with a multifaceted psyche capable of great depth and character. Your look is most likely a mask designed to keep people at arm's length and to prove to society that you're different from the rest."

"Those are big words coming from someone who's already on his fourth drink and dresses like a hobo," Clare said, more than a little peeved.

"That's because I'm a complex being with a multifaceted psyche capable of great depth and character. My look is mostly a mask designed to keep people at arm's length and to prove to society that I'm different from the rest," Henry said with a smirk. "Don't judge a book by its cover."

Clare conceded defeat with a rueful shrug. "Touché, but for the record, there's nothing wrong with being different."

"I'll let you in on a little secret," Henry said, tapping the side of his nose. "We're all different, and we're all the same too."

"That's it. I'm out of here," Clare said, throwing in the towel, literally and figuratively. "See you all on Monday."

"See ya," Yvonne, the other bar lady, said with a negligent wave.

"Good luck with the exams," Henry added, a smile playing on his lips.

Clare rolled her eyes and grabbed her bag. She'd had enough of pseudo-psychology for the day. On her way out, she caught a glimpse of her reflection in the mirror. As much as she hated to admit it, Henry had a point. If she wanted to make a success in nursing, she'd have to tone down her look. The heavy make-up and silver jewelry would have to go along with the wild hair. *I'll be damned if I go blonde, though.*

She exited the bar with swift strides. If she could get home in time, she could order a Chinese take-away—her favorite.

A year ago, a Saturday night spent indoors would have seemed ridiculous to her party-going alter-ego. Now, she looked forward to a quiet night spent indoors with her books. She enjoyed nursing and wanted to make it a full-time career. It felt good to help others, and she wasn't squeamish. Blood and guts left her cold.

Clare stepped out onto the street and paused to get her bearings. It was getting dark already. Night came early now that winter was around the corner. A chill hung in the air, and she shivered beneath her thin jacket. *I'd better get home before I freeze to death.*

She turned the corner and headed toward her apartment. While calling a cab was an attractive proposition, her bank account disagreed. It wasn't that far anyway, and the exercise would do her good.

With her hands tucked inside her pockets and her collar pulled up around her ears, she navigated the streets. It didn't take long to notice something weird was happening. A couple of cop cars raced past, sirens blaring. Then she spotted several vehicles loaded to the brim. It looked like they'd crammed in the contents of their entire household, which struck her as odd. This was not the time of day or year to go on a vacation.

A man ran past her, elbowing her in the ribs, and she staggered. He never looked back, ignoring her existence, and she shook her fist at him. "Asshole!"

Before she could recover, another blow hit Clare in the back, and she almost fell. Catching herself against the lamp post, she stared after the person with her mouth hanging open. "What the effing hell?"

This time it was a woman in a business suit. Her eyes were wild, and she had her phone glued to her ear. She had the decency to look back and yell, "Sorry!" before continuing on her way, and Clare caught the tail-end of her conversation. "I'm telling you, Martin. It's the end of the world!"

Clare stared after the hysterical woman, one hand pressed to her bruised side. "End of the world? What is she talking about?"

With a shake of her head, she turned back in the direction of her apartment. Whatever was going on, she'd be better off behind a locked door. She lengthened her strides and half-walked, half-jogged two more blocks with every sense on high alert. A fire truck blared in the distance, and she was reminded of Mason. *I should give him a call later. We haven't spoken in a while, and he might know what's happening.*

Her mind drifted to the recent news about a viral epidemic gone wrong. Thousands of people were dying, and the WHO and CDC had rallied to the call. However, it hadn't reached the borders yet. At least, not as far as she knew. Had she missed something? Were they in the midst of an outbreak?

The sound of screams brought Clare to an abrupt halt. The glass display of the shop in front of her exploded outward, showering her with glittering fragments. She threw up both hands to shield her face and dropped into a crouch.

A man landed on the sidewalk, blood pumping from his neck. Clare stared at the fountain of bright red arterial blood. It pooled on the concrete, spreading outward in a rapidly growing puddle. Her mouth grew dry, and her hands shook. She had to help him, but at that moment, everything she'd learned deserted her in a rush. *It doesn't matter what you do. Just help him!*

Galvanized into action, she jumped upright and shook the fragments of glass from her clothes and hair. "Sir, hold on. I'm here to help."

His eyes rolled toward her, and he choked. His chest spasmed as his lungs filled with fluid, and she knew she had to hurry. With one hand, she pulled her phone from her pocket and dialed the emergency services. With the other, she searched in her bag for the wad of tissues she knew was there. *Call an ambulance and apply pressure to the wound.*

However, before she could move, a stranger launched himself through the broken window with a ferocious howl. He landed on top of the bleeding victim and tore into the man's wounded throat with his teeth. Shaking his head like a dog's, he ripped through flesh and sinew, chewing and swallowing with relish.

"Oh, my God," Clare screamed, her voice shrill with terror. A hand grabbed her elbow, and she whirled around with her bag held ready to strike.

"No, wait. Don't hit me!" It was a boy, a teenager, his eyes wide in his freckled face. "You have to run!"

"What?" Clare said, her mouth hanging open.

"No time to explain. Run before he comes after you next," the boy cried.

Without waiting for her to reply, he sprinted up the street, leaving her shocked and confused. A low growl caused the hair on the back of her neck to rise, and she slowly turned around.

The man on the ground was dead, his neck torn to ribbons, but that was the least of her problems. His attacker stared at her with a feral grin, his bloodshot eyes the same color as the blood on his shirt. He bared his teeth and growled again, his muscles tensed in readiness to leap.

Clare stumbled backward, her phone dropping from numb fingers to clatter to the ground. The crazed man launched through the air, his fingers reaching for her. With a cry, she hit him with her handbag, and he staggered to the side. She tossed the bag at his face and dashed around him while he clawed at the object.

Her feet pounded the pavement as she ran, pushing her body to the limits. She dodged around parked cars and swerved to avoid other runners. It seemed she wasn't alone in her plight. Twice she spotted people struggling with crazed and bloody attackers and concluded something was driving them nuts. *The sooner I get off the streets, the better.*

By the time her apartment block loomed into view, her legs felt like jelly. Her breath sawed in and out of her lungs, and sweat stung her eyes. With a cry of relief, she burst through the entrance and took the stairs three at a time. As she reached the door, she reached for her keys only to freeze as the shocking realization hit her. She didn't have them. They were still in her bag. The same bag she'd thrown at her attacker earlier.

A sense of defeat stole over her muscles, and she dropped to her knees. Screams echoed up the stairwell, but she couldn't find the strength to move. Her brain circled one futile question, unable to focus on anything else. *What now?*

42

What do I do now?

Then her eyes lifted, and she spotted an object fixed to the wall. Immediately, her brain jumped into gear, and she sprang to her feet. It took only three steps before she reached the article: A fire hose.

Clare tugged at the hose, and it slowly unrolled from its perch. A box on the wall next to it contained a fire ax, and she used the hose's brass nozzle to break the glass. Once she held the weapon in her hands, she cast around for the nearest window. It lay at the end of the narrow corridor and looked out onto the street below.

She ran toward it, taking the hose and ax with her. Although it was tough going, she didn't hesitate. From the stairs, the growls and snarls of the infected grew louder. She was running out of time.

Clare peered through the grimy dirt-stained glass to the pavement below. It was a long way down, three stories, and there was nothing to break her fall. If the hose was too long, she'd go splat. Plus, the area crawled with infected. Even if she survived the jump, she'd have to move fast to escape. Still, she had no choice. It was either that or get eaten alive.

She lifted the ax and smashed the window to smithereens. It exploded outward in a spray of glittering shards, and she cleared the edges with the blade. Next, she tore the curtain free from its moorings and flung it over the window sill.

With a few quick turns, she wrapped the fire hose around her middle. Peering into the street, she prepared to jump. But still, she hesitated. Clare hated heights and couldn't will her body to move.

Then the first zombie spilled into the hallway, and her heart leaped into her throat. The creature snarled at her and launched itself down the passage. More infected flooded into the corridor, rapidly filling the small space. It was now or never.

Clare closed her eyes, mumbled a quick prayer, and jumped. The ground hurtled toward her, and the wind whistled in her ears. Her skirt billowed upward, exposing her thighs, but that was the least of her worries. *Please, stop. Please, stop.*

The ground closed in, and she braced herself for impact. But with a brutal yank, her fall was arrested in mid-air. The hose tightened around her waist like a vice, and her breath left her lungs in a rush. The pain was intense, and she flopped around like a fish out of water.

The hose unraveled, and Clare dropped to the ground like a sack of potatoes. Black spots danced in front of her eyes, and she knew it was the end of the road for her. Powerless to move or catch her breath, she lay motionless as the undead closed in. Soon, she'd be one of them.

Chapter 6 - Robert

Robert had his face glued to the window the entire way to Clare's apartment. His gaze swept across the passing scenery, searching for her familiar face. She'd been to the station a couple of times looking for her brother, and she was not the kind of person you forgot in a hurry.

The truck swerved around a corner, and he braced himself against the dashboard. They narrowly missed clipping another car. The driver waved a fist at them and sped past. In the back, three little faces stared at them with frightened eyes. They resembled a row of chicks, and Robert hoped their dad got them to safety.

Mason swore under his breath as he navigated the road, dodging cars and people alike. His mouth was set into a thin line, and Robert guessed he was worried about Clare.

He understood the sentiment and turned his attention back to the world outside the cab. It was one of blood, fear, horror, and darkness. Everywhere he looked, people were either dead or dying. The yellow glow from the street lamps lit the scene in lurid detail, and the shadows seemed to throb with menace.

Zombies roamed the streets looking for victims, and sadly, there were many to go around. It was a terrifying situation. The infection had hit the city with little or no warning, catching its citizens off guard. Now, they were paying the price.

Robert's thoughts strayed to Amelia, and his gut churned, but he brushed it aside. As worried as he was about his wife, she was safe for the moment. Mason's sister was not.

"We're almost there. Clare's apartment is just around the corner," Mason said, his voice strained.

"We'll find her. Your sister is one tough cookie," Robert said, remembering Clare's intense gaze and fierce disposition. "She's a fighter."

"That she is," Mason agreed without taking his eyes from the road. "How are the kids holding up?"

Robert inspected the children with care. The girl had fallen asleep in her brother's arms, and her expression was peaceful. For the moment, at least. But the boy stared into the distance like a robot, and Robert nudged him on the shoulder. "Oliver? Are you okay?"

The boy glanced at him and nodded. "I'm fine, Sir."

Robert stared at Oliver for a few seconds. The boy was pale and sweaty, his expression blank. "Are you sure? Do you feel sick?"

Oliver shook his head. "No, Sir. I'm just tired."

"Well, try to get some sleep. We'll be at the station soon," Robert said in soothing tones.

"Thank you, Sir," came the solemn reply, and Oliver leaned back in his seat. His eyes closed, and Robert felt a touch of relief. *He's probably in shock. We'll get them both sorted out once we get back to the station. Poor kids.*

"We're here," Mason said moments later.

He slowed down and eased the truck closer before coming to a halt. He flicked the lights over to brights, and they inspected the apartment block on the corner. It was a nondescript structure consisting of four floors. The outside was painted a bland beige, and the lift hardly ever worked. But it was in a decent neighborhood and affordable.

Robert sucked in a deep breath. A couple of zombies wandered around the street looking for fresh meat. So far, they had yet to notice the people inside the truck and ignored the hunk of metal on wheels.

They were not the problem, however. The entrance stood wide open, and the security guard was nowhere in sight. The lobby was filled with infected, maybe a dozen or more. They fought among each other to get up the stairs, jostling for position.

"They know there are people up there, and they're on the hunt," Mason said, pointing at the upper floors.

"I hope for their sake they locked their doors," Robert replied.

"Right, but how do we get my sister out?" Mason said. "There's so many infected. What do we do?"

Robert hesitated. This was the same situation they faced with Amelia. There were too many infected for them to take on. It would be better to come back with reinforcements, but he wasn't sure Mason was ready to hear that yet. *Play for time. He'll realize it for himself soon enough.* "How do we know she made it back to her apartment?"

"She had to. We didn't see her along the way, and I'm sure she would've headed straight home after her shift," Mason said.

Robert prayed he was right. If Clare had made it to her apartment, she was safe for the time being behind a closed door. But if she hadn't, their chances of finding her were zero.

"Try calling her again."

Mason nodded and fished out his phone. After a couple of seconds, he shook his head. "Voicemail."

"Damn," Robert said with a shake of his head.

Silence fell, thick and heavy.

"We have to save her. She's all I've got left," Mason blurted out, his voice filled with desperation.

"Look, Mason. Maybe—" The sound of shattering glass interrupted him mid-sentence, and Robert searched for the cause of the noise. It didn't take long for him to spot the source: Clare's building.

Glittering shards of glass rained down from a window on the second floor. Suddenly, a woman stuck her head through the opening and looked down at the street. She placed what looked like a cloth over the rim of the windowsill before ducking back inside.

"What the hell is she doing?" Robert asked, gaping at the scene.

"Jump! She's going to jump!" Mason said, ramming his foot down on the accelerator.

"It's too high. She'll kill herself," Robert cried. Before they could reach the site, the woman hurtled through the opening, and he gasped with horror. "No, no, no!"

Time slowed down to a crawl as his adrenaline spiked. The woman had her arms wrapped around something, though he couldn't make out quite what it was. Her long black skirt fluttered upward around her pale thighs as she plummeted toward the sidewalk.

Just before she hit the ground, she stopped mid-air with a brutal yank. Her mouth opened in a soundless cry, and her arms flailed. A line was wrapped around her middle, and she spun like a top as it unraveled. She fell the last few feet and hit the concrete with a thump, where she lay unmoving.

Already, the infected had noticed and were closing in for the kill. Mason barreled through them with the truck while Robert gripped his ax, ready to jump out. The kids were wide awake, and Paisley was bawling, adding to the chaos.

The truck shuddered to a stop next to the woman, and Robert opened the door. Immediately, a zombie was on him, growling with hunger. He hacked at the thing's skull, cleaving bone. The infected fell away, but another quickly replaced it.

Hooked fingers clawed at his visor, and Robert punched the zombie in the face. Its nose broke with a crunch, and blood splashed onto his chest. He chopped at the infected, and the blade cut into the flesh between its neck and shoulder. A boot to the chest sent the zombie flying, and he hurried to the woman's side.

She was on her hands and knees, shaking her head. He reached down and grabbed her arm. As he yanked her to her feet, their eyes met. Robert's jaw hit the ground. "Clare?"

She gazed at him with confusion, both hands pressed to her ribs. "Robert? What are you doing here?"

"No time to explain," Robert said, dragging her toward the truck. He shoved her inside and clambered into his seat. As the door slammed shut, the truck sped away, and he hung on for dear life.

Paisley was still crying, and she'd curled up into a corner on the seat behind him. Oliver sat unmoving, staring into the distance like an automaton. It worried Robert, but he had to check on Clare first. "What was that? Are you okay?"

She shook her head with a pained grimace. "Ow. That hurt a lot more than I thought it would."

49

"What possessed you to jump like that? Are you crazy?" Mason asked, throwing her a wild look.

"They were coming up the stairs. What was I supposed to do?" she said. "I grabbed the fire hose and went for it."

"How did you know you wouldn't hit the ground?" Robert asked.

"I didn't," she said with a shrug. "But rather that, than getting eaten alive."

"You're nuts; you know that?" Mason said.

"Thanks, bro," Clare replied, shifting in her seat. She hissed with pain and clamped her arms around her middle. "I think I cracked a few ribs."

"I wouldn't be surprised," Robert said, reaching for his backpack. "Here. I've got something for the pain."

He handed her a bottle of painkillers and water before turning his attention to the kids. Paisley sobbed nonstop, curled into a fetal position, and his heart went out to her. "Hey, sweetie. Please, stop crying."

Paisley shook her head, and he reached over to pat her hand. "It's going to be alright, I promise."

A low growl caused him to freeze, and the hair on the back of his neck rose. He slowly turned his head, and his gaze locked with Oliver's. The boy stared at him, his eyes filled with blood and menace.

"Oliver?" Robert whispered as ice flooded his veins. With his free hand, he reached for his ax. His fingers curled around the handle, and his muscles tensed. At the same time, his mind was in turmoil. *This can't be happening. He's just a kid. I can't kill a kid.*

"Oliver, please. Don't do this," Robert begged.

The boy snarled, and his lips peeled back to expose his

canines. Oliver was no more.

Chapter 7 - Susan

Susan crouched behind a car wreck, hidden by the smoke that billowed from its smashed radiator. It filled the air around her with a grayish haze barely penetrated by the glow of the street lamps. Far above her head, the moon shone like a silver beacon, fat and full. Normally, she'd pause to appreciate its beauty, but it was cold—a distant onlooker to the pain and suffering below its gaze.

She shifted from one leg to the other and tightened her grip on her fire ax. Already, its blade was smeared with crimson, and blood spattered her uniform. It boggled the mind to think she'd killed a person, another human being. Yet, here she was, prepared to kill again.

A shrill scream blasted her eardrums, and she winced. It was the sound of pain, or rather, extreme agony. Susan didn't look for the source. It was already too late to help. Once bitten, it was over.

It hadn't taken her long to figure out what was going on. She'd watched enough zombie movies with her son, Noah, to recognize the signs. The only difference between these infected and those onscreen was their speed. These zombies were fast, and they had no problem chasing people down like frightened little rabbits.

Her thoughts wandered to Noah, but there was nothing she could do for him at the moment. He was far away, working as a crew member on some billionaire's private yacht. She could only hope that he was safe. She'd taught him as well as she could, but now it was up to him, and she had to trust in his ability to survive.

Susan dared to take a quick look up the street. She was only three blocks from the fire station, but it might as well have been three hundred. The area was infested with zombies, and they were hungry. *Damn it. What now?*

Suddenly, a familiar siren blared, and a fire truck raced down the street. For a moment, she was tempted to flag it down, but there were too many zombies around. The vehicle raced past her hiding spot, and she craned her neck to get a look. A flash of bright blonde hair in the passenger window was all she got, and she surmised it was Ellen. That meant Rick was the driver. The two were best friends and always went out together.

Susan didn't waste additional time or effort on them. They were probably on their way to save friends or family. Or maybe they were out looking for the other truck. Either way, she was on her own. *It's up to me to get my ass to safety—nobody else.*

A knot of infected ran after the vehicle, drawn by the noise and flashing lights. More followed, and within minutes, the street had cleared. Relief flooded her veins. *This is it. This is my shot!*

Susan jumped to her feet and sprinted up the road, sticking to the shadows. At the same time, she kept an eye out for more zombies. But none jumped out at her, and the street was empty except for a couple of mangled corpses. They had yet to reanimate, and she gave them a wide berth.

The going was tough. Her heavy boots dragged at her limbs, and her helmet kept bouncing around on her head. She held it in place with one hand while the other clutched her ax. It pulled her off-balance, though, and slowed her down. "Damn it. I must've grabbed the wrong helmet. If the captain finds out, he'll have my head on a platter."

Susan fell silent when she realized that the captain would never find out. Nor would he say anything to her ever again. He was dead.

She winced at the memory. It still felt unreal to her. One moment, she was helping George with the hose, and the next, a bunch of crazies attacked from nowhere.

***

Susan bent down to pick up the hose and dragged it toward the burning house. The building was a flaming inferno, and the heat enveloped her even from a distance. She chewed on her bottom lip, worried about Robert and Mason. If they didn't get out soon, they wouldn't be coming out at all. "George, you'd better hurry up. We need to get water on that blaze."

"Almost there," George replied as he connected the hose to the fire hydrant.

"What's the hold-up?" Captain Schmidt bellowed.

"We're almost ready, Sir!" Susan replied, taking up her position on the lawn.

"Move your asses," the captain replied.

Suddenly, a wild scream caused Susan to pause. It came from the ambulance, but she couldn't see what was happening. "Captain?"

"Stay where you are," the captain said, moving toward the

noise. "I'll check it out."

"Okay," Susan replied with a curt nod.

A couple of people ran past, hauling ass down the road, and she frowned. Usually, onlookers were curious about a fire, and they'd stop and stare with morbid fascination. Something was wrong, and the hair on the back of her neck prickled. *What's going on?*

Then, Captain Schmidt yelled out. "What the hell? Get off me!"

She whirled toward him, and her jaw hit the ground. Three men had the captain pinned to the ground. One had latched onto his helmet while the other two tore at his clothes. Their teeth were bared, and they gnashed at the air like rabid dogs.

Before she could make a move, the captain's angry bellows turned into an agonized scream. One of the men had managed to pull off his glove and was chewing on his fingers. Blood spurted, and cartilage crunched as the other joined the feast.

"What the f—!" Susan cried, dropping the hose. "Captain!"

She pulled out her ax and ran toward her superior. She'd barely taken three steps, however, when a wild-eyed woman appeared out of nowhere. With an ear-splitting shriek, she attacked, and Susan was bowled off her feet.

She fell to the ground with the woman on top of her. The ax was pinned between them, and Susan couldn't get it free. The woman wriggled about like a worm on a hook, and she snapped at Susan's visor with her teeth. Spit drooled from her lips, and her eyes were shot through with crimson. "Get away from me!"

The woman paid no attention, and her vicious growls sawed through the air. The sound caused Susan's knees to go weak, and she shook her head from side to side. Zombies. It had to be an outbreak, just like in the movies she'd watched with Noah.

The thought of her son flashed through her mind, and she realized she had to fight. She had to survive. It was what she'd taught him. The way she'd raised him, and she could not let this sick woman get the best of her. "That's enough!"

With a roar, Susan shoved the woman away and scrambled to her feet. She raised the ax above her head and brought it down on the woman's skull. It cracked open like an egg, and brain matter spilled from the wound.

Susan wrenched the ax free and turned back to Captain Schmidt, but it was too late. He was buried beneath a squirming knot of humanity, and his blood stained the tar.

She whirled around, looking for her teammates. "George? Where are you?"

But George was gone, and the rest were down. More infected were coming toward her, and she knew she had no choice. *I have to run.*

With a final look at the horrifying scene, Susan fled, leaving it all behind. At the same time, the fire inside the burning house reached its peak. The flames billowed outward, bathing the world in lurid orange and red—a fitting tribute to the dead.

***

Susan sobbed, and grief lay heavy in her heart. Her captain and teammates were gone, eaten by zombies. George was missing. Robert and Mason had probably died inside the house, waiting for help that never came—burned alive by the flames she should've doused with the hose.

Her boot hooked on a concrete slab, and she stumbled. For a second, she wanted to stop and just… *just what? Give up? I can't give up.*

With a determined grunt, Susan pushed herself forward. She had to keep going. She couldn't afford to let the memories get her down. Neither the captain nor her team would've wanted that. The station was only one block away—only one block.

Chapter 8 - Robert

Oliver snarled, and a thin stream of drool spilled from his lips. If the eyes were the windows to the soul, Oliver's was a bottomless pit of horror and death. Nothing remained of the boy he'd once been, and Robert knew that he was gone. In his place was a mindless monster—a killing machine.

Even so, Robert didn't know if he could bring himself to kill the boy. *He's just a kid. An innocent kid.*

But there was nothing innocent or childlike about the way Oliver stalked him with his predatory gaze or the way his muscles bunched in readiness to attack. Everything about him screamed danger. From his bloodshot eyes, bared canines, to the way his fingers dug into the backrest.

"Please, don't do this, Oliver. You have to be in there somewhere," Robert pleaded.

"What's going on?" Clare cried, her eyes wide. "Is he turning?"

"What's happening?" Mason added, his hands clenched on the steering wheel.

Robert ignored them both, his full attention locked on the boy. He dared not look away, not even for a second. Swallowing hard on the knot in his throat, he raised the ax, nerving himself to strike.

Oliver launched himself at Robert with a vicious growl. Robert swung the ax and hit the boy on the temple with the handle. It was a short chopping blow that momentarily stunned the child.

Taking advantage of the slight reprieve, Robert grabbed Oliver by the collar and dragged him across the seat and onto his lap. At the same time, he reached for the door, planning to toss the boy into the street. *Rather than kill him.*

But the ax hampered his efforts, and he couldn't get a grip on the handle. Loathe to drop his only weapon, he hesitated. Oliver writhed in his lap, hissing and spitting like an enraged cat. He scratched and clawed at Robert's visor, trying to get to the flesh underneath.

Panic coursed through Robert's veins, and he knew he had to do something fast. Something he really didn't want to do. Gathering his courage, he raised the ax, prepared to strike. This time, he'd go for the kill. *I'm sorry, Oliver, but I've got no choice.*

However, Oliver was as slippery as an eel, and he wriggled free from Robert's grip. Sensing easier prey, the boy launched himself at Clare, his teeth snapping at her flesh. She screamed and scrambled away from the rabid child, bumping into Mason.

Caught off-guard, Mason wrenched the steering wheel, and the truck swerved across the road. Robert was thrown to the side, and he lost his grip on the ax. It tumbled to the floor, and raw terror filled his mind. He feared not for himself but for the people under his care. As the senior firefighter present, they were his responsibility, and he'd let them down. *I should've killed the kid when I had a chance.*

But empty regrets wouldn't save them now, and he threw

himself at Oliver. The boy had latched onto Clare's jacket, and he was perilously close to ripping out her throat. She screamed like a banshee, her voice melding with Paisley's bawls. Together they created a duet of terror, the perfect backdrop to an awful situation.

Robert wrapped his arms around Oliver and pulled him off Clare. She continued to kick and scream, buffeting the hapless Mason. The truck zigzagged across the road, narrowly missing the cars and other obstacles in the street.

"Clare, get off me," Mason cried, struggling to keep control.

She shook her head, unable to calm down. "I can't; I can't. He's going to get me!"

Robert had Oliver in a bear hug, pinning the boy's arms to his sides. The infected child struggled against his grip, roaring with rage. He possessed a kind of strength Robert had never encountered in a child before, and he tightened his hold. However, the swerving vehicle made it difficult, and he planted one boot against the dashboard to steady himself.

It was an impossible situation, and he knew it couldn't last. Sooner or later, Oliver would get loose again, and this time, he'd hurt or kill someone.

Then, he spotted his fire ax tumbling around on the floor. It was just out of reach, and he calculated the distance. Clenching his teeth, he prepared to go for it. It was a risky move, but he didn't have much choice.

Robert let go of Oliver with his left, holding onto the boy with his right. He reached for the weapon, straining to get it. His fingers brushed against the handle, and he tried to drag it closer. His muscles quivered, and sweat beaded his forehead and stung his eyes. *Almost there. Almost.*

A sudden turn of the truck sent the ax rolling out of range, and he swore. "Damn it!"

At the same time, Oliver twisted around and latched onto Robert's shoulder. His teeth sank into the thick material of Robert's suit, and he ground his jaws together. The fabric resisted his efforts, but that didn't faze the boy. Not when the warm, living flesh he craved was just beneath the surface. He gnawed and chewed with a vengeance, and Robert cried out in agony.

Without realizing what he was doing, he lashed out. His fist connected with Oliver's jaw, and the boy's head snapped back. Before he could bite down again, Robert planted his hand on the child's forehead and pushed back as hard as he could.

A sickening snap followed a loud crunch, and Oliver went limp. His head flopped around on his broken neck, and his eyes rolled in their sockets.

Shocked by what he'd done, Robert dropped the boy. He stared at the body, struck by how fragile and defenseless Oliver looked. "I killed him. He was just a kid, and I killed him."

Clare took the opportunity to escape. She jumped onto the back seat and gathered the hysterical Paisley into her arms. "Hush, sweetie. Hush."

Robert saw none of this, his gaze fixed on Oliver's. To his utter dismay, the boy wasn't dead. Despite the broken neck, his mouth gaped open and shut like a fish on land.

"Is he still… alive?" Mason asked, staring at the boy's corpse. "How's that even possible?"

"I… I don't know," Robert said, shaking his head. His brain refused to process it all, and he found himself frozen to the spot, unable to move.

Suddenly, Clare screamed. "Mason, look out!"

Robert looked up, straight into the headlights of an oncoming vehicle. Mason slammed on the brakes, and the wheels screeched as the truck slid across the tar. The sound of a blaring horn filled the cab, followed by a terrific crash.

The impact tossed Robert through the air like a rag doll, and he smashed into the windshield shoulder-first. His body dropped onto the dashboard below before rolling off and landing on the seat with a thump.

Robert groaned. It felt like every bone in his body was broken, smashed into tiny little bits. Blood filled his mouth, and his breath hitched in his throat as he struggled to breathe. Darkness encroached on his vision, thick and oppressive. The last thing he remembered before passing out was the smell of burning rubber and Paisley's frantic cries.

***

Joe used to be an average kind of guy before the apocalypse. Nothing special. If you asked his boss or his co-workers, he was a bit of a loser. Joe Schmoe, they called him, a nickname that didn't bother him much. Who cared as long as he had a roof over his head and could pay the bar tab he racked up every night?

Then the apocalypse dawned, and he became Joe, the zombie. For the first time in his life, he was good at something. Real good. His mother might even have been proud if she was still alive to witness his transformation.

Reborn, Joe the zombie stalked the streets like a man-eating crocodile. He pounced on his unsuspecting victims and ripped them apart with savage glee. They breathed their last as he tore into their quivering flesh, seeking out the juiciest morsels. Only living meat could sate the bottomless hunger that ruled his existence.

So, when a red, metal monstrosity barreled past him in the street, he paid it little heed. He was too busy stuffing his face with his latest victim. But a tremendous crash drew his attention, and he abandoned his meal in search of greener pastures.

As he drew closer to the now-stationary red monster, the screams of a little girl reached his ears. Saliva filled his mouth, spilling over his lips in streams of sticky drool. His pace quickened until he reached the truck.

He searched for a way in, clawing at the smooth metal that lay between him and the delicacies inside. If he'd had a functioning brain, he might have joked that he was craving canned meat.

But that didn't matter. While he didn't possess the ability to think or reason anymore, he was driven by the relentless urge to feed. He would never stop, never sleep, and never give up until he got what he wanted: Flesh.

Chapter 9 - Ellen

Ellen stared at the scenery that flashed before her eyes. It played like a movie on a reel, and it felt just as unreal as the silver screen. She remembered the first time she watched a horror at the tender age of ten. She snuck out of her room to crouch on the stairs, shivering with ghoulish delight when she caught a glimpse of the television. Ten minutes later, she was back in her bed, hiding under the covers. Nightmares filled with blood haunted her for weeks afterward, and even now, she wasn't fond of slasher movies.

This was worse.

Much, much worse.

Dark figures ran amok, chasing their victims down with single-minded determination. They were one with the night, pouncing from the shadows in search of flesh and blood. The streets pulsed with menace, and the city's beating heart lay exposed.

Screams, sirens, car horns, and alarms rose above the chaos and melded into a killer chorus. It was the sound of the end. The sound of the apocalypse. It illuminated the stark reality of the situation, a reality her mind struggled to grasp. "I can't believe this is happening."

"Me neither," Rick said, shaking his head.

He swerved past a pile-up at an intersection, and she twisted in her seat to get a better look. Infected people swarmed the crashed vehicles, and she caught a glimpse of stranded survivors fighting for their lives. "We have to go back. We have to help them."

"We can't. It's just the two of us, and we're not armed," Rick said.

"We have our fire axes," she said, gripping hers with one determined hand.

"Do you think it's enough?" he asked with a pointed look. "Besides, we have our orders."

"Screw orders. People are dying out there!"

"I'm sorry, Ellen."

"This isn't right. We're supposed to save lives, not look the other way."

"I know," Rick said, staring ahead. His expression was closed, but she knew him well enough to know he felt as conflicted as she did.

Ellen fell back into her seat, feeling sick. Nothing was as it should be. It was all upside down. People were killing and eating other people; the authorities were notably absent; cars fled the city in droves, driven by the desperate; riots broke out on every corner, and looters took what they wanted. Meanwhile, the police department tried to maintain order, but years of poor funding left them unable to respond with enough force to halt the infection's spread. The city was doomed from the start.

"I'm worried about my family," Ellen said after a while.

Rick glanced at her. "They're not answering your calls?"

She shook her head. "No, they're not."

"My brother isn't answering either," Rick said. "All I get is his voicemail."

Silence fell across the pair, thick and oppressive.

"I wonder how the others are faring out there. George, Susan, Robert, and Mason," Ellen said, changing the subject.

"I don't know. I hope they're all still alive and making their way back to the station," Rick said.

"It's a nightmare," Ellen said. "We've lost the captain, Briggs, and White. How many more?"

"I won't let those things near you, Ellen," Rick said, surprising her. Though they were close friends, he wasn't the sentimental type. Emotions weren't his thing, as evidenced by the sardonic twist to his lips and sharp gaze.

"Thanks, but I can hold my own," she said.

"I know, but I've got your back."

Ellen smiled despite the horror surrounding them. Rick always had her back, and she knew she could count on him. "So, who's first on the list?"

"The captain's wife. She's terrified, according to Theresa," Rick said.

"I'm not surprised. She just lost her husband to a mob of flesh-eating monsters, and her kids are on a different continent. She's all alone, the poor woman."

"Well, we should reach her house in the next few minutes," Rick said. "If we can get through these streets, that is."

Rick's words proved prophetic. As he turned a corner, he had to slam on the brakes. The truck slid to a screeching halt, and they stared in dismay at the jam-packed street ahead.

"Oh, my God. We'll never get through that," Ellen said, perched on the edge of her seat.

The road was filled with bumper-to-bumper traffic as far as the eye could see. Horns blared, lights flashed, and enraged drivers shouted at each other to move—all in vain. Nobody was going anywhere. That much was obvious.

"Guess we'll have to take a different route," Rick said. He shifted into reverse and glanced at the rearview mirror. "Here goes."

Rick reversed, but before he'd gone more than a few yards, he had to stop again. A minivan loaded to the brim with a small family and their possessions roared up behind them. The driver opened his window and leaned out. "Get out of the damn way!"

"Go back. The road forward is blocked," Rick replied, waving at the man to reverse.

The driver ignored him, leaning on his horn. Rick tried again with no success. Panic had robbed the man of his common sense, and the ear-splitting noise of his horn filled the cab. Finally, Rick gave up and closed his window.

Ellen sighed with relief as the outside world faded away. The cab became a cocoon, a haven from the chaos and death outside. But it couldn't last. They had to get out of there. "What do we do now?"

"Now, we go around them," Rick said. He edged the truck forward at a sharp angle and shifted into reverse. They crept backward, and Ellen held her breath. *I hope this works. Please, let it work.*

The tail end touched the minivan's bumper, and Rick swore. "Shit. There's not enough room."

The driver waved a fist at them. "Hey, that's my car, you asshole!"

Another vehicle rolled up behind the minivan, followed by another and another. With each passing second, their chances of escape grew slimmer. Each driver was as desperate as the next one. They leaned on their horns and screamed insults at each other. Frightened kids cried in the backseat, shushed by fearful mothers.

"We're completely boxed in," Ellen said, her heart sinking into her stomach.

Rick slammed his fists on the wheel. "I knew I shouldn't have come this way. This exit leads to the freeway, and I should've known better."

"It's not your fault," Ellen said. Her mind worked feverishly to find a solution. Finally, she settled on a plan and reached into the cubbyhole for a flashlight. Next, she opened the door and jumped out.

"Ellen, no! What are you doing?" Rick cried.

Ellen removed her fire ax from her belt. Hefting it in her right hand, she said, "I'm getting us out of here."

"Get back insi—"

She slammed the door shut, cutting Rick off in mid-sentence. With determined strides, she headed toward the minivan. The driver stopped shouting and blinked at her with surprise. "What do you want?"

"I want you to calm the fuck down, Sir," she said. "The road ahead is blocked, and you're not helping."

His face reddened, and he blustered. "You can't speak to me—"

"I'll speak to you any way I damn well like. It's the apocalypse if you haven't noticed," Ellen said, standing her ground. "Do what I say, and we might get out of here. If not, I'll reverse that truck right over you. Got it?"

"Listen to her, honey. She's a firefighter," his wife said, laying one hand on his forearm.

The man hesitated. One glance at his terrified kids decided

the matter, and he nodded. "Alright, lead the way."

"Wait for my instructions," Ellen said.

She strode toward the next car and the next, speaking to each driver in turn. One by one, she convinced them to listen. Simultaneously, she blocked further incoming traffic, flashing her torch at them as a warning. Her uniform saved the day. People were used to obeying those in charge, relieved even. It was easier than being responsible for their own lives, and it gave them someone to blame when things went wrong.

Once Ellen reached the end of the line, she lifted her hand and waved. One by one, the cars reversed and drove off in search of an alternate route. The road cleared, and the driver of the minibus graced her with a curt nod before he raced away.

"No need to thank me, Sir. It was my pleasure," Ellen shouted after him. With a shake of her head, she flashed her light at Rick. "Come on, come on. The coast is clear."

Ellen stepped onto the curb as Rick edged the firetruck past her. He backed up until he had enough room to turn and rolled down his window. "That was some stunt you pulled."

"Thanks," she replied, flashing him a broad smile.

"It wasn't a compliment," he said, his expression taut.

"Yeah, I figured that," she said.

"Just get your ass back inside the—"

Something hit Ellen with the force of a freight train. She flew to the side and crashed into a lamppost. Her head hit the metal post, and she saw stars despite the protection of her helmet. Her jaw snapped shut on her tongue. A coppery taste filled her mouth, and pain shot through her ribs.

Before she could blink, it was there. A thing. One of the monsters. It gnawed at her vizor, smearing blood and saliva across the clear plastic. Its hands gripped her by the collar, and Ellen was helpless against the assault. Her ax was gone, and so was her flashlight. She was unarmed and vulnerable.

Bit by bit, Ellen's helmet slipped backward, and the thing's snapping teeth got closer to her flesh. Its stink invaded her nostrils, and vicious growls filled her ears. She sagged against the post, her knees turning to jelly. It was just a matter of time.

Chapter 10 - George

George clung to the dashboard as the truck they'd commandeered careened through the zombie-infested streets. A sharp turn flung him against the window, and his head smashed into the glass. Stars filled his vision, and he smothered a yelp. "Watch it, will you?"

Bobbi didn't bother to answer. Instead, she swerved around a knot of infected. The bumper clipped a straggler, and the zombie tumbled across the hood. It landed in front of George, hanging on for a few precious seconds. Long enough to snarl at them through broken teeth. Its eyes were inhuman, an empty abyss. A yank of the wheel caused it to lose its hold, and it flew off into the night, much to his relief.

George sank deeper into his seat, wishing he had suckers attached to his ass. Bobbi Todd did not take any prisoners. That much he'd noticed in the short time he'd known her. *Maybe I should try to reason with her.* "We won't make it to the station if we crash."

"We'll make it," Bobbi said, her expression one of fierce determination.

George decided to stay silent for the time being and pray they didn't have an accident. He studied his new companion from the corners of his eyes, wondering what he'd let himself in for. While she seemed capable, Bobbi also appeared a tad self-serving. Selfish, even. *Let's pray I'm wrong.*

Strands of dark-blonde hair framed her face, escaping from the tight knot at the nape of her neck. It curled around the collar of her flannel shirt. The shirt was accompanied by jeans and hiking boots, practical gear for a practical kind of woman. Her skin bore a light tan, and the corners of her eyes were creased. The outdoorsy type, he decided. "Do you garden?"

"Huh?" she asked.

"You look like you spend a lot of time outside."

Bobbi hesitated for a moment.

"You might as well tell me," George said. "Since we're stuck together."

"Alright," she conceded. "I grow my own vegetables, and I raise chickens. I've got three dogs too. All rescues. Is that enough information for you, or do you need more before we can be best buddies?"

George noticed the edge in her voice and frowned. "What happened to them? Your animals?"

"What happened?" Bobbi asked. "The damn zombie apocalypse happened. I woke up this morning to a ruckus. By the time I got outside, it was too late. They were... they were torn to shreds by the neighbors. Zombies. Both of them."

"I'm sorry," George said. "What about your neighbors?"

"I killed them. Stuck them both with a pitchfork. Serves them right. Never liked them much anyway," Bobbi said, her expression grim.

George shuddered. "I saw three of my fellow firefighters die before I ran for it. I'm a coward."

"You're alive," Bobbi said. "Could you have helped them?"

"No," George admitted.

"Then stop whining."

George felt his temper flare, but he kept it in check with an effort. Starting an argument for nothing wouldn't help anyone.

"Check the cubby hole," she commanded.

"Why?" he asked, feeling the tiniest bit rebellious.

"Have you got something better to do?" she asked with a pointed look.

"Fine," he grumbled, popping the compartment open.

A gun fell out, and he grabbed it. It slipped from his grasp and tumbled into the footwell, where it rolled around between his feet. "Shit!" George scrambled to pick up the gun, handling it like a hot potato. "It's a gun."

Bobbi rolled her eyes and took the gun from him. "Relax. The safety's on."

She tucked it into her belt and focused on the road once more. "We're almost there. Here's hoping your station is still standing."

"It will be," he said with absolute certainty. Although he was the newest recruit, he knew his fellow firefighters, and he knew they'd be on top of the situation. Especially Theresa. She gave him the chills sometimes, but she was tougher than nails.

"We'll see soon enough," Bobbi said, tearing past a minivan loaded to the brim with a small family and their possessions.

Suddenly, she slammed the brakes, and the truck slid to a screeching halt. The smell of burning rubber filled the cab, and George nearly went through the windshield. With his face smashed up against the glass, he bellowed, "What did you do that for?"

"Look," Bobbi said, pointing at a stationary fire truck a few yards ahead. "Isn't that one of yours?"

George stared at the vehicle, and a frisson of excitement ran down his spine. "It is one of ours."

"Looks like someone's in trouble," Bobbi said, pointing at two figures struggling on the sidewalk.

George gasped when he recognized one of them. "That's Ellen!"

Ellen was pressed up against a lamp pole by a zombie, and it clawed at her gear with relentless ferocity. It snapped at her face and neck, growling with frustration when her helmet got in the way.

"We've got to help her," George cried, reaching for his ax.

"Yeah, I suppose we do," Bobbi said with reluctance. She pulled the gun from her belt and checked the load.

"Hurry," George said, opening his door.

Before he could move an inch, another firefighter leaped out of the fire truck ahead and ran to Ellen's assistance. It was Rick, and he brandished his ax like a club.

With a wild yell, Rick struck at the zombie's unprotected skull. The blade failed to penetrate the bone, sliding to the side. It sheered off a chunk of the infected's scalp, and putrid blood spewed from the wound.

With a snarl, the zombie abandoned Ellen and grabbed Rick instead. It gripped his arm and snapped at his hand like a rabid dog. Rick screamed with pain, and the ax dropped from his useless fingers, clanging to the ground.

Ellen dropped into a crouch before launching herself at their attacker. She jumped onto the zombie's back and wrapped her arms around its torso. Locked together, they wheeled around on the sidewalk like a drunken couple out for a night of fun. She bashed it on the head with a fist but to no avail.

The infected never faltered, clawing at her arms with hooked fingers while George watched in frozen horror.

"Come on," Bobbi cried, jumping out. She sprinted around the truck and beckoned to George. "Move your ass."

Her words acted like an electric shock, and George ran after her like a bullet shot from a gun. He overtook her in three strides and reached Ellen's side in seconds. With his free hand, he yanked her from the zombie's back and flung her to safety. His ax whistled through the air in an overhead blow, and the blade cleaved through bone. Grayish-pink brain matter spewed from the horrendous injury, and the zombie dropped to the ground with a thud.

Heaving for breath, George turned to Ellen. "Are you alright?"

She nodded, her eyes wide. "Rick! He got bitten!"

George whirled around and stared at Rick, his heart in his throat. "Your gloves?"

Rick stared at him with a stark expression. Slowly, he exposed his injured hand to the light. Blood dripped from two mangled fingers, the bones splintered and broken. "I wasn't wearing any. It all happened too fast. There wasn't time."

"Ah, shit," George said, his arms dropping to his sides.

"No, it can't be," Ellen said, tears streaming down her cheeks.

Silence fell as the trio surveyed each other, the cold realization of Rick's imminent death sinking in.

Suddenly, Bobbi Todd was there, shoving George to the side. "Move over."

She grabbed Rick's hand and studied the damage, ignoring his pained protests. "It's just the pinkie and the ring finger. You don't need all of your fingers, do you?"

Rick gaped at her. "Er, what?"

75

Rolling her eyes, Bobbi turned to Ellen. "Give me your ax."

Ellen didn't move, her head shaking from side to side in complete denial of the situation. "No, no, no. Not Rick. Please, not him."

"Take mine," George said, offering Bobbi his weapon.

"I can't use that," she scoffed. "It's full of zombie blood. Give me your ax, girl."

"My ax?" Ellen said with faltering tones. She patted her belt. "I don't know, I…."

"She dropped it when she got attacked. It's over there," Rick said through gritted teeth.

Bobbi scooped up the fallen ax and handed George her gun. "Keep watch for more zombies, okay?"

"Okay, but I'm not a very good shot," George said.

"Wait until they're close. Point and squeeze the trigger. Squeeze, don't pull," Bobbi said. "Got it?"

"Got it," George said with a nod.

The weapon felt cold and heavy, an alien thing that delivered fearsome destruction. However, it gave him confidence, and he pointed the muzzle at the looming shadows.

"Ellen, do you have something to wrap his hand with once I've chopped off the fingers?" Bobbi said

"Chopped off his fingers?" Ellen repeated, her cheeks devoid of all color. "You can't do that."

"Why not? Would you rather see him turn into one of those monsters?" Bobbi asked with cool logic.

"No, of course not, but…."

"Then figure something out," Bobbi demanded. "We'd better move fast before more infected show up for the party."

"Will it work?" Rick said, pulling his hand free from Bobbi's grip.

"How should I know?" Bobbi said. "It makes sense, though. Cut it off before the infection spreads."

"And if it doesn't work?" he said, his eyes narrowed.

"Then you die, but it's worth a shot, isn't it?" Bobbi said.

"Alright. Do it," Rick said with a curt nod.

"There's a first aid kit in the back of the fire truck," Ellen said, appearing to shake herself awake.

"Great. Get ready to treat him," Bobbi said.

"Okay," Ellen said with a relieved look. She ran toward the vehicle and opened the back. The trauma kit was at hand, and she dug out antiseptic, gauze, and bandages. "I'm ready."

Bobbi removed her belt from her jeans. She wound it around Rick's wrist and pulled it tight. So tight that the flesh bulged around the leather strap. Next, she dragged him to his knees and placed his hand on the concrete with the fingers splayed. Raising the ax in the air, she said, "On three."

"Just get it over with," Rick said.

"Three!" With a short, sharp motion, Bobbi chopped off the two injured fingers.

Rick grunted with shock and surprise as blood flowed from the stumps. He staggered to his feet, supported by Bobbi, and she led him toward the waiting Ellen. They climbed into the back, and Ellen immediately set to work stemming the flow of blood.

In the meantime, George watched it all with a weird sense of calm brought on by a feeling of responsibility. His friends and teammates needed him, and he couldn't fail them. With that goal in mind, he focused on their surroundings instead of Rick's plight. The last thing they needed was another ambush by a bunch of zombies. On high alert, he patrolled the area.

When he crossed the junction of streets, he noticed movement in the far distance. A group of figures moved closer, their actions erratic but fast. *Zombies.*

"Bobbi, we need to go," he said, the hair on the back of his neck rising. "We've got company."

"Are you two set?" Bobbi asked Ellen and Rick.

"I've got him," Ellen said, wrapping a wad of gauze around Rick's bleeding stumps.

"Ow," he muttered.

"See you back at the station," Bobbi said, slamming the door shut.

"Bobbi, we need to get out of here now!" George cried.

"Way ahead of you," she answered, jumping into the front of the fire truck.

George ran toward the driver's side with a sense of profound relief. The zombies had halved the distance, and their howls shivered through the night. They were like wolves, roving the streets in packs, and he did not think one gun would be enough to stem the tide. Not by a long shot.

He climbed behind the wheel, feeling better once sealed inside the cab. He handed the gun back to Bobbi and started the engine. "I don't know about you, but I'm just about done for the night."

"Agreed," she said, lying back in her seat. "Let's get the hell out of here."

George turned the fire truck back toward the station, ready to end the nightmare he found himself in. Hopefully, they could regroup and develop a plan once they were back home.

Home.

It was strange to think of his workplace as home, but he realized that that's what it had become. A home filled with family and friends, and together, they'd face whatever came their way.

Chapter 11 - Robert

Joe, the zombie, clawed at the smooth red metal that separated him from the humans behind its opaque surface. A little girl's screams filled him with morbid excitement, and he snarled with frustration when the barrier wouldn't give way. Two more zombies joined him, but even their combined efforts delivered zero results.

It was the smell of blood, thick and heavy, that drew him away from the truck. He lifted his head and sniffed. The delicious scent formed an invisible trail, and he followed it with growing enthusiasm.

His path carried him past the front of the red metal monster toward a smaller vehicle. Its nose was all scrunched up from the crash, and steam curled into the air from the broken radiator. One headlight was smashed, but the other lit the scene in garish detail.

A man lay across the hood, impaled on the shattered glass of the windshield. He groaned, and blood poured from his many injuries. It flowed onto the road like a crimson river, beckoning to Joe and his fellow infected.

Joe's shuffling gait sped up when he spotted his next victim, and he pounced on the defenseless man with savage glee. His teeth tore into the man's cheek, and he gorged on the delicate flesh.

When the other zombies joined in, he growled and swatted at them with his fists. They snarled back, but the tension between them subsided as they settled down to feast on their unwilling prey.

Hoarse screams issued from the man's lips as his bones were laid bare to the light, ignored by his attackers. They possessed no sense of right or wrong. No pangs of sympathy stirred their unbeating hearts. They cared only about the aching hunger that filled their every waking moment with torment and suffering. A need that could never be satisfied. It would never relent, driving their rotting bodies ever onward in search of more.

And more.

And more.

***

Robert's mind slowly rose to consciousness. He fought his way to a waking state, swimming through layers of pain and darkness. Gradually, he grew aware of his surroundings: Paisley's hysterical screams, the constant clamor of a car horn, the glaring light that streamed into the cab, and the pain that fizzed through his nervous system.

With care, he lifted his hand and touched his aching skull. A knot the size of an egg grew on his forehead, a lump of throbbing agony. He lay crumpled up in a heap, his head and shoulders wedged into the footwell. His eyelids fluttered open, and he recoiled with a sharp cry of horror. "What the fuck?"

Mere inches from his face was Oliver's. The boy stared at him with dead eyes, his skin the color of ash. His limbs were splayed out like a broken doll's, and his head twisted at an ugly angle. Worst of all, his mouth never stopped moving. The boy's jaws snapped open and shut, over and over, forever in search of sustenance.

Robert scrambled upright, ignoring the pain that shot through his spine. He couldn't stand being face-to-face with Oliver. It was too much. A toxic mixture of fear and grief galvanized his movements, and he found himself cowering in the corner of the cab. Frozen in place, he could do nothing but stare at Oliver's undead corpse.

Behind the wheel, Mason stirred. His groans snapped Robert out of his funk, and he shook himself with renewed vigor. *Come on, Robert. Wake up. People need you. Your friends need you.*

He started with Paisley. The girl was wrapped up in Clare's arms, bawling her lungs out. She looked unhurt. Frightened, but not injured. A small mercy. "Paisley, sweetie. Please, stop crying. Everything's okay."

She didn't look convinced, and how could he blame her? Not after everything she'd been through. Her scrunched-up face was the color of beetroot. Tears and snot ran down her face in silver streaks. On autopilot, he pulled a handkerchief from his pocket and wiped her cheeks. Her cries rose to a fever pitch, and he pleaded, "Please, stop screaming. I'm begging you. It's okay, I promise."

She clutched the handkerchief with tiny fingers and smothered her face in the cloth. It muted her cries and offered a measure of relief to Robert's beleaguered ears. With a deep sigh of relief, he turned to Clare. "Clare? Can you hear me?"

Her eyes were closed, and she didn't answer. He tipped her back in her seat, and her head lolled around on her neck. She was completely out of it, and a frisson of fear shot through his veins. *I hope she... dear lord, if she's been bitten... I can't kill again.*

With searching fingers, he examined her exposed skin. She appeared to be unharmed, and he couldn't find any bite marks or other wounds. "Thank God."

He slumped back in his seat and turned to Mason. "Mason? Buddy, are you okay?"

Mason raised his head with another deep groan and blinked into the light. "Why is it so bright?"

"It's the headlights from the car we crashed into," Robert said.

Mason's head swung toward him, his gaze confused. "Crash? What crash?"

"Don't you remember what happened?" Robert asked with growing concern.

"No."

Robert examined Mason's head and found a deep cut inside the hairline. Blood ran down the side of his face and soaked into his collar. "Damn it, Mason. You're hurt."

"I am?" Mason said, still bewildered.

"Yeah, and I think you might have a concussion."

"A what?"

"A concussion," Robert repeated.

"It hurts," Mason said.

"Hold on while I find my bag," Robert said.

He found it between his feet and rummaged through the contents. Not for the first time, he was grateful he carried the thing with him wherever he went. While most people thought he was paranoid, he believed in being prepared.

At the bottom, he found a small towel. After folding it into a thick wad, he pressed it to the gash on Mason's head. "Hold this, and lie back. No sudden moves, got it?"

"Got it," Mason repeated, pressing the cloth to the wound.

At that moment, Clare shot upright with a gasp. "What's happening? Mason? Robert?"

"We crashed, but we're okay for the moment," Robert said in soothing tones. "Are you hurt?"

Clare thought about it before shaking her head. "I'm fine.

What about Mason?"

"He's got a gash on his head," Robert replied. "And I think he might have a concussion."

"Don't you have a first-aid kit?" Clare asked with a worried frown.

"There's a trauma jump kit in the back," Robert said.

"I'll get it," Clare said, her body tensed for action.

"Hold up. It's too dangerous out there. We're drawing attention," Robert said. He pointed to his window. Already, a few zombies clawed at the truck's body with eager moans. "Besides, your brother's okay for now. I think our best option is to head straight to the station. He can get the care he needs there."

"Are you sure?" Clare asked. She pointed at Oliver, her expression pinched. "What about him?"

"I'll take care of him," Robert said, his heart heavy with sorrow. He reached for his helmet, removing it from the bracket. After checking that his gear was in place, he picked up his fire ax and hefted it with one hand.

"What are you doing?" Clare asked.

"I'm going to jump out, and I'm taking Oliver with me. As soon as I'm out, I need you to move Mason over," Robert explained. "I'll run around and take his place. The sooner we get to the station, the better."

"What about the zombies?" Clare asked.

"I can handle them, and my gear protects me," Robert answered with cool confidence. "Are you ready?"

Clare nodded. "I'm ready."

Robert reached for the door but froze when hoarse screams filled the air. "What the hell?"

He craned his neck to look for the source of the sounds. To

his horror, he saw that the infected had found a new victim, the driver of the other car. They crawled across the hood, ripping the man to pieces in front of his disbelieving eyes.

"I think I'm going to be sick," Clare mumbled over his shoulder, her face the color of bleached bone. "Can't we help him?"

"I'm afraid not," Robert said. His next thought caused him to cringe with shame, but it was the truth. With the zombies distracted by their new meal, he had a small window of opportunity. *I'd better make the most of it.*

Robert shoved the door open and jumped out. Reaching into the footwell, he grabbed Oliver and heaved the boy onto the pavement. It went against everything he stood for to dump the child like he was nothing but trash, but there was no choice. It had to be done. "I'm sorry, Oliver. I really am."

He turned away, but a new set of screams caused the hair on the back of his neck to rise. *Please, no. Not another victim.*

Robert looked at the crashed car where the zombies still tore at the driver's flesh. Inside the vehicle, a woman tugged at her seatbelt. She appeared to be stuck, and her expression was panicked. One of the infected had already noticed her plight and was attempting to crawl through the smashed windscreen. Luckily, the corpse of the driver hampered its efforts. The woman still stood a chance, but only if she had help.

Indecision paralyzed Robert for a brief moment, but not for long. Saving people was his job. More than that, it was his calling. He jumped over Oliver's corpse and charged toward the car with his ax raised to strike. "Hold on. I'm coming!"

The woman saw him, and relief flooded her features. "Help! Please help me. My baby…"

The shock caused Robert to falter. *Baby? There's a baby too?*

85

The knowledge caused a rush of adrenalin to spurt through his veins, and he sprinted forward with renewed determination. He couldn't let the infected win this round. Not again. They'd already taken too much from him that day. He and everyone else he knew. *This time, it's my turn.*

Chapter 12 - Susan

Susan dashed across the intersection in a low crouch. She dropped down behind a mailbox and took a peek around the side. At the far end of the street, a bunch of infected milled about. They blocked the way to the station, and she had to figure out how to get around them without being spotted.

For several moments, she studied them with morbid fascination, cataloging their strengths and weaknesses. It felt important, and an old saying came to mind: Know thy enemy.

The zombies were on the prowl, looking for fresh victims. Their movements were stiff and jerky, and they lacked coordination, but they could run surprisingly fast. They were not very smart, though, and easily distracted by noise—a fact she could use to her advantage.

But, their sense of smell was acute. They sniffed the air, lifting their heads to catch the scent of their prey. Luckily, she was downwind, and they couldn't smell her where she hid. The same could not be said of their eyesight. They kept tripping and falling over everything, including their own feet. It made sense when one looked at their bloodshot eyes. Excessive bleeding probably caused damage to the optic nerves. Irreversible damage.

A snort nearly exploded from her lips, and she stifled it with a grimace. *Irreversible damage indeed. They're dead!*

The minutes ticked by while Susan planned her next move. Getting past the infected wouldn't be easy. Still, she was determined to do it and assessed the terrain with a keen eye. Across the street, a long line of stationary cars were parked along the curb. She could use them as cover right up to the mob of zombies. After that, she didn't have a clue but decided to tackle that problem when she got to it.

Taking a deep breath, Susan dashed across the street and hid behind the first car. Her heart raced in her chest, and her stomach churned. The thought of being seen filled her mind with terror, and she tried not to envision what would happen if she was caught. *Keep it together. You're almost there.*

After a quick look around, Susan scurried toward the next vehicle and the next. When she reached the last car in the line, she stopped. With her back pressed to the door, she searched for a way forward.

Her heart sank.

There was no more cover in sight. No vehicles, no mailboxes, no trash cans. Nothing but an open road. *Shit, what now?*

The infected were horrifyingly close. She could hear their shuffling feet scraping across the tar. Now and then, one of them would groan plaintively. They sounded almost sad, but that did not fool her. It was hunger, plain and simple.

With her fire ax clutched to her chest, Susan tried to think of a plan. But her mind came up blank, and she couldn't seem to focus. It was an impossible situation, made worse because salvation lay so close at hand. The station was only half a block away, but it might as well have been miles.

Suddenly, she saw movement in the corner of her eye. A

couple of zombies had drifted toward the car, and they were coming around the corner. She was seconds away from being discovered. *Oh, crap.*

Susan dropped to the ground and rolled underneath the vehicle with not a moment to spare. A pair of dirty feet rounded the front of the car and shuffled toward the spot she'd occupied seconds before. There they paused, joined by a second set dressed in expensive Italian loafers.

She waited and waited, but neither zombie seemed inclined to move on. Finally, Susan realized she'd have to do something or risk being found and torn to pieces. She removed the cell phone from her pocket and switched it on with care.

The screen came to life, and she blinked back a tear. Her son looked back at her, a cheerful grin fixed on his face. He was like that, always smiling and happy. An optimist. It was the thing she loved most about him.

With deep regret, she pressed her lips to the screen. *Goodbye, Noah. I hope you survive, and I pray I get to see you one more time before I die. If not, live. Live for me, my son.*

Before she could change her mind, Susan set her speaker to full volume and set the alarm. She counted down the seconds, her heart in her throat. A second before it went off, she tossed the phone into the street. It skittered across the tar and settled close to the middle of the road. The alarm blared, a noxious melody meant to wake the dead.

Susan grinned. *Pun intended, suckers!*

A mad scramble ensued as the infected honed in on the tinny sound. They congregated around the phone and swiped at it with their hands. The two zombies next to her car joined in, and the way forward became clear. *Now!*

Susan crawled out of her hidey-hole and shot to her feet.

Drawing on her last reserves, she sprinted toward the station. Her feet pounded the pavement, and her breath sawed in and out of her lungs.

Behind her, a cry went up as the infected noticed her flight. They set off in full pursuit, and she had to push even harder to stay ahead. A stitch took up residence behind her ribs, and she pressed one hand to her side. Gritting her teeth against the stabbing pain, she pushed forward. *Come on, come on. Faster!*

Susan dodged around a car wreck and jumped over an abandoned suitcase on the pavement. Each obstacle slowed her down, and her desperation grew with every step. A glance revealed that the zombies had gained on her.

They numbered at least twenty or more, and their howls cut through the air. Like a pack of wolves, they hunted her down. All it would take was one misstep, one mistake. If she fell, it was all over, and she'd be ripped to pieces within seconds.

The station loomed ahead, bright lights flooding from the windows on the upper floor. It beckoned to her with its promise of safety, and she renewed her efforts. Ten yards, twenty yards, thirty, forty, fifty.

At top speed, Susan slid to a stop in front of the entrance. She yanked at the handle, but it was locked, and the windows were shuttered. Nothing moved within, and she hoped it wasn't abandoned.

With both fists, Susan banged on the door and shouted. "Open up. It's me, Susan." When no one answered, she tried again. "Theresa, please. It's Susan."

The zombies had halved the distance between her and them, and she knew she had precious moments left to live. She pummeled the door with all of her strength, splitting the skin on her knuckles. Blood flowed from the wounds and trickled down her wrists, but she didn't care. "Please, somebody!"

A sob bubbled up her throat, and her voice grew hoarse with her screams. "Open up, damn it!"

The mob of infected were only a few yards away now, and she had a choice to make. Run or fight. Both options meant death. She was too tired to run much farther, and there were too many for her to kill. With a shake of her head, she acknowledged the inevitable. *It's over.*

Steeling herself against the horror to come, Susan turned to face her attackers. She raised her fire ax with trembling hands and said, "Come on you undead horrors. I'll take a few of you with me, at least."

The infected drew closer and closer. So close she could stare into their bloodshot eyes. Baring her teeth, she prepared to strike.

The door behind her opened. Before Susan could blink, a pair of hands yanked her inside. Darkness fell across her vision as the door slammed shut again, and the rattle of chains sounded as a lock clicked in place. Someone dragged something heavy across the floor, blocking the entrance.

"What the—" Susan cried. "Theresa?"

"Sh, it's me. Back away," Theresa whispered.

"Oh, thank God," Susan said, slumping with relief.

"It's okay. Come with me," Theresa said in a soothing voice.

Susan allowed her to lead away, glad to leave the outside world and its monsters behind. The zombies howled with frustrated hunger and hammered the door, but the entrance was secure, and she knew she was safe. For the moment, at least.

Chapter 13 - Robert

Joe, the zombie, kneeled on the hood of the car, enjoying the feast before him. The man's garbled pleas for help fell on deaf ears. Neither Joe nor the other zombies cared. Even if they wanted to, it wasn't possible. The virus that animated their dead brains had shut off the parts that controlled emotions, memories, thought, and reason. Everything that made them human.

He stuffed another morsel into his mouth, and a sensation of relief washed across his being. The feverish hunger that plagued his existence abated for a brief moment.

It didn't last.

It never did.

His victim's struggles faded, his injuries too great to sustain life any longer. The impact with the windshield had caused his brain to hemorrhage. The glass had sliced into his abdomen, and the three zombies on the hood had stripped his flesh to the bone. With a sigh, he blew out his last breath.

Joe grunted. Death didn't excite him. It was life he wanted. Screams from within the car drew his attention, and he spied the woman inside the metal box. She writhed in her seat, and her movements drew him like a moth to a flame. There was the living, breathing flesh he craved.

He crawled toward the hole in the windshield, slipping in the driver's blood. When another zombie got there ahead of him, he yanked it back with a vicious snarl. The woman belonged to him.

With a single-minded purpose, he pushed through the hole. The razor-sharp glass cut into his hands and face. It peeled the skin back from his cheeks, revealing the bones underneath. The woman's cries grew hoarse with terror, and she tugged at the belt that held her in place. Joe's movements sped up in anticipation of the kill to come. She was his, and there was no escape.

***

Robert ran toward the crashed car with his ax held, ready to strike. His booted feet thudded on the pavement, but the zombies took no notice. They were too focused on their next meal, the woman trapped inside the vehicle. She screamed with terror, and her frantic struggles increased tenfold. "Help me! Please!"

"I'm coming," Robert yelled.

He reached the crumpled car and honed in on the nearest infected. With a short, chopping blow, he cleaved through its skull. The blade cut into the brain like a hot knife through butter. Clotted blood and brain matter spewed from the grievous wound and spilled across the infected's collar. His shirt had been white once, part of a business suit. Now it was the same color as his tie. Crimson.

Without pause, Robert wrenched his weapon free and turned toward the next zombie. It twisted around and snarled at him with bared teeth.

"Come on then," Robert said, taunting the creature.

With a vicious growl, it launched itself off the hood and straight at Robert. Its hooked fingers reached for him, ready to latch onto anything it could grab.

Robert watched the thing close the distance with a shrewd

gaze. At the last possible moment, he stepped aside. The infected missed him by a couple of inches and crashed to the pavement. It rolled across the ground with an enraged howl, landing face-down in the dirt.

He stepped on the zombie's back and pinned it to the ground. It struggled against his weight but to no avail. With a wild yell, he ended its undead life with a swift blow from the ax. It stilled, its muscles slackening into the true death.

"Help me, please," the woman cried again.

Robert looked up, and he blanched. *Oh, no!*

The third and final zombie was nearly through the hole. It slithered toward the defenseless woman like a poisonous serpent. The creature looked grotesque. A horrid beast summoned from the pits of hell.

Its skin had peeled away from its flesh like a ripe melon, and the quivering muscles were laid bare. The left cheek was cut to the ear, exposing the teeth in a mocking grin. Drool spilled from its lips in a silver stream to mingle with the blood from its last meal.

"Hold on," Robert cried, sprinting toward the door. He reached for the handle, but the woman shook her head. "Not me. My baby. Help my baby first."

"But…" Robert said with hesitation. The zombie was almost upon the woman. Another wriggle or two, and it would have her.

"Please," the woman begged. "Save Sebastian."

Their eyes met for a brief moment. Hers was a deep forest green, earnest and clear. She knew what she was asking, and she was willing to take the risk.

"He's all I have left," she added, her gaze traveling to the corpse of her husband.

"Alright," Robert conceded.

He whirled to the back of the car and yanked open the door. His gaze roved across the backseat, looking for a baby's car seat. There was nothing except a plastic box wedged inside the footwell. Strange sounds emitted from within, a mixture of yowls and hisses. "What the hell?"

He picked up the box but nearly dropped it when a claw swiped at him through the bars. "A cat? Sebastian's a cat?"

"Could you hurry up?" the woman cried. She had one foot planted on the zombie's shoulder and the other on its face, holding it at bay. "I can't keep this up forever."

With a muttered curse, Robert pulled the cat carrier out of the car. He placed it on the ground before opening the passenger side. "Try to hold still."

"Um, that's impossible at the moment," she said in a shrill voice, battling with the infected.

The zombie grabbed one of her feet and chewed on the boot with ghoulish delight. When it realized it was eating rubber, it abandoned her shoe and lunged for her calf. The woman screamed and threw herself back, straining against the seatbelt. The infected got a mouthful of her jeans and ground on the tough fabric, hungry for the fresh meat beneath the tough exterior. "Get it off! Get it off!"

"Give me a second," Robert cried, sweat beading his forehead.

"I don't have one. Hurry the hell up."

Robert sawed at the seatbelt with the blade of his ax. It wasn't easy, and the rough material resisted his efforts. Finally, he made it halfway through. With short chopping blows, he severed the rest. "Yes!"

The woman tumbled into his arms, and he yanked her from

the wreckage. She flopped to the ground with an undignified yelp before scrambling to her feet. "Sebastian!"

Robert paid her no head, occupied with the infected in the car. It crawled across the seat, gnashing at the air. Its relentless drive was terrifying.

With a grunt, Robert swiped at the creature's head with his weapon, but the angle made it hard to land a solid blow. The blade glanced off the zombie's head, shearing off a piece of the scalp. He tried again with zero results.

The zombie kept coming.

"Oh, for goodness' sake," the woman said, popping up at his side.

She gripped the carrier's handle in one hand and shoved Robert aside with her shoulder. Before he could protest, she slammed the door shut. It smashed into the infected's face, sealing it inside the car.

"Come on," she said, running toward the firetruck. "There are more of those things coming our way."

Robert cast a bemused look at the infected trapped inside the vehicle. A couple of its front teeth had broken when the car door smashed into its face. It howled with frustrated rage, its gap-toothed grin granting it a comical look.

More infected answered its cries. They appeared from every shadowed corner and flooded the street by the dozens. Their feet pounded on the pavement, headed straight for him.

"Oh, shit." Robert dashed toward the truck.

The strange woman was there before him. She shoved the carrier inside and climbed into the cab. Her face was pale but determined, and she waved at him with fierce gestures. "Move it!"

Robert jumped into the driver's side with seconds to spare.

Within moments, the truck was surrounded, and the sound of beating fists filled the interior. Angry faces filled the windows, and a couple climbed onto the hood.

Clare gripped his arm. "Get us out of here. Now."

"With pleasure," Robert replied.

He turned the key in the ignition, praying the engine would start. It rumbled to life, and he jammed it into reverse. He freed the truck from the wreckage with a screech of metal on metal and shot down the road.

Infected went flying as he crashed through the mob. Several zombies landed under the wheels, and the vehicle shook as it crunched over their bodies. At last, they were free, and he set a course for the station.

As the mob faded into the distance, he glanced at the woman. "What's your name?"

"Andrea," she replied. "Andrea Beatrice Reed."

"Well, Andrea. Maybe next time, you'll think twice before asking me to risk my life for a stupid cat." Anger filled him at the thought of the close call he'd had. *I could've died back there, damn it.*

Andrea lifted her chin, and her cheeks flushed with fiery blood. "Sebastian's life is worth just as much as mine or yours."

"Don't be ridiculous. We almost became zombie chow back there because of that creature," Robert said. "You lied to me. You said it was your baby."

"And I'd do it all over again in a heartbeat," Andrea said, much to his chagrin. "Besides, I didn't lie. Sebastian is my child. He's part of my family."

Robert snorted. *Crazy cat lady!*

He glanced at the animal in question. It was a Maine Coone. Tufts of hair sprang from the tips of its ears, and its striped gray fur was thick and long. It was a handsome creature, but at that moment, nothing more than an annoyance. "Just be glad I don't toss you and your damn cat onto the curb."

"Don't you dare touch Sebastian," Andrea warned, her eyes narrowed to slits.

Before Robert could answer, Clare cleared her throat. "This is not the time to argue. Mason needs medical care, and Paisley just lost a brother. Pipe down, both of you."

Robert reigned in his temper, realizing he was lashing out at an innocent woman. *She must be scared out of her mind, and I'm making it worse.* "I'm sorry."

Andrea gave a tight nod. "I apologize as well. It's been a trying day, both for Sebastian and me."

"I think it's safe to say none of us will ever be the same after this," Clare said.

"No, we won't," Robert said. He glanced at Paisley's grief-stricken face and Mason's pained grimace. "Hold on. We'll be at the station soon. It's not far."

"Thank God for that," Clare said, turning back to her charges.

As the scenery flashed past his window, Robert reflected on everything that had happened. Nothing had gone as expected, and he wondered what more the night had in store for them. Only time would tell.

Chapter 14 - Rick

Rick could do little but grit his teeth against the pain on the way back to the station. The truck hit an obstacle, and he yelped when his amputated fingers bumped against the side. "Shit, that hurts."

"I'm sure it does," Ellen replied with a hint of acid in her voice. She waved her hand at the first-aid kit next to her. "I can give you something for the pain."

"I know, and as I've already said, I don't want it," Rick replied. He wiped one hand across his brow, not surprised to find it covered in a film of cold sweat.

"You're a jackass," Ellen said, folding her arms across her chest.

"No, I'm not."

"Yes, you are," she insisted.

"Fine, I admit it," he conceded.

"So take the damn medicine," she cried.

"Okay, but not the heavy stuff. I want to be in my right mind in case something happens," Rick said.

"You wouldn't be much use with your hand like that anyway," Ellen reasoned. She jabbed a shot into his upper arm and watched him closely. "That's better, right?"

"Much better," Rick said as the searing pain in his stumps

faded. He still wasn't happy, though, and showed her his sternest frown.

She ignored it and him, fussing over his bandages. He wasn't surprised. Ellen never listened to anyone but herself. It was one of the things he liked about her. Like. It was such a tepid word. Not at all the way he felt about her.

Rick shook his head, convinced the meds were making him loopy. He'd long since resigned himself to squashing his feelings. She'd made it clear she viewed him as a friend only. Maybe even an older brother. He didn't know which was worse.

"Are you okay?" she asked, her face hovering inches above his.

He swallowed, his mouth suddenly dry. "I'm fine."

She smiled, and he watched as the corners of her eyes creased. She had a dimple on one cheek, and he itched to caress it. Maybe… maybe she wouldn't mind. Not with the way she was looking at him now. "Ellen?"

"Yes?" she asked, leaning closer.

The air between them sparked, and he went in for the kiss. Suddenly, the truck swerved to the side. A loud thump sounded from the front, followed by another two along the side. The wheels drove over something, or several somethings, probably zombies.

Rick rolled to the side and reached out to brace himself with his injured hand. Big mistake. A stab of pure agony shot through his nervous system, and he swore.

"I'm sorry!" Ellen cried, grabbing him by the shoulders. She steadied him until the truck smoothed out, a worried frown on her forehead.

"It's not your fault," Rick said through gritted teeth once the worst of the pain subsided.

"Try to rest, okay?" she said, covering him with a blanket.

"Alright," Rick said, leaning back. Now was not the time to tell Ellen how he felt. He had other concerns, such as missing two fingers and becoming a zombie. Possibly.

Wouldn't that be the worst? To become a flesh-eating monster after all the things he'd overcome in his life: A deadbeat dad, a depressed mother, poverty, the struggle to put himself through school and the academy.

"Don't do that," Ellen chided.

"Do what?"

"Overthink things," she replied.

"I'm not."

"Yes, you are. Sometimes, things happen, and there's nothing you can do to change it," she said.

"Maybe, but I don't believe in fate. I believe in these," he said, raising his two hands.

"Then believe in it now," she said. "You'll be fine. You're not turning into a zombie. I promise."

"Pinky swear?" he said with a grin, holding up the hand with the missing fingers.

"Glad to see your sense of humor is still intact," she said with a low chuckle.

"Of course. It's the end of the world. When will there ever be a better time to joke about shit?" Rick said. It made him happy to make her smile, but his words had the opposite effect than he intended.

Instead, she shivered. "Do you really think so?"

"Think what?"

"That it's the end of the world?" She looked through the window to the outside world.

He followed her gaze and had to admit it looked pretty grim. Flames licked at the sky, casting the city in a lurid orange glow. Shadowy figures raced through the street, screeching and howling, while innocents screamed for mercy. The town was dying, and there was little they could do about it.

"Come here," Rick said, waving at Ellen with his uninjured hand. She moved to his side, and he pulled her close. While he couldn't help the city, he could comfort her. "It's going to be alright. You'll see. It's not the end. It's just the beginning of something new."

"Something new? Like what?" she asked, her voice small.

"That we'll have to wait and see, but whatever comes, we'll face it together," he said, squeezing her tight. "Deal?"

Ellen nodded. "Deal."

She snuggled close to him, and silence fell as the truck made its way to the station. There was no need for words, after all. Not when they had each other.

Chapter 15 - Robert

Robert drove toward the station, his entire focus on the road ahead. They couldn't afford another mishap, and he needed to get them all to safety. Thankfully, it wasn't far, and he reckoned they'd get there in about twenty minutes.

His mind traveled back over the past few hours. It was hard to believe so much had happened in such a short time. The dead walked the streets, feeding on the living. Those who survived the initial attacks had to navigate a city in ruins, an unrecognizable place. Everywhere he looked, chaos met his eyes.

An abandoned police barricade blocked one of the main roads. The officers were nowhere in sight, but there was blood aplenty to give evidence to their fate. A car had driven through the front of a shop, and shards of glass glittered in the light like diamonds.

Rioters poured from the entrance of an electronics business, carrying flat-screen TVs and other useless equipment. Several more looted the inside of a stranded ambulance, running off with drugs and IV bags. Random shots rang through the air, and a stray bullet clipped the fender of the fire truck.

It was shocking how fast humanity descended into anarchy, though Robert knew he shouldn't be surprised. History proved that disasters often brought out the worst in people.

Fire exploded through the windows of an office block, and he thought of his wife, Amelia. He had to believe that she was still alive and well. To think otherwise was to invite insanity. Thirty-two years. That's how long they'd been together, having met when he was only twenty-three. A lifetime ago.

After a few miles, Robert dared a quick look at the other occupants inside the truck. As much as he wanted to rescue Amelia, he was still responsible for their lives. Abandoning them was inconceivable.

Paisley had stopped crying, but she stared into the distance like a robot. Her silence bothered him more than her earlier hysterics, and he hoped she wouldn't suffer from permanent psychological damage. Not that he could blame her if she did.

Andrea was quiet as well. She looked out the window with Sebastian's carrier clutched on her lap. Her lips were compressed, and her eyes glittered. For a moment, his heart went out to her. She'd also lost someone that day. Someone close to her.

Finally, he studied Mason and Clare. Mason sat hunched in a corner with the towel pressed to his head wound. It bled profusely, typical of a cut on the scalp, and his face was pale.

Clare fussed over him, her brows furrowed with concern. "How much further?"

"We're almost there," Robert replied.

"You said that five minutes ago," she replied, her voice tart.

He eyed her in the rearview mirror. "It'll be okay, Clare. I promise."

She sighed. "I'm sorry. I'm just worried about my brother."

"I know. This is one crazy situation," Robert said.

"Tell me about it," Andrea said, turning toward them.

"Where were you when this all went to hell?" Robert asked, trying to make conversation.

"At the vet," Andrea said. She stuck one finger through the bars of the carrier and cooed at her cat. "Sebastian needed his booster shots. I was on my way home when some random guy attacked me."

"What did you do?" Clare asked, clearly interested.

"I tripped him and ran as fast as I could," Andrea said. "And let me tell you, running with an eight-pound cat in a carrier is not easy."

"You were on foot?" Robert asked, perplexed.

"Yes, the veterinary practice is only two blocks from my apartment, and my car is in for a service," Andrea said.

"But you were in a car when I found you," Robert protested. "Or rather, when you crashed into us."

"Those things were chasing me, and this guy cut them off and told me to get in," Andrea said. "We probably wouldn't have made it if it wasn't for his help."

"So, that wasn't your husband back there?" Robert asked.

"No," Andrea said.

"Huh," Robert said with rising irritation. He'd managed to push aside his dislike for her when he thought she'd lost someone dear. Now, that dislike returned in full force. It wasn't rational or even her fault, but he couldn't shake the feeling.

"Does it matter?" Andrea asked, zeroing in on his emotions with laser accuracy.

"It doesn't," Robert said with a shake of his head.

"It's clearly bothering you," she mused. "Let me guess. You were feeling sorry for me before, and now you don't."

"Something like that," Robert admitted with reluctance.

"Remember one thing. I never lied to you. I never said he was my husband," Andrea said. "And I do feel sorry for what happened to him. I have a heart, you know?"

"All right, I get it," Robert said with a sigh. He didn't want to argue the point, especially when he had no foot to stand on.

At that moment, he rounded the corner and spotted the station straight ahead. The familiar structure beckoned to him, and a mixture of intense relief, joy, and weariness flooded his being. He was both happy and exhausted. *I'm just about ready to call it a night.* "We made it. We're here."

Clare leaned forward, her expression eager. "Thank God. I was beginning to think we'd never get here in one piece."

"Me neither," Robert said.

He drove toward the building, noting its shuttered appearance. The windows and doors were closed, and only a couple of lights shone from the upper floor. It looked deserted, but he knew that wasn't the case. Theresa would not have left without notifying him. *Unless... unless the infection got in somehow. Maybe they're all dead.*

Robert shook off the morbid thought. It wasn't true. It couldn't be. It was just a figment of his overactive imagination. *Everything will be okay.*

He stopped the fire truck in front of the big rolling doors that led to the parking bay. A cautious look up and down the street showed him it was quiet for the moment, but he knew it wouldn't last. *We'd better hurry.*

He reached for the radio. "Theresa, are you there? Over."

When nothing happened, he tried again. This time, his voice was tinged with desperation. "Theresa, it's Robert. Please, come in. Over."

Static crackled on the line, and a voice came on. "Robert? Where are you? Over."

"In front of the station," Robert answered. "I need you to open up for us. Over."

"Are you alone? Over."

"No, I have Clare, Mason, and two others with me. Over."

"Have any of you been bitten?" Theresa asked. "Over."

"Oliver, the little boy, was infected, but he… I took care of it. Over," Robert said, swallowing the sudden lump in his throat.

"Are you one hundred percent sure none of you are infected?" Theresa said. "I can't let you in if that's the case. Over."

"I understand, and we're not infected," Robert said. "Over."

"How about the area around the doors? Is it clear? Over."

Robert looked up and down the road once more. It was dark, and he struggled to make anything out in the gloom. The only light came from the moon overhead and a couple of street lamps." Clare, Andrea. Do you see anything?"

"No," Andrea said with a brief shake of her head.

"Me neither," Clare added.

"Are you sure? Nothing is lurking in the shadows?"

"Not that I can see," Clare said. "And my eyesight is pretty good."

"Alright. Thanks." Robert raised the radio to his lips. "Theresa, it's clear for now, but you'd better hurry up. Over."

"Stand by. Out," Theresa said.

The metal door in front of the truck began to open, and bright light chased the darkness away. The heavy metal sheet lifted slowly. Too slowly for his liking. He kept looking around, expecting a mob of zombies to appear at any moment. His heartbeat sped up, and sweat beaded his forehead. *Please,*

please, please. I don't think I can handle any more surprises tonight.

Four people dressed in full gear and carrying axes ducked through the opening. They ran out into the open, surveying the area. When nothing happened, they waved at Robert to proceed. He took a deep breath and gripped the wheel with both hands. The engine ran without a hitch, and he eased the truck into the open bay.

Theresa awaited him inside, with a clipboard clutched to her chest like a weapon. Her gray hair was pulled back into a severe knot that complimented her steely eyes. She ducked down and checked underneath the truck before doing a full inspection of the entire vehicle.

Finally, she rapped on the window. "Come on. What are you waiting for? Get out."

"Yes, ma'am."

Robert obeyed her summons and jumped out. One by one, he helped the others out as well until they formed a small knot of humanity. They looked a little lost, and his heart went out to them. Clare supported her injured brother while Paisley looked haunted, and Andrea clung to her cat.

None of that mattered, however. They were safe. Safe and uninfected. A sense of elation replaced the despair that weighed down his shoulders, and he smiled. "We made it, guys. We're safe."

Chapter 16 - Theresa

Theresa watched as the fire truck rolled into the open bay. Once it stopped, she ducked down and checked the undercarriage before making a brief circuit around the vehicle. While some might call her paranoid, it was the end of the world, and she'd be damned if she cut corners. She'd handle the apocalypse the same way she handled everything else: With cool and calm efficiency.

Once Theresa was satisfied, she nodded at the four guards that stood by for her orders. "It's clear. Close her up."

"Yes, ma'am," the nearest replied with a quick nod.

The guards closed the bay door, and it slammed shut with a loud boom. They secured it in place with heavy locks and chains. It was a system they'd worked out earlier to ensure no infected got in. It wasn't foolproof, and she knew the plan needed work, but it would do for now.

"Anything else, ma'am?" a guard asked.

"No, thank you," Theresa said, waving them away. "We'll be right up. Make sure the coffee's hot."

"Yes, ma'am," they chorused.

She turned to Robert's window and rapped on the glass. "Come on. Get out. What are you waiting for?"

He climbed out of the vehicle, followed by the rest of his

group, and she studied them with sharp eyes. They looked tired and shell-shocked, but she ignored that fact for the moment. First, she had to make sure they posed no danger to her station.

Her station. It was strange to think of it that way, but the moment she'd heard about Captain Schmidt's death, she'd assumed the mantle of responsibility. Not because she wanted to but because she had to. Besides, she was the most qualified for the job.

"What happened to your head, Mason?" she asked.

"I hit it on the steering wheel," Mason replied.

"You had an accident?"

"We did. A head-on collision."

Theresa eyed the fire truck, relieved to see there was very little damage to the front. Obviously, the other party took the brunt of the blow. "You can tell me about it later."

"Theresa, what—" Robert began.

"Not now, Robert. We can talk after you and the rest of your group pass your inspections," Theresa said.

"Inspections?" Robert asked, his brows furrowed.

"I need to make sure you're clear of infection."

"I told you we weren't infected," Robert protested.

"I believe you, but it needs to be done nonetheless."

"But why?"

"People lie. Especially when their lives depend on it."

"I'd never lie about something like that," Robert said.

Theresa sighed. "This isn't about you, Robert, but about all of us."

"What do you mean?"

"Every time one of us goes out, we will have to pass inspection and decontamination upon return. It makes sense and will ensure the infection doesn't hitch a ride inside," Theresa explained. "The last thing we need is an outbreak within these walls."

"But…"

"There will be no exceptions, Robert. If I start bending the rules for you, I'll have to do it for everyone else as well," Theresa said. "Do you understand?"

After a few seconds, Robert nodded. "I understand."

"Follow me," Theresa said, waving at the group.

They trailed after her to a far corner of the parking bay. A white linen curtain cordoned off one section of the room. Next to it stood a wooden table and a couple of chairs.

"What's that?" Robert asked.

Theresa halted in her tracks and turned around. "This is where I'll check you for infection. Who's first?"

A strange woman carrying a cat in a carrier stepped forward. "I'll go first. I'm not afraid."

"Good. Step inside, and I'll be right in," Theresa said with an approving nod.

"What about Sebastian?" the woman asked.

"The cat?" Theresa asked. "Just put him down over there. No one will harm him."

"Thank you."

Theresa waited a few minutes before she stepped into the cubicle and quickly checked the strange woman for injuries. Afterward, she jotted down the woman's details on her clipboard: Andrea. Mid-thirties. She appears fit and healthy—frame of mind - unknown.

"Thank you for your cooperation," Theresa said, pointing to a second cubicle equipped with wipes, sanitizer, and a couple of bins. "Please clean your hands with the sanitizer."

"Alright," Andrea said.

"Did you get any blood or bodily fluids on you?" Theresa asked.

"I kicked a zombie in the face."

"Then you should take your shoes off and clean them," Theresa said, pointing at the wipes.

Andrea wiped and sprayed her shoes, then checked her clothes for good measure. Once she was done, she said, "I'm clean."

"Thanks," Theresa said. "Who wants to go next?"

"I'll go, but can Paisley come with me?" Clare asked. "She's terrified."

"Of course," Theresa said.

After a quick examination, they sanitized and checked their clothes. Paisley's shirt had some of Oliver's blood on it, and it went into the bin. Theresa gave the child a spare t-shirt of hers to wear. It was too big, so they knotted it around her waist, but it was better than nothing.

"Right. Robert and Mason, you're up," Theresa said.

"Do we really need to do this?" Robert said. "Mason's injured, and he needs medical care."

"All the more reason to make sure he's not been bitten," Theresa said. "And dump your contaminated gear and weapons into those bins when you sanitize."

"Fine," Robert said with a grumble.

While Theresa understood how Robert felt, how they all felt, she was not willing to compromise. Down that road lay disaster, and nothing good could come from it. Now was not the time to give in to emotion and sentiment. What mattered was the numbers. Numbers never lied.

Five people. Four adults and one child.

That meant five beds, five lockers, and five extra mouths to feed, not including the cat. Tucking the radio into her belt, she made a few notations on her clipboard. Already, there was a long list of things to be done and supplies to be procured, and it would only grow as the hours passed. Her brain ran through the many variables and calculations on autopilot, assessing the ever-changing situation.

Once Robert and Mason were done, she patched up the wound on Mason's head. After a quick check-up, she said, "He looks okay. It doesn't seem like he has a concussion."

"Are you sure?" Clare asked, her tone anxious.

"I can't be a hundred percent sure. It would be best to keep an eye on him," Theresa said.

"I'm fine," Mason said, swatting at Clare, who hovered above him. "Look after Paisley. She needs you more than I do."

"Is she all right?" Theresa asked, eyeing the little girl. "She's very quiet."

"She's not okay," Clare replied, taking Paisley's hand. "But she will be in time. Won't you, my sweet?"

Paisley said nothing, her eyes huge.

"Are you guys hungry?" Theresa asked, changing the subject.

Immediately, the group's glum expressions lightened up, and she smothered an inward smile. People were predictable, and managing them was easy if you catered to their needs. Food, water, shelter, and a little bit of attention. The belief that they were needed and part of a whole, even if it was just an illusion. "Right this way."

The kitchen was crowded with people. The four guards had removed their helmets and sat at the table drinking coffee. There was candidate Timothy, the newest member of the crew. Next to him sat Ruby. A seasoned firefighter, she'd been off-

113

duty but made her way to the station the moment the infection hit the town. With her, she'd brought Elijah, her husband, and Benjamin, a next-door neighbor.

Theresa was glad for their presence. Without them, ensuring the safety of the station would've been a lot harder. When the crisis hit, she'd been alone except for Timothy, Ellen, and Rick. Ruby, Elijah, and Benjamin's arrival had been a blessing.

The last person at the table was a recent addition: Susan. She'd recovered from her dangerous trip through the zombie-infested streets and relaxed in a chair with a mug of coffee clasped in her hands.

The moment Robert and Mason spotted Susan, they rushed over with glad cries. The three embraced, and Theresa took the opportunity to pour coffee for everyone except Paisley. For the little girl, she scrounged up a juice box instead.

Once the reunion was over, she introduced everyone to each other and gestured to the table. "Have a seat, folks. I'll rustle up a quick dinner while you all get acquainted."

"Thank you, Theresa," Robert said, dropping into the nearest chair. "It's been a long day."

"Indeed, it has," Mason said, rubbing his forehead.

"Does it hurt?" Clare asked.

"Of course, it hurts," he answered with a frown. "Now stop fussing over me."

Clare rolled her eyes and leaned back in her chair. "Whatever."

After a quick meal of ham sandwiches, Theresa made herself a cup of tea from her personal stash of Earl Grey. She vastly preferred it over coffee and sat down with a sigh of satisfaction. "Well then, let's hear all about it."

Robert frowned. "Are you sure?"

"Yes, and don't leave anything out. The more information we have, the better," Theresa said with a firm nod.

"I'll put Paisley to bed while you lot talk," Clare said, standing up. "She's exhausted, and she doesn't need any more information."

"I'm sorry. I should have thought of that," Theresa said with a touch of dismay. "Down the hall, the first door on the left. I'm afraid we'll have to share. There are only two dorm rooms available, each equipped with bunk beds. The first one is for us ladies, the second for the men."

"That's fine with me," Clare said, leading Paisley away by the hand. "Come on, sweetie. Time for bed."

"Can I be excused, as well?" Andrea asked, standing up. "I don't have much to add to the conversation, and Sebastian needs attention. Do you have something for him to eat? And a couple of bowls for food and water? Maybe something I can use as a litter box?"

"Actually, the station had a resident cat until recently," Theresa said. "We had to put him down, the poor thing. Cancer."

"I'm sorry to hear that," Andrea said, shaking her head. "What was his name?"

"Pumba."

"Pumba?" Andrea asked with a chuckle.

"Yes, he was rather fat. My fault, I'm afraid. I suppose I spoiled him," Theresa said, her expression softening at the fond memory. "But I kept his things just in case. There's dried food, a couple of cans, food bowls, and a litter box in that cupboard over there. I'm not sure about litter. If there's none, you can use the newspapers in the meeting room. It's not ideal, but we can get proper supplies later on."

115

"Thank you," Andrea said, taking what she needed from the cupboard. Before she left, she paused. "You don't have to worry about Sebastian. He's well-behaved, and he won't be a bother."

"Let's hope not," Robert said, glowering at the cat in question.

"I'm sure it will be fine, Andrea. If you want, you can sleep in the office. There's a couch inside, and you can shut the door. I understand Sebastian might need to acclimatize to his new surroundings first."

"That would be wonderful, thank you," Andrea said with a faint smile.

After she left, Robert looked at Theresa. "Why are you so nice to her and that damned cat?"

"Because that cat is all she has, and Andrea might prove to be a useful member of our community in the days to come," Theresa said. "Besides, I like cats."

"Community? You talk like we're all there is. Like the city is doomed," Robert said.

"Isn't it?" she asked. "You've seen what's happening out there. The infection, the fires, the traffic, and the death."

"We've all seen it," Robert said.

"That is not the worst, however. The worst is the lack of response from the government and emergency services," Theresa said. "That is what tells me this isn't temporary. We are looking at years of recovery."

Silence fell across the table, grim and thick. The truth of her words was both undeniable and depressing.

"Where were we?" Theresa asked, determined to keep the group's spirits up.

There was much to be done and little time to do it. Moping

about wouldn't help anyone, least of all the people at the station.

"It's a long story," Robert said, dragging a tired hand across his face.

"Start at the beginning," Theresa said. Before he could continue, however, the radio at her waist crackled, and she grabbed it.

"Theresa, are you there? Over."

"I'm here. Who is this? Over?" Theresa replied.

"It's George. Over."

"George? He's alive?" Robert exclaimed, jerking upright in his chair.

"Where are you, George? Over," Theresa asked.

"We're coming in hot and heavy. Be ready to open up for us. Over," George replied, his voice strained.

"We? Who's we? Over," Theresa said.

"Ellen and Rick plus a woman named Bobbi. Over," George explained.

"Are any of you hurt or infected? Over."

"Rick got bitten, but we cut it off. Over," George said.

"You cut it off? What do you mean? Over," Theresa cried, shocked by the statement.

"I'll explain later, but you need to get ready. We're right around the corner, and there's a bunch of zombies on our tail. Over."

"We'll be ready. Out," Theresa said, jumping up. At the same time, she looked at Ruby, Timothy, Elijah, and Benjamin. "Get ready for a fight, guys."

"What about us?" Robert asked, glancing at Mason and Susan. "We can help."

"Stay here, and hold the stairs if any infected get past us,"

Theresa said with grim determination. "You're the last line of defense."

"All right," Robert said, and Mason nodded his agreement.

A mad scramble ensued as Ruby, Elijah, and Benjamin grabbed their helmets and fire axes. They rushed down the stairs with Theresa hot on their heels and paused inside the parking bay. In the distance, they could hear the roar of the fire truck drawing closer. In its wake came the howls of the infected.

Determined to do her share, Theresa laid down her clipboard and picked up an ax. This time, it wouldn't be as easy as it was with Robert's arrival. This time, they'd have to fight for their survival.

Chapter 17 - Robert

"Mason, warn Andrea and Clare. Tell them to lock their doors and open for nothing and no one but us," Robert said.

"Will do," Mason said, rushing down the hall.

Robert exchanged a grim look with Susan. "Are you ready for this?"

"Are you?" she asked with a crooked grin.

Her teeth shone like ivory against her dark skin, and her curls formed a halo around her head. She looked tough and prepared for action, and he knew she'd have his back. She always did, even in the hairiest of situations. Once, she'd pulled him out of a burning clinic after the roof nearly collapsed on top of him. He'd been lucky to escape with his life that day, and it was all thanks to her.

Mason returned moments later. "I told them."

"Good," Robert said with a curt nod.

He jammed his helmet onto his head and secured it beneath his chin. Next, he pulled on his gloves and picked up his ax. His eyes fell on the blade and the rim of dried blood that encrusted the edge. Bile rose up his throat, and he had to swallow hard to keep his nausea under control. *How many people have I killed today?*

He didn't want to know the answer to that question. With

a shake of his head, he moved toward the top of the stairs. He hefted his weapon in one hand and planted his feet in a solid stance. Nothing would get past him. Of that, he'd make certain.

Seconds later, Susan and Mason joined him, dressed in full gear and armed with their axes. A shiver ran down his spine when the howls of the infected drew closer, but he stood firm. So did Mason, despite his injury. While he might be young, he was no slouch and had plenty of courage to spare.

A hint of smugness filled Robert's mind. The zombies had the advantage of numbers, but the firefighters had each other. After weeks, months, and years of fighting disasters and risking their lives for each other, they functioned like a well-oiled machine. Nothing would get them down as a team, not even the undead.

The sound of the garage doors lifting grabbed his attention. He leaned over the railing and looked down into the parking bay. Timothy, Ruby, Elijah, and Benjamin stood in a row at the entrance, their shoulders hunched against the incoming attack.

The bright lights of the fire truck flooded the bay, and its engine idled steadily. The doors had reached chest height when the first infected slammed into the metal. The door shook, and a loud boom echoed throughout the station. More bodies rammed into the sheet of metal before the first zombie ducked underneath.

Immediately, the team below jumped into action. They hacked and slashed at the incoming infected, and corpses tumbled to the concrete floor. Clotted black blood formed puddles on the ground, and Robert held his breath as he watched his teammates fight. *Come on, come on. You can do this.*

His palms grew sweaty, and his shoulders tense while he waited. Adrenalin rushed through his veins, and he longed to throw himself into the fray. But the others held their own, and it looked like the flood of infected was slowing down. Even Theresa jumped in to help, taking down a couple of stragglers.

"They're winning," Mason said with a grin, but he sobered when the situation took a sudden turn for the worse.

An infected woman jumped onto Ruby with an unholy shriek, and they tumbled to the ground. Elijah cried out with horror, struggling to reach his wife, but a sudden surge of infected blocked the way. "Ruby!"

Benjamin launched himself at the struggling duo, and he tackled the infected woman in a flying leap. They rolled across the floor in a tangle of arms and legs. The zombie hissed and clawed at Benjamin's helmet. She managed to hook her fingers into the strap and yanked the helmet off.

Immediately, she snapped at his throat with her bared teeth, and he was hard-put to fight off her frenzied attack. With his hands pressed against her chest, Benjamin cried out, "Help me!"

Ruby scrambled to her feet but fell once more when a zombie grabbed her ankle. She hacked at the creature's head with her ax but failed to get in a solid blow. "Shit, I can't… Elijah!"

Elijah fought his way across the floor, but his progress was achingly slow. For each zombie he took down, two more took their place. "Hold on. I'm coming."

Timothy was backed into a corner, unable to help. Theresa jumped forward but danced back again when an infected rounded on her with a vicious growl. It swiped at her with meaty fists, and her ax went flying. Caught off guard, she backpedaled into the workbench behind her and grabbed her clipboard. She whacked the infected across the head with the flimsy wood, and it shattered into pieces.

Angered, the zombie tipped back its head and roared. It sprang on her, and they crashed into the bench. Theresa went down with the infected man on top of her. Tools and equipment scattered around them, adding to the chaos.

"They need help. I'm going in," Robert shouted, unable to stand still any longer.

"What about the stairs?" Susan asked, grabbing his arm.

He shook her off. "You hold the line."

"No, wait," Mason said, reaching out.

Robert ignored his pleas and took the steps two at a time. He landed next to Theresa and lifted his ax overhead. With a grunt, he brought it down onto the skull of her attacker. The blade split the bone like an overripe melon, and putrid brains spattered from the gash.

"Ugh," Theresa cried, shoving the corpse aside. She crawled to her feet and waved him away. "Help Benjamin. I'll be fine."

"I'm on my way," Robert said.

He tried to pull his ax free, but it was stuck fast. With a growl of frustration, he abandoned the weapon and grabbed a wrench instead. Whirling the heavy tool like a club, he forged through the crowd of infected.

He booted one zombie in the knee, and it snapped like kindling. A quick blow caved in its head, and he barreled through two more. They fell over like bowling pins, and he smashed their skulls with quick blows.

Benjamin still had a death grip on his attacker's shirt, keeping her teeth away from his flesh. He was clearly weakening, however, and his hoarse cries carried to Robert's ears. "Help me, please!"

"I'm almost there. Hold on," Robert replied.

"I'm trying, man, but this is one crazy-ass—"

Suddenly, a wild yell cut across the noise in the parking bay. Rick and Ellen appeared from the back of the fire truck. Ellen wielded her ax while Rick used his fists and boots. He shoved, stomped, booted, and smashed his way to Benjamin's side. Ellen followed in his wake, dispatching his victims with her blade.

Rick tossed Benjamin's attacker aside and stomped on her neck. The fragile spine snapped like a twig, and she collapsed onto the ground like a broken doll. Without pause, he helped Benjamin to his feet, and they retreated into the parking bay.

Timothy joined them after taking care of his own attacker, his face speckled with blood. He cast a look around and grinned. "Who's next?"

He needn't have bothered. The fire truck's window rolled down, and a volley of gunshots rang out. Three zombies fell to the hail of bullets, and Elijah dispatched the last remaining two. As quickly as it began, it was over, and a thick silence descended over the survivors.

During the lull, George and a strange woman exited the truck and entered the bay. Rick cradled his hand to his chest, a bloodied bandage wrapped around the limb, while Ellen hovered next to him, her cheeks pale.

Breathing hard, Robert stared at the surrounding destruction. It was hard to believe they were all still alive. Corpses littered the concrete floor, and his boots squelched through puddles of blood. Pieces of flesh and severed limbs lay strewn about. The walls were splashed with grayish-pink brain matter and other unnameable fluids. Even worse, the putrid muck coated their clothes, skins, and weapons in a layer of filth.

The sight was enough to make anyone sick, but the smell was something special. Many of the infected were ripe with decay, but even the fresh zombies added their unique stench to the mix. Voided bowls, old blood, and flayed flesh swirled together to form a unique aroma that had Robert's eyes watering.

"Holy shit, that's ripe," he muttered, swallowing hard on the vomit that threatened to exit his stomach.

"It most certainly is," Theresa said, dusting off her clothes with a business-like demeanor. She surveyed the mess with raised eyebrows. "It seems we have work to do."

"Huh?" Timothy said, picking a piece of goo from his hair. "There's more?"

"You can't expect us to leave the place like this," Theresa said in cutting tones. "Ruby, Benjamin, and Elijah, please make sure no other infected make it inside while we're busy."

"Yes, ma'am," Elijah said with a quick nod, and the three moved toward the outer edges with their weapons held ready.

Benjamin scooped up his helmet and put it back on his head with a rueful grin. "That was close."

"Yes, it was, you dumbass," Elijah growled, punching him on the arm. "But thanks for saving Ruby."

"Don't sweat it, man," Benjamin said with a grin.

"Yes, well. Be more careful next time," Theresa said before turning to the strange woman with George. "I'd appreciate it if you could back them up with your gun, whoever you are."

"I'm Bobbi Todd, and I'll be happy to help, though I only have a few shots left," Bobbie said.

"It will have to do," Theresa said, her mouth drawn into a severe line. "Timothy, you and George can get rid of the bodies."

"How?" Timothy asked with a puzzled look.

"Drag them a few yards away from the station. We'll figure out a more permanent solution in the morning. The rest of you grab a mop, a bucket, and a boatload of sanitizer. We need to get rid of any trace of the infection. Any questions?"

Nobody challenged her authority, and Theresa took complete command of the situation. If Robert had wondered about her ability to lead them before, he didn't doubt it any longer. She was the right person for the job. For the first time, he had genuine hope that they could survive the apocalypse.

Chapter 18 - Ellen

Ellen scrubbed at the mess on the floor, the soap suds forming a bloody froth. It swirled across the concrete and created weird patterns. The repetitive motion freed her mind from its usual constraints, and she thought back over the past few hours.

So much had happened in such a short time, and she found it hard to process it all: The sudden onset of the infection, the way it turned ordinary people into monsters, the deaths, and the destruction of a town she'd come to love in the short time she'd been there.

But the worst was the moment Rick got bitten. At that point, she'd thought it was all over. Her best friend was dead, doomed to turn, and she'd be left behind. Alone. Slowly suffocating beneath the weight of her guilt and regrets. Guilt because he gave his life for hers. Regret because she never told him how she felt about him. *About us.*

Then Bobbi Todd stepped in, cutting his infected fingers off without so much as blinking. She was a strange and harsh woman, but Ellen owed her a debt she could never repay if it worked. *I hope he doesn't turn into one of those things.*

She glanced at Bobbi, studying her from beneath lowered lashes. The woman looked tough and fit. She was short with a wiry build and a deep tan that spoke of days spent outdoors. Her dark blond hair was tied back into a careless knot, and her practical clothing spoke volumes about her nature. She was a survivor. *But am I? I froze when Rick got bitten. Hell, he got bitten because of me. It's all my fault.*

Shame rose in her breast, and Ellen scoured the floor with renewed vigor. Anything to take her mind off her mixed feelings. She dunked the brush into the bucket and wrinkled her nose. The smell of bleach clogged her nostrils and caused her eyes to water. She was thankful for the gloves she wore, which kept the harsh chemicals away from her skin. Her knees ached, and her back grew sore, but there was no time to rest. They had to get the station cleaned before more trouble arrived.

Timothy and George dragged the last couple of corpses out of the station and dumped them into a large pile a few yards down the street. Come morning, they'd remove the bodies before they posed a serious health hazard. Ruby, Elijah, and Benjamin shadowed them, ensuring no more infected arrived to spoil the party.

With a final sweep, Ellen finished her section of the floor. She got up and dumped the contents of the bucket down the drain, watching as the filth swirled away. Sighing, she wiped her forehead with her sleeve, careful not to get any of the muck on her face.

Susan, Robert, and Theresa weren't far behind her, emptying their buckets as well. Afterward, they turned around to survey the parking bay. Most of the remains of the fight had been washed away, and it reeked of bleach. Still, the faint tang of blood and offal remained, much to Ellen's dismay. "What now?"

"Now, we spray all the surfaces with disinfectant," Theresa said, handing out a few bottles. "Robert can grab the hose and give it all a final wash."

"Alright," Ellen said, taking the disinfectant. "Let's get this over with."

She walked around the parking bay, spraying each nook and cranny. Nothing escaped her notice, and she made sure to do a proper job. The last thing she wanted was for the infection to linger inside the station.

It was a nerve-wracking job. The entire time, she was acutely aware of the yawning bay doors that opened onto the street. Despite the guards, she couldn't help but worry. The zombies were everywhere, and she half expected them to come howling around the corner at any moment. *I don't think I can handle more tonight, not after what happened to Rick.*

Ellen glanced at him, saddened to see him struck down. He huddled on a chair in a corner, his wounded arm held on his lap. His complexion was as pale as ash, and dark hollows lined his face. But when he caught her gaze, he smiled, and her heart leaped into her throat. *I have to tell him how I feel. I might not get another chance.*

Once she'd finished disinfecting the area, she dumped the empty bottle into the trash along with her dirty gloves. Robert took the hose they usually used to wash away accumulated dirt and oil and sprayed the floor. It was a relief to see the last remaining residues of the battle wash away. The water ran down the street and into the storm drain, taking the lingering scent of death with it.

"It's over," Susan said.

"For now," Robert added, shutting down the hose and rolling it back up.

When he was done, Theresa nodded at Ruby and the other guards. "Close her up."

The heavy garage doors slammed back into place, sealing them inside the fire station. The tight knot of fear in the pit of Ellen's stomach eased, and she walked toward Rick. "How do you feel?"

"I'm still me. So far. The boogeyman is still in the closet," he said with a rueful smile, and she found herself grinning in return. It was like him to make light of the situation.

"Does it hurt?" she asked, immediately regretting the question. "I'm sorry. Of course, it hurts."

Rick shrugged. "I'm just glad you're okay."

"Rick, I need to tell you something, something important, but I don't want you to freak out," Ellen said. She chewed on her lower lip as butterflies filled her stomach. Opening her heart to another person, even Rick, wasn't easy.

"What is it?" he asked with a frown. "Did you get hurt back there?"

"No, I'm fine. I just wanted to—"

"Right, folks. Gather around," Theresa said, clapping her hands.

Ellen sighed. "We'll talk later, okay?"

"Okay," Rick said with a nod.

"Now that the station is clean, we need to look after ourselves. Those of you dressed in gear, please take it off and dump it into that bin over there. We can wash and disinfect it in the morning," Theresa said.

"What about me?" Bobbi asked, looking down at her blood-spattered shirt. "I didn't exactly pack for this."

"I've got some extra clothes in my locker," Susan volunteered.

"Me too," Ellen added.

"So do I," Ruby said.

"You do?" Timothy asked, scratching his head. "What for?"

"What for? Are you serious?" Theresa asked with a raised eyebrow.

"We learned long ago that it's best to be prepared," Susan replied. "We spend half of our lives here. It's only natural that half our wardrobes would end up here too."

Theresa nodded. "Exactly, but first, we need to check ourselves for bite marks and scratches."

"Do we?" Ruby said with a groan. "I'm sure we're all fine. I could really use a hot shower and a cup of coffee right now."

"No exceptions, Ruby," Theresa said with a brisk shake of the head. "It has to be done. You can have a shower afterward. It will only take a few minutes."

"She's right," Bobbi said. "We can't be too careful with this… disease."

"What about him?" Benjamin asked, pointing at Rick. "He got bitten, didn't he?"

"Yes, but Bobbi cut off his fingers almost straight away," Ellen protested. She moved closer to Rick, determined to protect him no matter what.

"Even so, he needs to be quarantined," Theresa said.

"For how long?" Ellen asked, dismayed.

"I'm not sure. The infection seems to take hold quite quickly. Forty-eight hours should be enough," Theresa said.

"Forty-eight hours!" Ellen cried. "That's ridiculous. He's in pain, and he needs help."

"And he'll get it. Along with a shower, food, and a bed just like the rest of us," Theresa said in a placating tone of voice.

"But—" Ellen began.

"No buts, Ellen. We can't take any chances," Theresa said.

"It's okay," Rick said, taking Ellen by the arm. "I'll be fine. I promise."

"I'll stay with you," she said.

"No, you won't. I can't risk turning on you," Rick said. "Besides, it's only two days."

"Are you sure?" Ellen asked.

"Of course. I'm a big boy," Rick said, his eyes twinkling.

"Where will we keep him?" Ruby asked.

"We can lock him up in the equipment room for now," Theresa said.

"That's fine by me," Rick said.

With a consensus reached, the group sprang into action. The firefighters stripped off their contaminated gear and dumped it into the bin. They disinfected their weapons and put them within easy reach. After a thorough exam to make sure no one had been bitten, they took turns to shower and get dressed in fresh clothes.

Afterward, Theresa took care of Rick's hand while Ellen prepared a bed for him. Susan made coffee and doled out ham sandwiches to those who hadn't eaten yet. Finally, they locked Rick inside the room with a bucket for a toilet and a bottle of water.

"See you in the morning," Ellen said, her heart breaking in two.

"I'll be here, I promise," he replied with a wink.

"You'd better be," she said.

Walking away was hard. Maybe the hardest thing she'd had to do all day, but she had no choice. As Ellen walked up the stairs, she prayed he'd still be human in the morning. Still the Rick she'd come to know.

"He'll be okay. You'll see," Susan said with a comforting smile. "Rick's tougher than all the rest of us put together."

"I hope you're right."

In the kitchen, Theresa was doling out orders. "It's late, and we all need to get some rest, but we should post a guard just in case something else happens."

"I'll take the first shift," Timothy said with the enthusiasm of youth. "I'm not tired."

"What about the families of Briggs and White?" Robert asked. "Weren't they on their way here?"

"I haven't heard from them in hours, and there's no point waiting any longer," Theresa said. "If they do arrive during the night, we can deal with it then."

"And the captain's wife? And my wife, Amelia?" Robert said, his expression taut.

"We can't help any of them now, Robert. Tomorrow is another day," Theresa said.

"You make it sound so easy," Robert replied.

"It's not, but we won't be of use to anyone if we're dead. Plus going out there half-cocked and exhausted is tantamount to suicide," Theresa pointed out.

"She's right, Robert," Ellen said. While it was hard to swallow, it was the truth. "Let's get some rest, and tomorrow we can kick some zombie ass. Deal?"

After a moment, Robert nodded. "Deal."

As Ellen crawled into her bed, she wondered what the next day would bring. She'd sounded so confident back there, talking about kicking ass. *But the truth is, I'm scared. I'm scared for all of us.*

Chapter 19 - Robert

Robert woke up the following day feeling like he had a hangover. His eyes were swollen, and his head throbbed with every beat of his heart. With a groan, he dragged himself out of his bunk bed and surveyed the room. Dawn was still an hour off, but he couldn't sleep any further. *I might as well get up.*

Benjamin, Elijah, Timothy, and Mason still lay in their beds, fast asleep. Robert made his way to the window and pulled aside the thick curtain. Outside, darkness reigned, and the street below was quiet. Nothing moved—nothing except a lone plastic bag blown along the sidewalk by the early morning breeze.

A streetlamp on the corner flickered. Something flitted past the light and ducked into the shadows of a side alley. Something fast. He stared at the spot for several seconds before giving up. Whatever it was, it was gone.

Robert dropped the curtain back into place. The thick material acted as a divide, sealing them back inside their safe haven. With everything happening in the city, the station was an oasis in a sea of chaos.

With a big yawn, he shuffled toward the men's bathroom and opened his locker. The interior was neat and orderly, a reflection of his nature. Each item had a place: A spare outfit, fresh socks, clean underwear, a pair of sneakers, a comb, deodorant, two-in-one shampoo and body wash, a toothbrush, toothpaste, floss, a roll of Super C's, multivitamins, and a couple of protein bars. In addition, there was his carry bag with its supplies, which he shoved to the side for the time being.

After brushing his teeth, Robert grabbed the soap and got into the shower. He cranked up the heat until the bathroom exploded into a cloud of steam, fogging up the mirrors. The stream of hot water cascaded across his shoulders and back, relieving the tension that knotted his muscles.

Still, he couldn't stop thinking about everything that had happened, and the events of the previous night kept playing over and over in his mind. But the worst of all was the gnawing sensation of worry in his gut. Anxiety and fear for his wife, Amelia. He had no way of knowing if she was still alive or not. All he had was hope. Desperate, all-consuming hope.

After a couple of minutes, Robert quickly washed and exited the shower. He didn't want to use all the hot water. Not with so many people in the station. Everyone deserved a turn.

After drying off, he dumped the wet towel into the laundry basket and pulled on a set of fresh clothes. He added his old clothes to the bin, wrinkling his nose at the tang of sweat and smoke that permeated the fibers. *I'll need to do a load of laundry soon or get some extra clothes from home.*

Home. It was such a small word. A mere four letters. Yet, it meant the world to him, and he wondered if he'd ever set foot there again.

He performed the rest of his ablutions, spraying deodorant, combing his hair, and popping a multivitamin before heading toward the kitchen. The light was on, and he encountered Theresa and Clare inside. A pot of coffee brewed in the corner, and the rich aroma teased his nostrils.

"Good morning, ladies," he said.

Theresa acknowledged him with a brisk nod. "Robert."

Clare poured him a cup of coffee and shoved it across the counter.

"Morning," she said with a sullen nod.

Her dark hair was pulled into a messy bun, and deep purple shadows lined her eyes. She looked pale without her usual makeup, and her Nirvana t-shirt was torn in several places. She'd swapped her long black skirt for a pair of jeans, and he guessed they belonged to one of the other girls at the station. Coupled with her old boots and leather jacket, she still managed to look rebellious.

"Thanks for the coffee," Robert replied. He pulled out a chair and sat down. "Sleep well?"

"Like a baby," Clare said with more than a hint of sarcasm. "You?"

"Not a morning person, huh?" he replied.

"You guessed it," she replied.

"She's always been like that," Mason said, slouching into the room. He rubbed one hand through his messy hair, blinking under the bright fluorescent lights. "Even as kids. I still carry the scar where she bit me when I tried to wake her up once."

Robert snorted. "Bit you?"

"Yeah, she's been known to kick and punch, too," Mason said.

"Stop talking shit, will you?" Clare said, eyeing her brother through slitted lids.

"Whatever," Mason said, pouring himself a cup of coffee.

135

"How's your head?" Robert asked.

"A lot better, thanks," Mason said, touching the bandaged cut with tentative fingers.

"And your ribs, Clare?" Robert said, turning to her. "You took quite a hit when you jumped out of that window yesterday."

Clare rubbed her middle and winced. "Don't remind me. That's one stunt I'll never pull again."

"Why didn't you tell me you were hurt when you came in last night?" Theresa said with a frown.

"It's nothing serious. Just bruises," Clare said, shaking her head.

"I'll decide what's serious or not, young lady," Theresa said. "We all need to be in fighting form for the days to come, or we won't make it. If one of you is injured, I need to know about it."

"Yes, ma'am," Clare acknowledged in a dry tone of voice.

"Where's Paisley?" Mason asked. "Still asleep?"

"Yeah, she's passed out cold, poor mite," Clare said.

"I'm glad to hear that," Theresa said.

"Yes, I'm sure she'll feel better after a proper night's sleep," Mason added.

"Wouldn't we all," Clare said, slumping across the table.

"Well, you need to get over whatever funk you're in," Theresa said. She glanced at her ever-present clipboard. "We have a lot of ground to cover today."

"Such as?" Clare asked.

"Saving Robert's wife, Amelia. I made her a promise, after all," Theresa said.

"A promise?" Robert asked.

"I promised I'd send you as soon as possible, and now's my

chance to keep my word."

"Have you heard from her since last night? Or the captain's wife? Anyone at all?" Robert asked.

"No, I haven't. The phone lines are still down," Theresa said. "I can't get through to them."

"What about the radio? Surely, there must be someone else left out there," Robert said. "The police or ambulance services?"

"I'll try to get into contact with them today," Theresa said, writing it down at the top of the list on her clipboard.

"Didn't you break your clipboard last night?" Robert asked.

"I got a new one," was the swift reply.

Robert noted the way she clung to the flimsy board as if her life depended on it. In a way, it probably did. Or her sanity, at least. It was her way of coping with the crazy situation. As long as she felt she had some control, it kept the wolves at bay.

"What about you?" Theresa said, breaking into his thoughts.

"What about me?" Robert asked.

"Have you got a plan? A strategy? The last we heard, your wife was trapped in her office building on the third floor," Theresa pointed out. "How are you going to get her out?"

"I don't know yet, but I'll think of something," Robert said.

"And who's going with you?"

"I am," Clare said, raising her head off her arms.

"You are?" Robert said, surprised.

"Of course. I can't let you and my brother run around out there alone, can I?" Clare said. "You need me."

"How did you know I was going?" Mason asked. Clare leveled a look at him, and he raised his hands to ward her off. "Sorry. Dumb question."

"I'd like to come too," Susan said, appearing in the doorway.

137

"You're going after Amelia, right? I can help."

"It seems you have your team, Robert," Theresa said. "I'll allow you to take the truck, but make sure you bring it back in mint condition. No scratches."

"Yes, ma'am," Robert said.

"And hose it off when you're done," she added with a shudder. "We can't let the infection get a free ride inside the station. The same goes for your gear and weapons."

Robert rolled his eyes. "Anything else?"

"Just bring Amelia back in one piece and unzombified, got it?" Theresa said.

"That's the plan," Robert replied.

"What about Paisley?" Clare asked.

"I'll look after her," Theresa said, sorting through her notes. "There's plenty to keep us busy here while the rest of you traipse around out there."

"You're putting her to work?" Clare asked.

"Can you think of a better way to take her mind off everything she's lost?" Theresa asked.

"No, I suppose not," Clare conceded.

"Besides, idle hands do the devil's work," Theresa added.

"Like I haven't heard that before," Clare mumbled beneath her breath.

"What about the others? The captain's wife? And Brigg's and White's families?" Mason asked.

"I'll send another team out to look for them," Theresa said. "Them and anyone else who still needs rescuing."

"That's a tall order," Robert said. "Why don't we swing by Brigg's house on the way to Amelia's office? It's on the same route."

"Alright. That would be great," Theresa said.

138

"Just be careful while we're gone," Robert said, swallowing the last of his coffee.

"We'll be fine. This place is like a mini fortress. It's got thick walls, barred windows, security gates, and the steel bay doors," Theresa pointed out.

"That's true, but still," Robert said, standing up. "You can't be too cautious."

"I'll keep that in mind," Theresa said, standing up. "Now, you'd better get going. I'll whip up a quick breakfast before you leave. We can't have you running around on empty stomachs."

"Thanks," Robert said, making his way toward the stairs. Theresa was right. They'd better get a move on. There was much to be done and precious little time to do it in. *Don't worry, my love. I'm coming for you. Just hold on.*

Chapter 20 - Amelia

Amelia couldn't take her eyes off the door. Her gaze clung to the square frame, committing each tiny flaw, even the smallest of variations in the battered wood to memory. During the long hours of the night, she sat, staring at the thing that had become to represent both her greatest fear and her greatest hope.

She thought back to the moment it all began. She'd been on her way home, ready to call it a day. She left her office at a brisk pace, her heels clicking on the floor. She nodded at any colleagues she passed along the way and got into the elevator. A push of the button and the door closed. A couple of seconds later, the motor hummed, and she dropped toward the ground floor and its foyer. Soft music played in the background, and all was as it should be. Ordered and predictable.

Her phone rang, and she frowned at the screen. It was Theresa, which was unusual.

"Amelia? Is that you? I can't believe I got through to you," Theresa said, her voice pitched just a little too high for comfort.

"Theresa? Is something wrong? Did something happen to Robert?" A familiar mixture of panic and fear churned in Amelia's breast. It was a sensation she loathed, but it came with the territory. Being married to a firefighter wasn't always easy, and she always wondered when she'd get the call. The one that ended her world. Hopefully, today wasn't that day.

"No, no. Robert is fine. At least, he was when I last spoke to him," Theresa said. "Where are you?"

"At the office," Amelia said. "I'm on my way out now."

"No, don't go outside. It's not safe," Theresa cried.

"What? What on earth are you talking about?"

The elevator came to a stop; the door pinged, and it slid open. Instantly, the world changed from peaceful quiet to raging chaos. Screams assaulted her ears, and she gaped at the scene that met her eyes.

People milled about in a panic, ignoring the hapless security guard who tried to keep order. A few pushed against the doors, trying to keep them from opening. Outside, a mob of howling crazies clamored around the entrance. They threw themselves at the transparent glass, not caring when they smashed their heads open. Still, they attacked, ramming the barrier over and over again.

Inside, it was just as terrifying. A woman screamed as a man ripped into her jugular, and her blood fountained into the air. Others stalked the space, their teeth bared in vicious grins. Whenever they encountered a fleeing person, they pounced and tore into their victim's flesh with gleeful abandon. A couple of shots rang out, and a man tumbled to the floor, a red flower blooming on his chest. Still more huddled against the far wall, too terrified to do more than sob with terror.

"Oh, my God! What's happening?" Amelia said, stumbling back until she was pressed up against the far side of the elevator.

Suddenly, a man stormed toward her and jumped inside.

141

His eyes were wild, and he smashed his hand on the elevator buttons. "Come on, come on! Close, you stupid piece of shit!"

Amelia gaped at him, unable to form a single coherent sentence. She vaguely remembered him from a meeting the year before. Evans. Michael Evans. While they worked for the same company, their paths rarely crossed. Not that it mattered now.

A young woman wearing thick glasses and a man in a suit followed Mike's example, barging into the elevator. An elbow hit Amelia in the stomach, and she doubled over with a gasp.

Through tear-filled eyes, she stared straight ahead, fixated on the mob of crazies who battered the doors. With a resounding crash, the glass shattered into a million glittering pieces. A flood of howling madmen streamed into the foyer, headed straight for them.

Two more people pushed their way into the open elevator, their screams of fright ringing in Amelia's ears. Someone smashed into her, and she fell to the side. Her phone clattered across the floor, and she scrambled to pick it up.

The faint sound of Theresa's frantic cries reached her ears. "Amelia? Amelia, answer me. What's happening?"

Amelia grabbed the phone but remained huddled on the floor. The crazies were getting closer and closer, and still, the doors of the elevator gaped open. *Please close. Please*, she silently begged.

"Close, damn it!" Michael yelled, bashing the buttons until she thought they would shatter. Just as the first crazy got within pouncing distance, the metal doors slid shut, and a sudden silence enfolded them.

"Thank fuck," Michael said, sagging against the wall.

He spotted her on the floor and reached out one hand. "I'm

sorry. Let me help you up."

Amelia blinked at his fingers, fascinated by the crimson stain across the skin. He noticed her attention and retracted his hand. "It's not mine."

She ignored him and pressed the phone to her ear. "Theresa? Are you still there?"

"Amelia! Are you okay?"

"I am for now. I'm in an elevator."

"Find somewhere safe. An office, a room, anything. Lock yourself inside. Don't let those things get to you."

"What are they?"

"It doesn't matter for now. What matters is that you stay safe. I'm sending Robert. You hear me?"

"I hear you," Amelia replied.

"Don't let them bite you, okay?"

"Okay," Amelia said.

The elevator doors pinged and slid open on a deserted floor she recognized as the third. Michael rushed out and waved to them. "Come on, guys. We need to get somewhere safe. We have to barricade the doors now before they come up the stairs."

After a second's hesitation, everyone followed him into the nearest office with Amelia right on their heels. As she ran, she shouted into the phone, "Tell Robert I'm on the third floor."

"What? The line's breaking up," Theresa said, her voice faint.

"The third floor. I'm on the third—"

The line died, leaving Amelia bereft and cut off from the only person she knew. There was no time to think about it, however. The crazies were coming, and they had to secure their position. It didn't take much in the end. The door was sturdy and made of steel. There were no windows that opened onto the stairwell and elevator landing. Only a bank of windows that provided a view of the outside world. A world she no longer recognized.

Amelia blinked back a tear. Her eyes burned from lack of sleep, but she didn't care. Outside, dawn had come, and with it, a new day. But still, she sat, tethered to the door that represented both death and life. It was the only way out. "Robert. Please come. I need you. I don't know how much longer I can hold it together. This time, I'm the one who needs rescuing."

Chapter 21 - George

George nursed a cup of hot coffee in his hands, watching as Theresa doled out instructions to everyone. The plan was simple: rescue anyone who still needed help, scavenge for supplies, secure the station, and attempt to contact other survivors, especially the emergency services.

"We have to salvage what we can of this city before it's too late," Theresa said, looking around the room. "We owe the citizens of Burlington that much."

Nods of assent did the rounds.

"Robert, Mason, Clare, and Susan are on their way to rescue Amelia and anyone else who might be trapped with her. On the way there, they'll stop at Brigg's home and check on his family. That leaves the captain's wife and White's family. Is there anyone else I'm missing?" Theresa asked.

"My family and friends are all back in South Africa," Ellen said with a shake of the head. "I tried phoning them, but I can't get through."

"What about Rick?" Theresa asked.

"His brother lives in Arizona with his wife and kids. They're on their own for now, unless we can get hold of them later," Ellen said.

"How is Rick doing, by the way?" George asked.

"He's fine," Ellen said, her voice sharp. "He hasn't turned into a zombie yet, if that's what you're wondering."

"I just wanted to know if he's alright," George said, put on the defensive. "He lost two fingers."

Ellen sighed. "Sorry, I didn't mean to bite your head off. I'm just worried about him, that's all."

"I understand," George said.

"We're all worried about him," Theresa said, her usually severe expression softening somewhat.

"I fixed him a plate of food and a cup of coffee," Ruby said, pointing to the kitchen counter. "And I'll treat his injuries as soon as I'm done here."

Though all the firefighters had extensive knowledge of first-aid, only Ruby, Robert, and Theresa were certified EMTs. Not that Theresa had worked in the field for years. A debilitating back injury benched her career, and she took over the office administration. Sadly, Briggs had been a fully qualified paramedic, which meant his loss was a bitter blow to the station.

"Thanks, I'll take this to him," Ellen said, collecting the cup and plate. She descended the stairs and dropped out of sight.

George turned his attention back to Theresa. She was going down the list on her clipboard, making notes. "I don't have any family here. Neither does Susan, I think. Her son is on some cruise ship, right?"

"That's right," Ruby said.

"Lucky bastard," George said.

"I don't know about that," Ruby said. "What if there's an outbreak on board? He'd have nowhere to go."

George blanched, picturing the scenario in his head. Ruby was right. He'd rather be here than stuck on the water with nowhere to run.

"Mason has Clare," Theresa continued. "George? What about you?"

"I don't have anyone," George said, dropping his eyes to the table. Guilt permeated his mind. It was a lie. He had family, but they were far away and out of his reach. He'd told no one the real reason he'd taken a job halfway across the country, and he wasn't about to tell them now. *I'm sorry, Nikki. Please forgive me.*

"It's just Elijah and me," Ruby said. "We were lucky to pick Benjamin up along the way."

"Timothy?" Theresa asked, turning toward him.

"I got hold of my dad. He got my grandma out of the retirement home in time. She's back at the farm with him and my mom, and they should be alright for now. The house is built like a fortress, and my dad's got guns. Lots of them."

"That's good to know, Timothy," Theresa said. "Is it a working farm?"

"It is," Timothy said. "My dad grows crops, and he raises livestock."

"That might come in handy later," Theresa said. "What about you, Bobbi?"

"I'm a widow. No kids," Bobbi said, volunteering nothing further.

"I see, and you, Andrea?"

"It's just Sebastian and me," Andrea replied.

"Poor thing," Theresa said. "How is he settling in?"

"He's struggling. It's a strange environment, and I think he can smell traces of the previous cat," Andrea said. "He'll need to stay in the office for a few days. Luckily, I've got his favorite toy and a bottle of Feliway hormone spray to help him feel at ease."

"So, you probably won't be able to go on supply runs any time soon?" Theresa asked.

"Not until he's settled in," Andrea said. "Is that going to be a problem?"

"Actually, I've got a job in mind for you," Theresa said. "One that doesn't entail leaving the office at all."

"Name it. I'd be happy to help," Andrea said.

"I thought we could move a bed and a locker into the office for you. That would set you up nicely," Theresa said. "Plus, there's a phone line, a radio, and high-speed Internet."

"Right," Andrea said with a frown. "You want me to call someone?"

"I want you to gather information. Find out who's out there. What's happening around the world? Where are the government and the army? What are they doing about the situation? That sort of thing."

"I can do that," Andrea said.

"You should try to contact other emergency services around the city, too," Theresa added. "It wouldn't hurt to look for likely places to raid either. We're going to need supplies. Lots of it."

"Got it," Andrea said with a brisk nod. "In fact, I'll start right away."

"Thank you," Theresa said.

"What about the rest of us?" George asked.

"As the only other EMT besides Robert and me, I'd like you to stay here, Ruby," Theresa said. "You and Ellen can help me organize the station. We need storage space for supplies and extra room for more survivors."

"Alright," Ruby said.

"Paisley can help us, right sweetie?" Theresa said, turning to the little girl in question.

Paisley nodded before taking another bite of her egg and toast. She hadn't said a word since she woke up and acted like a robot. She obeyed any commands given to her, nodded or shook her head when asked a question, and allowed herself to be handled like a doll. It was a problematic situation for all of them, and nobody knew quite what to make of the child.

Except for George. He recognized the signs of deep trauma and feared that a breakdown of some sort was in the offing. Paisley's reaction to the loss of her family and the horror surrounding it reminded him of his childhood. Once again, the specter of guilt raised its ugly head, and he thought of Nikki. *I couldn't stay. I'm sorry.*

"As for the rest of you," Theresa continued. "We need volunteers to check on White's family. They must be out there somewhere. And someone needs to fetch the captain's wife."

"I'll go," George volunteered, glad to be of service. Anything was better than sitting around doing nothing.

"I'll go with him," Elijah said, stepping forward.

"So will I," Bobbi Todd said.

"That's settled then," Theresa said with an approving nod. "But you'll need to clean your gear, both now and upon your return. The truck as well."

"Will do," George said.

"Timothy, you and Benjamin can clean and sanitize the rest of the equipment," Theresa said, gathering her papers.

"What?" Benjamin said. "That's a crappy job."

"No complaints," Theresa said in a brisk tone. "Everyone needs to pull their weight."

149

"But—"

"Not another word."

With a groan of despair, Benjamin dragged himself toward the stairs with Timothy right on his heels. They had a big job ahead of them. Several drums were full of uniforms and equipment that needed sanitizing, including another one full of boots.

Still, it had to be done, and George smothered a smile as he finished his coffee. Nobody refused an order from Theresa. Nobody. Her word was law.

Theresa gathered up her papers and clipboard. "Good luck on your mission, and be careful out there. We can't afford to lose more people."

"I'll be careful," George said.

"Don't worry about us," Bobbi added, standing up.

"Excellent. Because tomorrow, the actual work begins. Fortifying the station, gathering supplies, and forming a network of safe houses and survivors."

"You're planning ahead, I see," Bobbi said.

"Of course. The world as we know it is gone, and we can't count on the government to save us. This is it. We're it," Theresa said.

"You're right. It's up to us now," Bobbi said.

"As I said, be careful out there," Theresa said, coaxing Paisley to her side. "Come on, my sweet. We have work to do."

"See you later," George said, turning to Elijah and Bobbi. "Ready, guys?"

"We're ready," Elijah said, his dark eyes somber.

"Be sure to come back in one piece," Ruby said, pulling him in for a kiss.

"Don't worry, babe. I'm tougher than you think," he said

with a grin.

"Prove it," she replied with a glint in her eyes.

George strode away, making his way down the stairs. Open emotions made him uncomfortable. It was best to focus on the task at hand: saving the captain's wife and finding White's family. That was all he needed to know.

Chapter 22 - Robert

Robert's heavy boots crunched across the gravel that lined the walkway to the door. The smell of disinfectant filled his nostrils. His gear reeked of the stuff, and he wondered if he'd been a tad overzealous earlier when he cleaned it. *Maybe use a lighter hand next time,* he thought with a rueful shake of the head.

In front of him loomed the entrance to a house—Brigg's old home. The front door yawned wide open, and a smear of blood marred the cream-colored paint. It boded ill for the fate of Brigg's family, but Robert needed to make sure there were no survivors.

Mason waited in the truck, ready for a quick getaway while Susan and Clare followed close on his heels. The suburb was quiet so far, with not a single hint of zombies. That didn't mean they weren't around, however, and Robert was ready for anything.

After a careful look around, he closed the distance. When he reached the bottom of the steps, he nodded at Clare. "You wait here. Warn us if any zombies show up and cover our rear, but don't be a hero."

"I'll do my best," Clare said with a tight nod.

She looked a little off in the gear he'd given her, but it was the best protection he had to offer. The thick material, helmet, boots, and gloves were an excellent defense against zombie bites, while the ax was an efficient weapon. Still, she looked swamped in the heavy outfit, and he made a mental note to get her something better for future excursions. *Not just her. Everyone, firefighter or not, will need protective clothes in the months to come.*

He left her there at the bottom of the steps and continued upward to the entrance. A quick examination of the blood revealed that it was old. Dried and crusty. Whatever had happened there, it had been a while already.

"Ready, Susan?" Robert asked when he reached the door.

"Go ahead. I've got your back," Susan said.

Robert gave the door a nudge, and it creaked as it swung open on unoiled hinges. He winced, certain a zombie would come raging out at any second. But nothing happened.

A couple of seconds passed before he stepped inside. Immediately, a thick wave of decay hit him in the face. His eyes watered, and he was suddenly grateful for the smell of disinfectant on his clothes. It took the edge off, at least.

"Oh, man. That's rank," Susan said in a low whisper.

"Uh-huh. Something died in here," Robert answered. *Or someone.*

"Be careful," she warned as they moved deeper into the house.

Robert nodded, acutely aware of the danger they were in. His eyes roved across the dim interior of the foyer, noting the smears of dried blood on the walls. In the living room, a trail of rust-red droplets led across the carpet and into the kitchen.

Robert inched forward but stopped when he saw a pair of feet sticking out from behind a counter. A woman's feet clad in jogging shoes. He took a few more steps and rounded the corner. Brigg's wife lay in a thick pool of blood, her skull caved in with a wheel spanner. The weapon lay discarded nearby, covered in blood and brains.

The stench was almost unbearable, and a cloud of flies rose from the corpse to buzz around his head. He waved them away with a grimace of disgust and stumbled back. "Susan. I think we found Mrs. Briggs."

Susan drew up beside him and shook her head. "Poor woman, but what about the kids?"

"I don't know," Robert said. And he didn't want to know, not after Oliver.

"They had two boys, right?" Susan asked.

"I think so," Robert said.

"We need to look for them."

"I know."

With supreme reluctance, Robert moved toward the hall with its bedrooms. Two open doorways reared their ugly heads, and he turned to Susan. "You take the left. I'll take the right."

"Alright," she whispered and moved across the hall. She halted inside the opening; her ax held ready to strike. A single, breathless moment passed before she glanced at him across her shoulder and whispered, "Nothing."

Robert nodded and headed past her toward his chosen room. His mouth was dry, and his heart heavy as he approached the half-open door. As he got closer, a strange noise reached his ears, and he faltered. It sounded familiar, and his gut roiled when he realized what it was. *Not this. Not the kids.*

Susan came up behind him and shot him a fearful glance. Swallowing hard, he forced himself to continue forward. The noise grew louder, and it reminded him of those animal shows he used to watch—the ones where a pride of lions tore through a freshly killed carcass.

As he entered the room, Robert jerked to a stop. Bile rushed up his throat, and he fought to remain calm. It was his worst nightmare all over again, and the memory of Oliver's undead gaze came back to haunt him.

Splayed out on the thick carpet lay one of the Brigg boys, his eyes lifeless. A trickle of blood ran from his mouth and pooled beneath his cheek. The smell of copper pennies hung thick in the air and coated Robert's mouth until he thought he'd never be free of it.

Beside the dead child's corpse sat his brother, older by three years. The boy dug into his sibling's stomach with intense focus, tearing free morsels of flesh and innards. He stuffed these bites into his mouth and swallowed without bothering to chew. He was no longer human, just a mindless eating machine.

He's eating his own brother, Robert thought, the errant thought buzzing around in his brain while shock and horror held him immobile. The boy paid him no attention, too focused on the feast at hand to notice anything else.

Behind Robert, Susan approached on silent feet. "End it, Robert."

When he did nothing, she nudged him and said, "You have to. You know you do. You can't leave them like this."

"I know," Robert said, looking away long enough to collect himself. He had no choice. Raising his ax, he stepped forward.

One blow.

That was all it would take.

Minutes later, he stumbled toward the truck, trying to

155

ignore the blood splattered across his chest. He felt cold and empty inside, but he still had one more mission to accomplish that day. The most important one of his life: Rescuing his wife. *I'm coming, Amelia. I'll save you. I swear it.*

Chapter 23 - Amelia

"Come on, Amelia. You need to rest," Michael Evans said, tugging on her arm.

She looked away from the door and blinked at him. His voice seemed to come from a great distance, and it took a moment for her to regain her focus. "What?"

"You need to rest. You've been up all night," Michael repeated, coaxing her to her feet.

"I'm not tired," Amelia replied.

"At least have something to drink," Michael said, offering her a glass of water.

Suddenly aware of a raging thirst, Amelia grabbed the glass and gulped it down. Wiping a hand across her wet lips, she sat down in the nearest chair. "Thank you."

"Your phone… does it work?" Michael asked, taking the chair opposite her.

"No signal," she said, shaking her head. "Yours?"

"Nope," he said.

"None of our phones work," the other woman said from a corner in the room. Her sandy hair was cut into a short bob, and gold-rimmed spectacles glinted against her pale skin. "My name is Jane."

"Hi, Jane. I'm Amelia," Amelia replied in a dull voice. She

wasn't genuinely interested in the others but supposed she had to make an effort. "Do you work here?"

"No, I was grabbing a coffee from the shop on the corner when... when all this happened," Jane said. "I ran to the nearest building, this one, and Sam followed me."

"Sam?" Amelia asked.

"That's me," the other guy in the room said. He was young with tousled hair and a sprinkling of freckles across his nose. He wore a Starbucks uniform with a nametag that read Bob.

"But your tag," Amelia said.

"I don't like it when strangers know my real name," Sam said.

"Interesting," Amelia said, her attention wandering almost immediately. She stared out of the window at the world outside. It looked like a war zone. Plumes of smoke rose into the sky across the city. Buildings burned, consumed by raging fires caused by panic and accidents.

Crazed cannibals wandered the roads searching for fresh victims. Stray dogs and cats lurked in alleyways, rummaging through the overflowing trash for food. Now and then, a car raced past, crammed to the brim with survivors and their belongings. Some made it, and some didn't. All semblance of order was gone, and nothing remained of the Burlington she'd once known and loved.

Her thoughts wandered to Robert, and she wondered where he was and what he was doing. *He has to be on his way. He'd never abandon me. Unless... unless he's dead.*

But no. It wasn't possible. He was still alive. To believe anything else was unthinkable.

"We should start planning an exit strategy," Michael said. "We can't stay here."

"Why not?" Jane asked. "Those things are out there."

"Yeah, it's safer inside," Sam said.

"But for how long?" Michael asked. "We've got no food, only water, and who knows how long that'll last before the pipes run dry?"

"He's got a point," Jane said.

"Maybe," Sam said in a doubtful tone.

"I say we arm ourselves with whatever we can, pick a safe destination, and make a run for it," Mike said.

"Safe? How would we know where it's safe?" Sam said.

"Common sense," Michael said. "The police station, for starters. Or a bank. Even a house with solid walls and strong doors."

"It's an idea," Sam said, frowning.

"There are knives in the kitchen," Jane said.

"If we could get to my car, we m—" Sam began.

"No," Amelia said. "We have to stay here."

"Look. I know you're scared, but if we work together, we can make it out of here," Michael said, leaning toward her.

Amelia leveled a flat stare at him. "I'm not afraid."

Michael smiled, a tentative curl of the lips as he attempted to win her over. "You understand that we can't stay here indefinitely. We'll starve."

"My husband will rescue us," Amelia answered.

"Your husband?"

"Yes, Robert. He's coming. I know he is," Amelia said.

"Look, lady," Sam said from his corner. "Whoever your husband is, he's probably dead by now. Nobody's coming for us."

"You're wrong," Amelia said with absolute certainty. "He's not dead, and he's on his way to rescue me."

"How do you know?" Michael asked. "Were you able to contact him?"

"No," Amelia said. "But I spoke to Theresa at the station earlier."

"Station?"

"The Fire Department," Amelia said.

"Wait. Your husband's a firefighter?"

"Yes, and he knows where I am," Amelia confirmed.

"But, how can you be sure he's coming?" Michael said.

"Because he's right there," Amelia said, pointing out the window into the street.

In the distance, a hint of crimson moved their way, and she instantly knew it was Robert. A warm glow suffused her body, a mixture of relief and gratitude. Theresa had kept her promise. *Thank God.*

"What?" Michael cried, jumping up.

He rushed toward the window, followed by Sam and Jane. Together, they stared out into the zombie-infested street. It looked much as it always had except for one significant fact. A big red firetruck was navigating its way up the road.

"Is that Robert? Your husband?" Jane asked.

"Yes, I'm sure it is," Amelia said with a sharp nod.

She pressed her face to the glass and watched as the vehicle weaved through the stationary traffic and knots of undead humanity until it reached the building. It inched past the shattered glass entrance with its foyer filled with zombies.

The wheels kept rolling, drawing closer and closer. Unable to contain herself, Amelia slammed both hands against the window. "Robert! Robert, I'm over here!"

The truck stopped in the middle of the street right across from her, and a hand waved back through the half-open window. She squinted at the figure and whooped for joy. "It's him. I'm sure of it."

Glad cries rose from the others around her, and Amelia flashed them a happy grin. Her trust in Robert had been vindicated, and she knew everything would be alright. *We're saved.*

The buoyant mood that reigned inside the office lasted five seconds before despair set in again. As the firetruck idled in the road, undead figures swarmed toward it like flies drawn to carrion. The zombies inside their building stayed put, refusing to give up on the victims trapped inside.

"How are they going to get us out?" Michael asked, turning away from the window. "The stairs and corridors are overrun with those things. They'd need an army to rescue us."

Amelia chewed on her lower lip. "Don't worry. Robert will think of something. He always does."

"No offense, lady," Sam said. "Your hubby might be a firefighter, but that doesn't make him a hero."

"Wait and see," Amelia said, her voice sharp.

The four of them stood together, waiting for the truck and its occupants to make a move. Suddenly, the vehicle shifted forward and to the side before changing direction. After several such maneuvers, the truck had done a one-eighty and stood parked with its back toward the building.

Amelia watched with bated breath as it inched onto the sidewalk. There wasn't a lot of room, and the truck clipped the rear of a parked car while narrowly avoiding a street lamp.

Finally, it stopped a few feet away from the building, and a sudden realization hit her like a lightning bolt. "The bucket! They're going to use the bucket."

Michael glanced at her. "The bucket?"

"Yes, is there a window that opens?" she asked, looking at the bank of clear glass that separated them from the outside. "Anything?"

"No, there aren't any," Michael said.

"Damn," Amelia said, looking around the room. "Then we'll just have to make one."

"It's not that easy. This is safety glass," Michael said, shaking his head.

"We'll see about that." Pursing her lips, Amelia walked toward the far side of the room and grabbed the fire extinguisher. With a grunt, she lifted it above her head and smashed it into the window.

It hit with a dull thud before bouncing off, and she staggered back on unsteady legs. Not a crack marred the smooth surface of the glass, and she growled with frustration. "Stupid thing."

But, she wasn't about to give up and tried again and again. Each blow sent vibrations running down her arms and into her spine until her joints ached. "Break already!"

Gritting her teeth, Amelia raised the metal cylinder above her head. Bunching her muscles, she intended to hurl it with all her strength. Alarmed, Jane and Sam ducked, but Michael grabbed her arm.

"Whoa, tiger. Let me try," he said, taking the extinguisher from her. He waved to Sam. "Come on. I need help."

Sam picked up a heavy chair, and they took turns bashing the window while Amelia and Jane watched anxiously from the side. Suddenly, the entire sheet of glass shattered into a million tiny pieces. The glittering shards rained down across the carpet and spilled out into the street.

Michael yelled with triumph and dropped the extinguisher with a thump. "We did it."

"Yeah, you know it!" Sam cried out.

"Careful," Jane said. "Don't cut yourselves."

"Don't worry. It's tempered glass. No sharp edges," Michael said, picking up a piece. He rolled it between his fingers before tossing it aside.

A sudden gust of wind swept through the office, and Amelia shivered. She pulled her thin jacket tighter around her body, wishing she'd worn something warmer. With care, she edged closer to the opening and peered down at the sidewalk below. It was a long way down.

Her stomach leaped into her throat, and she took a step back. Heights weren't her strong point. She focused on the firetruck instead in an attempt to control her nerves. She prayed Robert had a plan. The undead surrounded his vehicle, and no one could get out and walk toward the ladder.

That didn't stop Robert, however. After a couple of seconds, he climbed out of the window and onto the roof. It was a tense couple of moments. At the sight of living flesh, the zombies around the truck went nuts. They reached upward with eager arms, clamoring to get hold of Robert's feet and legs.

"Is that your husband?" Michael asked.

"That's him," Amelia said, and never had she felt prouder than at that moment.

"He's one brave son of a bitch," Sam muttered as an undead's fingers scraped the bottom of Robert's boots.

"That he is," Amelia said.

To her relief, he made it onto the roof without mishap. Seconds later, a second person followed him. Amelia thought she recognized Susan, though it was impossible to say for sure. Not that it mattered. The only thing that mattered was that Robert wasn't alone, and Amelia and the rest were rescued.

Together, Robert and Susan crawled across the boom. With careful movements, they climbed into the bucket. Once inside, they shouted down to the cab, and the boom cranked into gear. It lifted up until it reached Amelia's level.

As Robert got closer and closer, a mixture of joy, relief, and love bubbled up inside Amelia's chest. It was good to see his face again, and she allowed herself to drink in the sight. To her, he represented safety, warmth, and familiarity. Everything she craved after the horror of the past day.

Tears pricked her eyelids, and she reached out to him with one hand. "Robert, you came!"

"Amelia. Just hold on," he said and turned around to speak to Susan. They conferred for a couple of seconds before Susan nodded and hunkered down inside the bucket. Robert moved toward the edge of the bucket until he stood with his lower body pressed against the side. With Susan providing a steadying hand, he reached outward. "Come on, Amelia. You first."

Amelia edged forward until her toes were on the edge. The bucket was only three feet away from the window, but it looked like a chasm to her. A divide that seemed as big as the grand canyon. "I can't do it. It's too far."

"Yes, you can, sweetheart," Robert said, holding out both hands. "I've got you. I promise."

Amelia shook her head, unable to make herself move. "What if I fall?"

"You won't."

"You don't know that," Amelia said, looking down again. It was a long way to the ground, and her stomach churned.

"Come on, sweetheart. You can do it," Robert urged.

But Amelia simply couldn't do it. To buy time, she pointed

at Jane. "You go first."

"Are you sure?" Jane said with barely repressed eagerness.

"I'm sure. Go ahead," Amelia said, stepping back.

"What are you doing?" Robert cried. "I'm right here."

"Take them first," Amelia said.

"No!" Robert said, shaking his head.

"Please, Robert. You know I'm afraid of heights," Amelia said, her voice softening. "Maybe if I see them do it first, it won't be so scary."

Robert hesitated for a couple of seconds before he nodded. "Fine. How many are there with you?"

"Three."

"Alright. Let the first one come out, but hurry," Robert said.

Jane stepped forward until she could go no further. After a quick look over her shoulder, she jumped across the gap. Robert grabbed her and hauled her into the bucket.

"One down," Robert said, motioning to Sam, who stood next in line.

Sam jumped across the gap with barely a hitch, making it look easy. With four people inside the bucket, it was becoming crowded, and Susan helped them climb out onto the boom.

"Wait there," she instructed.

Together, they clung to the metal railings suspended high in the air. At least they were safe from the grasping hands of the infected, a small bonus.

"Are you ready to try it yet?" Robert shouted, turning back to Amelia.

"Maybe," Amelia said, inching forward.

"You can do it," Michael said. He nodded toward the waiting Robert. "Just don't look down."

"Okay." Scraping together her courage, she readied herself

to jump. But at the last moment, she pulled back. "You first, Michael."

"Come on, Amelia," Michael said, urging her on. "You can do it."

"I know, but…." Amelia shook her head. "I'll go after you. I promise."

Michael blew out a breath. "Fine, but I'm holding you to that."

"Deal," Amelia said, motioning him forward.

Michael leaped across the gap and hauled himself into the bucket with Robert's help. Together, they waved to her. "Come on. Your turn."

"O… okay," Amelia said, inching forward. She glanced down, and the ground below seemed to call to her. Her stomach lurched, and her mouth went dry. "It's too far."

"Sweetheart, look at me," Robert said.

She raised her eyes to his.

"Don't look down. Just focus on me, and nothing but me," Robert said.

"I… I'm trying," she said.

He held out both hands. "I won't let you fall. I'm right here, ready to catch you. All you have to do is jump."

Taking a deep breath, Amelia focused on his face. She drank in every familiar feature. Every line, wrinkle, and gray hair. "I… I can do this."

"Yes, you can, sweetheart. Just jump," Robert urged.

As she prepared to leap, a crash caused them to look up in shock. Glass rained down from a broken window two or three stories up. A man's head popped through the opening. "Help, please help. They're breaking in. They're coming in!"

Robert waved at him. "Just hold on. We'll come to you."

"Hurry, they're almost through," the man shouted, his voice shrill with fear.

Robert looked at Amelia once more, his expression strained. "Honey, you have to jump. Now."

"But… that man," Amelia said.

"Forget about him and focus on me. You need to jump," Robert said, waving her on. "Now!"

"Alright." Amelia sucked in a couple of deep breaths, closed her eyes, and jumped. For a second, she was suspended in the air. Open and vulnerable. *Oh my God, oh my God, oh my God!*

With a shriek, she landed in Robert's arms. He grabbed her and held on tightly, much to her relief. "I've got you, sweetheart."

"Robert," she mumbled against the collar of his jacket. His familiar scent flooded her nostrils and soothed her fear. She was safe.

But it was not to last.

Above her head, the other survivor shouted. "They're inside. They're inside!"

"Hold on," Robert said. "We're on our way."

"I can't. It's too late. I'm coming to you."

"No!" Robert cried out in horror. "Wait for us!"

"I can't. They're… argh!" The man jumped through the window with a wild yell, his arms and legs flailing.

He hurtled toward Amelia and Robert, missing her by a mere inch. His knee thudded into the railing, and his elbow struck her on the head. Grasping fingers tore at her hair, and she felt herself slipping from Robert's grasp. "Robert!"

"Amelia, no!"

He caught her hands in his but almost lost her when the jumper grabbed hold of her legs. Amelia screamed as the

167

jumper's fall was arrested with a brutal yank. It felt like she was being torn in half, her ligaments stretched to the limits.

Robert was dragged halfway out of the bucket and would've gone over if not for Susan. He hung onto Amelia like a leech, knowing her life depended on it. "Don't let go, sweetheart."

"I'm trying," Amelia said through clenched teeth. Already the muscles in her arms burned with the effort, and her body swung through the air like a pendulum.

The man who'd jumped had a death grip on her legs, and he screamed like a banshee. In the bucket, a mad scramble ensued as Susan and Michael attempted to pull Robert back up. The added weight made it difficult, as did the man's kicking and screaming.

As they tried to pull her up, Amelia could feel Robert's grip slipping. Bit by bit, her fingers pulled free from his. Panic set in, and she knew she didn't have much longer.

The same realization hit Robert, and he shook his head. "No, no, no! Hold on!"

"I can't. We're too heavy," Amelia cried.

"Get rid of him," Robert said.

"You mean…" Amelia trailed off. She glanced down at the man who clung to her, and their eyes met.

"No, you can't," the man cried when he heard Robert's words. "Please, I have kids. A wife. A family."

"Amelia, you have to," Robert said. "If you don't…."

He didn't need to finish the sentence as her hands slid down another millimeter. It was now or never. She had to choose. It was her life, or they'd both die. *Can I do it? Can I kill an innocent person? A father? A husband?*

"I… I'm sorry," Amelia whispered.

"No, please," the man begged, tears pouring down his face.

He clawed at her legs and tried to haul himself up higher.

Closing her eyes, Amelia kicked out with both feet. When that failed, she kneed the stranger in the face. One knee hit him flush on the nose, and the cartilage broke with an audible crunch. Blood sprayed from the injury, and the man's grip loosened. With a final twist and turn of her waist, Amelia dislodged him.

With a wail of despair, he plunged to the ground. To Amelia, his fall lasted an eternity. Their eyes clung together as time slowed down to a crawl. His were filled with fear, shock, and accusation—hers with guilt and shame, but even worse, relief.

Finally, he hit the pavement with a sickening thud. Bones snapped, and blood misted the air. Broken and helpless, he lay on the unforgiving concrete, an unwilling sacrifice. His screams rose higher and higher until they cut into Amelia's brain. "Help! Help me!"

"I'm sorry," she choked through a web of tears. "I'm sorry!"

Zombies swarmed his body and tore into his flesh while he still breathed. They ripped him apart, and the awful screams ceased abruptly. Within seconds, little remained of the stranger but a bloody corpse. Whoever he'd been in life, he was no more in death.

Bitter tears stung Amelia's lids as Robert, Susan, and Michael hauled her to safety. Their cries of concern echoed around her head, but she hardly heard them.

At that moment, she knew nothing would ever be the same again. Her hands, once clean, were stained with blood. It was a sickening realization. A revelation of the lengths she'd go to live. And the worst of it all was the knowledge that she'd do it again if she had to. She'd choose herself—every single time.

Chapter 24 - Robert

Robert crushed Amelia to his chest. "Thank God, you're safe."

Amelia clung to him, her face buried in his jacket. "I killed him. That man. I killed him, Robert."

"Don't think about it, sweetheart," he said.

"But… it's my fault," she said with a choked sob.

Robert glanced down at the corpse splayed out on the pavement. Zombies swarmed over it like a pack of hyenas, tearing it apart with their bare hands. Already, there was little left of the stranger, and he doubted there would be enough to reanimate afterward. "No, it's not your fault. He chose his fate."

Averting his eyes, Robert focused on the task at hand. "Come on. We need to get inside the—"

Suddenly, a body hurtled past the basket. Robert looked up in shock and reeled backward. "What the hell?"

Zombies were falling from the broken window of the story above them. The same window the stranger jumped out of seconds before. Now the undead crowded through the shattered opening, pushing and shoving in their eagerness to reach the fresh prey below.

"Amelia, watch out!" Robert yelled, grabbing her arm.

He yanked her aside and shoved her behind him. A woman

plunged toward them, arms outstretched. She hit the basket with a thud, and her ribs snapped like kindling. Tumbling the rest of the way, she landed on the pavement with a sickening crunch.

More followed, and Robert knew they were in serious trouble. One of the undead would get lucky and land on top of them. It was just a question of time. "Susan, can you get to the cab?"

"What do you need?" she replied.

"Tell Mason to get us away from the windows," Robert shouted, watching as three more bodies plunged to the ground.

"I'm on it," Susan said. With haste, she climbed down the boom and hurried across the roof of the truck.

Robert herded the rest of them out of the basket and onto the boom. "Get back. It's not safe." He helped Amelia over the side, his heart thudding in his chest. "Hurry!"

A dull thump sounded behind him, and he whirled around. A hand closed around his ankle, and a set of teeth clamped down on his calf. A pulse of agony shot up his leg and set his nerves alight. "Get off!"

A zombie lay in the bottom of the bucket, one arm bent at a grotesque angle. The creature gnawed on his calf like a dog on a bone.

Robert yanked the ax from his belt and chopped at the zombie's head. The blade sunk into the skull, but the wound wasn't deep enough. With a muttered curse, he wrestled the weapon free and struck again. *Thunk!*

Metal grated on bone. It was a sound he was getting used to hearing, but he dreaded it. Blood spewed from the gash, and brain matter splattered onto his boots. The infected stiffened,

171

its gaze almost accusing.

For a moment, it looked human again, and it reminded Robert of Oliver. The creatures used to be people once. Guilt filled his being, and he looked away.

"Robert, are you okay?" Amelia cried, grabbing his arm. "That thing bit you!"

"I'm okay," Robert said. "It didn't get through the suit."

"Watch out!" Amelia screamed. She pulled him back as two more zombies rained down from the sky. One of them hit the bucket with a clang and disappeared into the crowd below. The other crashed inside with a dull thump.

It dragged itself toward them, its face twisted into a caricature of its former self. Robert backed up, herding Amelia away from the thing. The undead creature followed, relentless in its pursuit of warm flesh.

"Oh, my God. Oh, my God!" Amelia screamed. "It's coming right at us."

"I've got this," Robert said, lifting his ax.

He aimed at the zombie, ready to strike, but the truck roared to life. Susan had made it down the boom and across the roof of the vehicle. Following her orders, Mason drove forward and away from the rain of corpses.

The vehicle lurched forward, and Robert lost his balance. Falling to one knee, he lost hold of the ax. It clattered to the edge of the bucket and teetered on the edge.

"No!" Robert cried as it slipped over the side, lost to a mob of hungry undead. "Shit!"

"Robert, watch out!" Amelia warned.

He pulled back as the zombie lunged at him, but he was too slow. It slammed into him, and cold fingers groped at his helmet. He struggled to get the thing off him, but it was as

172

slippery as an eel.

Suddenly, it disappeared when a hand gripped its collar. With an angry roar, Michael tossed the infected over the side and helped Robert to his feet.

"Thanks," Robert said, scrambling upright.

"No, problem," Michael said with a quick nod. "We should be okay now."

The truck had moved forward, out of reach of the falling zombies.

Robert heaved a sigh of relief, but a shrill scream cut him short. He whirled around and spotted Jane clinging to the roof of the fire truck. She'd climbed down the boom and tried to make her way across the top toward the waiting Susan. Somehow, she'd slipped, and a zombie had hold of her foot. With fierce determination, it dragged her toward its gaping mouth.

Sam jumped forward and grabbed her around the waist, but his feet had no purchase on the slippery metal roof. Bit by bit, he was dragged down with Jane. Throwing a wild look around, he screamed, "Help us!"

Robert pushed past Amelia and Mike, sliding down the boom as fast as he could manage. His boots hit the roof of the vehicle, and he lunged at the struggling duo. As he reached out to grab Jane, she was yanked down into the mob. Sam followed, sliding right up to the edge.

Sam tried to pull back, but it was impossible. Jane had a death grip on his arms, and he screamed as his shoulders threatened to pull free from their sockets. "Ah, it hurts! Someone help!"

"I'm coming," Robert cried, crawling closer on his hands and knees.

It was already too late for Jane. The undead crowded around her and tore through her flimsy clothes. She screamed as they dug into her midriff and tore into her chest cavity like she was made of wet tissue paper. Blood bubbled up her throat and spilled down her chest, a crimson river of death. Still refusing to let go of Sam, she uttered a final plea. "Help me!"

"I can't," Sam cried. "You're killing me. Let go."

Her blood spattered his face, spraying from her lips. Then she was gone, rent from his grasp. He slid forward, unable to stop himself from falling. Robert grabbed him and hauled him to safety. They fell onto the roof in a tangle of limbs, breathing hard.

Robert extricated himself from the younger man and got to his feet on legs that felt like jelly. He stared down at the crowd of zombies below his feet. There was no sign of Jane. It was as if she'd never existed.

"Robert," Amelia said, tugging at his arm. "Robert, we have to go."

Still numb with shock, he nodded. "Alright."

Turning around, he guided Amelia, Sam, and Michael across the roof toward the cab. One by one, they crawled toward the far end, each trying to ignore the undead below.

They reached the cab where Susan waited, and she helped Michael down through the window. He dropped out of sight, and she waved to Sam. "Come on. Your turn."

He hesitated, looking at the crowd of zombies that reached for them with bloodthirsty fingers. "I can't."

"Yes, you can," Robert said. "Just be careful."

"What if I fall?"

"You won't," Robert said.

"I'll make sure of it," Susan said with a kind smile.

"O… okay." Slowly, Sam inched toward the window.

"That's it. Keep going," Robert coaxed, watching his every move.

Sam disappeared through the window, followed by Amelia and Susan. Finally, it was his turn.

Robert slipped over the edge, and, for a second, he hung in the air. The undead tried to grab him, but he was just out of reach. Hands from within the truck pulled him through the opening, and he dropped into the seat next to Clare. The others had climbed into the back, including his wife, Amelia.

Clare leaned over him to close the window, and the snarls and groans from the mob outside faded away. Mason retracted the bucket, and it clanged into position. Silence fell over the people inside the cab. They were safe, but it didn't feel like a victory.

Clare tried a tentative smile. "You did well out there. You and Susan saved everyone."

"That you did," Mason agreed.

"Maybe, but we lost that girl back there," Robert muttered.

"Her name was Jane," Sam muttered, his expression stricken. "She was nice, and I let her go. I should've held on tighter."

"It wasn't your fault. Neither of you," Susan said. "She slipped. I saw it happen. Those damned court shoes she wore were her end."

"It's not like we knew to dress for the apocalypse," Sam said, curling into a ball on his seat.

"None of us did," Amelia said.

Robert sucked in a deep breath. "Can we go home now? Please?"

"Let's go," Mason said. With a roar of the engine, he bulldozed through the crowd of zombies and set off for the station.

"Where is home now?" Amelia asked, leaning over the back of his seat.

"Home is wherever you are, sweetheart," he replied, reaching back to grip her hand.

Amelia smiled. "You saved me. I knew you would."

"Until death do us part," Robert replied.

The ache inside his chest was gone, at last, filled by her presence. He'd missed her more than he'd thought possible. He could look to the future now—a future with her by his side.

Chapter 25 - Mason

Mason glanced at the occupants of the truck before looking over at Robert. He tightened his grip on the steering wheel and asked, "Back to the station?"

"That's right," Robert said with a frown. He nodded at Amelia, Michael, and Sam. The trio of survivors looked shell-shocked and stricken after the horrific loss of Jane. "We need to get these folks home."

"Wait," Clare said, leaning forward.

"What's wrong?" Robert asked.

"We can't go back. Not yet, anyway," Clare said.

"Why not? We've done everything we set out to do today," Robert said.

"I know, but we can't go to the station empty-handed," Clare said. "As it is, we've got three extra mouths to feed."

"I'm sure we can last a few days," Mason protested, not sure what his sister was getting at. He wasn't keen on tackling any more than he already had.

"Sure, but what about clothes, towels, bedding, blankets, toiletries? That sort of thing?" Clare asked.

Mason mulled over her question. "She has a point, Robert. We don't have enough of any of that stuff."

"So, what do you suggest we do?" Robert said. "I lost my ax

back there, and we haven't got any guns."

"I still have my ax," Clare said, her expression determined. "So do you, bro."

Mason grunted in return.

"And me," Susan said.

"This is a bad idea," Sam said from the back. His eyes were wide, and his voice trembled with fright.

Michael shushed him. "She's right. We can't live on air. We need supplies, and we might as well get them while we're out here."

"No," Sam said, shaking his head. "You saw what happened to Jane." He rubbed at the specks of blood on his face. Jane's blood.

"You don't need to go in, Sam. You can stay in the truck. Right, Robert?" Amelia said.

"Of course. I wouldn't expect you newcomers, to endanger yourselves," Robert said, "Leave it to us."

"No, thanks. I'll do my share," Michael asserted.

Mason's estimation of the man rose considerably. Whoever he was, Michael was no slouch.

"You're not armed," Mason pointed out.

"My mind's made up," Michael said. "Sam can stay here with Amelia if he wants to. I don't blame him after what he's just been through, but I'm going."

"We'll keep an eye out for zombies," Amelia said. "If we see any, we'll blast the horn."

"Thank you, sweetheart," Robert said, hugging her tight. "As long as you're safe."

"I'll stick close to you guys until I can get my hands on a weapon," Michael said. "If you don't mind."

"We'll be glad to have you," Robert said. "We're all in this together, after all."

"It's decided then?" Clare said, looking from one to the other. "We're going to look for supplies?"

"Yes, we are," Robert said. "The question is, how do we go about it?"

"Going from house to house will take too long, and it's too dangerous," Mason said. "We need to hit one place and hit it hard."

"In and out," Clare agreed.

"What about that camping place three blocks from here?" Susan said. "They'll have everything we need, including weapons."

"If they haven't been looted yet," Robert said.

"Or overrun by zombies," Mason added.

"It's worth a shot, right?" Clare said.

"We can take a look," Mason agreed, taking the next turn-off. He thought about the place in question, trying to remember as much as he could about it. While not overly familiar with the shop, he'd been there a couple of times in the past.

It lay on the outskirts of the business district and sat on top of a low hill. The parking lot was wide open, and the front doors were automatic. With any luck, it wouldn't be overrun. *And we could sure use a bit of luck right about now.*

A few minutes later, Mason cruised up the hill, avoiding a couple of cars parked on the sidewalk. There wasn't a lot of traffic, nor did he spot any people, and his hopes rose. But he tamped it down, telling himself not to get too excited. Not yet, anyway. Anything could lie ahead. That much he'd learned in the short time he'd spent in the apocalypse.

After crossing an intersection, he turned into the parking lot and drove toward the long, low building ahead. Its zink roof gleamed in the mid-afternoon sun, and the whitewashed walls were stark against the backdrop of trees that ran behind it.

The lot was littered with stationary cars, abandoned goods, and overturned carts, and he slowed the truck to a crawl. Weaving through the debris, he noticed the congealed puddles of blood on the tar and the crimson smears on the scattered vehicles. A baby carrier lay on its side, the interior empty, and he averted his eyes. People had died here. Lots of people, and he could almost taste the fear and panic in the air. "Are we sure we want to do this?"

"It'll be the same everywhere we go," Clare said, her tone grim.

"She's right," Susan said. "Besides, we're here now, so we might as well take a closer look."

"Alright," Mason said with a shrug. Despite his misgivings, he drove closer to the camping shop. The sign loomed large against the blue sky, announcing to the world that they could cater to everyone's camping needs, no matter how big or small.

"Does it all look like this?" Michael asked, seeming downcast. "The whole city, I mean?"

"As far as we know," Robert said. "Do you have any family?"

"No, not really, and it doesn't matter anyway," Michael said, shaking his head. "What's left of my family lives far from here."

"And you, Sam?" Robert asked.

Sam shrugged. "A girlfriend."

"Have you spoken to her?"

"Not since all this started," Sam replied with a glum look.

"Maybe we can look for her once we're finished here," Robert suggested.

"Yeah, maybe," Sam said, sinking lower into his seat.

Silence fell inside the cab, broken only by Amelia's sudden question. "Where are all the zombies?"

"Huh?" Mason asked.

"Shouldn't there be a bunch of zombies around?" she added, pointing to a trail of blood on the ground. "Sick people. Bitten people."

"She's right. There should be a bunch of the things wandering around here somewhere," Robert muttered. He twisted around in his seat, trying to get a better look.

"Maybe they left," Clare said.

"Left?" Mason echoed, flashing her a dubious look.

"Think about it," she said. "This place was hit yesterday, same as the rest of the town."

"Yeah, so? Get to the point, sis," Mason said, growing impatient. His head hurt, his stitches itched, and he was in no mood for games.

"My point is, what do zombies do once they've turned?" Clare said, throwing him a mean look. "They go hunting, bro."

Understanding dawned, and the frown on his forehead smoothed away. "You're right. They wouldn't hang around once all the food was gone. They'd go looking for more."

"Er, how sure are you two about that?" Susan said, her voice heavy with doubt.

"It's the kind of behavior we've seen from them so far," Clare said with a shrug. "They're restless, and they never stay in one spot for long."

"Maybe, but I'd rather not take a chance on that," Robert said, still studying the lot.

"There must be some way we can che—" Susan said.

Suddenly, the truck drove over a bottle of soda, and it popped. The sound was as loud as a gunshot and echoed throughout the space before fading into the distance.

Mason slammed on the brakes, and the firetruck slid to a halt with a screech of burning rubber. "What the hell?"

"Look where you're going," Robert said, his voice laced with irritation. "Now everything and anyone within a ten-mile radius knows we're here."

"Sorry," Mason said, and his cheeks flushed with hot blood. Mortified, he pressed one hand to his chest and waited for his frantic heartbeat to return to normal.

"Look on the bright side," Clare said. "If there are any zombies around, the noise is sure to draw them out."

"See? Not all is lost," Amelia said, her fingers digging into Robert's forearm. "Apologize to Mason, dear."

Robert grimaced. "Okay, okay. I'm sorry."

"It's cool, man," Mason said, his eyes fixed on the shop entrance.

A thick silence fell over the cab until Clare squirmed in her seat, ever restless. "See anything, bro?"

He shook his head. "It's quiet in there. No movement."

"So, are we going in or not?" Clare said.

Mason rolled his eyes. "Patience, Clare."

"We haven't got all day," Clare pointed out. "The sooner we get this over with, the better."

Mason blew out a deep breath and unclenched his hands from the wheel. He reached for his fire ax and gripped it tightly. "Alright, let's go. Robert, you and Michael stick close to Clare and me until we hit the weapons department. Susan, you guard our rear. Sam, Amelia… sit tight."

Everyone nodded. The plan was simple enough, and no further explanations were needed.

Opening the door, Mason dropped to the ground with a

thud. He paused and looked around, making sure that nothing stirred in the vicinity. Once he was confident that all was clear, he adjusted his mask and gloves. With everything in place, he jogged toward the building.

Michael and Robert followed close on his heels, with Susan at the rear as planned. Together, they closed in on the shop. The doors swooshed open as they approached, and a blast of air-conditioned air welcomed them inside.

As the doors slid shut behind them, Mason paused to study the interior. The building was a simple affair: A one-story with no stairwells, elevator banks, or hidden nooks and crannies to make things more difficult. The aisles were ordered, the wall and tiled floors gleamed, and soft music played in the background.

Even so, there were signs aplenty of the death and destruction that had enveloped the city only a day before. Smears of blood marred the pristine tiles, abandoned carts, and hand baskets littered the floor, and the tills were empty. Not a soul moved, and the atmosphere was one of desolation.

Mason cleared his throat and shouted, "Hello!"

"What are you doing?" Robert hissed, his expression alarmed.

"Checking for zombies," Mason said with a shrug. "I'd rather know if there are any around now while I can still make a run for it."

"Speak for yourself," Robert said with a grunt. "I'm too fat to run."

Mason snorted. "Don't talk crap. You passed your physical earlier this year, same as me."

"Boys, boys, stop arguing, please. We've got company," Clare said, pointing at the aisles across from them.

"Company?" Mason said, his voice rising a few octaves.

Ghostly figures stepped out of the shadows, and low growls filled the air. His eyes widened as he scrambled to count them all. One, two, three, five, six…eight. Nine. "There's nine of them. Do we run, or do we fight?"

"Run," Robert said, taking a step back. "I'm not armed, and neither is Michael."

Michael shook his head and ran toward the nearest display. He yanked down the signboard, a placard attached to a slim pipe inserted into a foot piece. Tossing aside the sign, he pulled the pole free from its base and whirled it like a baton. "This will do. I say we fight. There are five of us, and only nine of them. We'll never have it this easy again."

"Are you sure?" Mason asked, watching as the zombies slunk toward them. "There are ten of them now."

Robert hesitated for a brief moment, then nodded. "They have to come at us over the tills. We can use that to our advantage."

Clare grinned. "They're not very good with obstacles. Everyone, grab a cart."

Mason found himself smiling in return. "This just might work."

"Of course, it will," Clare said, her eyes shining. "This is the apocalypse, and we're the survivors. Time to fight or die."

"Fight, preferably," Mason said, grabbing a nearby cart. Gripping it with one hand, he looked around. "Ready?"

"Ready!" the group replied.

With his ax raised above his head, Mason yelled, "Charge!"

As one, the group forged ahead, pushing a row of carts ahead of them. With howling cries, the zombies attacked. They threw themselves over the abandoned tills and crashed to the floor on the other side. As the infected scrambled to their feet, they tripped over the debris that littered the floor. One slipped in a puddle of cooking oil, while another tackled two of his kind in his haste to get to the humans first.

The two turned on him, snapping at his face and snarling like rabid dogs. Within seconds, the zombie lay prone on the floor with his head bent at an awkward angle. Thick, black blood poured from the bites that marred his face.

"One down, nine to go," Mason shouted, running as fast as he could.

A terrific crash sounded as the two groups collided, and the zombies went down beneath a wall of wheeled carts. They rolled around on the floor, unable to regain their feet.

Mason rode right over one before whirling around to finish it off with his ax. The edge sunk into the infected's skull with a dull thunk, and its face contorted into a death spasm. Planting one boot on its shoulder, he wrenched the blade free and looked for another victim.

A zombie sprang at him, launching itself into the air from a low crouch. Mason swung the ax, and the blunt end connected with the creature's shoulder. Caught in mid-air, it slewed to the side and crashed to the floor. Without hesitation, he followed and finished it off with a quick chop of the blade.

Clare whooped out loud as she kicked a zombie in the chest. The unfortunate creature toppled over into the arms of another, and the snarling duo went down. She crushed their skulls to a pulp with short chopping blows, her teeth bared in a vicious grin. "Take that, and that, and that!"

Mason winced as blood spattered across her face and clothes until she looked like a zombie herself. He grabbed her by the arm and pulled her away. "Clare, they're dead. They're dead."

185

She looked at him with blank eyes, and he was reminded of another time when he'd found her bloodied and pale. She hadn't recognized him then either, and he felt as if he faced a stranger instead of his own flesh and blood. "Clare! Snap out of it!"

She blinked, and Clare was back. The moment passed as if it had never been, and she pulled free from his grip. "What? I'm good, bro."

"Sure you are," Mason muttered, watching as she threw herself back into the fight.

But it turned out the brawl was over.

Susan stood with two corpses at her feet, an avenging angel with an ax dripping blood onto the floor. Michael leaned over another body with a bent pipe in his hand, and Robert had gone to town on a zombie's head with a handbasket. The plastic had exploded into chunks, mingling with the bone and brains that marred the shiny tiled floors. The last infected lay squashed beneath a cart and a collapsed display, and Susan quickly finished it off.

Once the zombies were dead, a breathless hush descended over the group. Mason did a quick tally. "Is everyone okay? No wounds, no bites, nothing?"

The others inspected themselves.

"I'm good," Clare said, wiping the blood from her face.

"Yeah, I'm getting too old for this shit," Robert said with a groan as he straightened up. His spine crackled as the joints clicked back into position.

"Me too," Susan echoed, her chest heaving for breath and her shirt damp with sweat.

"I'm still alive," Michael said.

Mason grinned. "Welcome to the end of the world, folks.

186

This is it, and we're the main attraction."

"Haha, very funny," Robert said.

"Someone's feeling a little grumpy," Mason teased.

"And someone's going to get a taste of my fist in his mouth," Robert said, frowning at him.

"That's enough," Clare said, pulling the brakes on the budding argument. She tossed her dark hair, and her look spoke volumes.

"Fine," Mason said, giving way.

"Sorry," Robert added.

Michael grinned until she turned on him, one delicate eyebrow raised. "You were saying, Michael?"

He sobered up fast. "Er, you can call me Mike."

"Mike, it is," Clare said, stomping her feet and settling her gear back into place.

Mason swallowed a chuckle. His sister had always skirted a fine line when it came to her disposition. Sometimes, she was a bitch out of hell, and at others, she'd give you the shirt off her back.

He wiped the blade of his ax on the nearest zombie's shirt and wrinkled his nose at the smell that emanated from the corpse. A few extra items popped onto his shopping list: Vaporub, air freshener, cologne, and a couple of neckties to tie around his mouth. That, plus a whole lot of other stuff.

Clare must've read his mind because she grabbed a cart and said, "Time to shop!"

"Oh, God," Robert said. "This is going to take forever."

"You're telling me," Mason said, but he was secretly glad to spend more time in his sister's company.

They hadn't been very close lately, each too busy with their schedule. It was a shame. At one point, they'd forged a strong

187

bond. It was them against the world after their parents died in a freak fire caused by faulty wiring.

At first, the accident drove them apart. Clare descended into a self-destructive haze while he blamed himself for it all until he got a call from one of her so-called friends.

Mason thought back to that night. The night he'd found her beaten and bloody on the bathroom floor of a seedy nightclub. That had been the turning point in their relationship. He'd picked her up and raced her to a hospital. After that, they'd worked through their loss and their grief together. They became a unit.

He'd since gone on to become a firefighter, and she enrolled in nursing school. The future looked bright even if they didn't see much of each other. Now they had the chance to rectify that, and he looked forward to it even if it was the end of the world.

Chapter 26 - Clare

Clare picked her way through the bodies, examining each with morbid fascination. They looked human. They were human. Yet, they weren't. Their bloodshot eyes held no emotion, no life, and nothing remained of their former selves. Or, so she hoped. "Do you think they know what they are?"

Mason looked at her, his expression somber. "What do you mean exactly?"

"Do you think they're trapped inside their bodies? Unable to help themselves?" Clare said.

"Now that's an awful thought," Susan said with a shudder.

"Agreed. If that were true, it must be horrible," Mason said with a shake of the head. "Poor things."

"It would be worse if the sickness twisted them into these monsters and made them want it," Susan said. "Or even enjoy it."

Clare pulled a face, revolted by the thought. "I'm sorry I broached the subject. It's much easier to think of them as mindless zombies unable to think or feel anything."

"Yes, indeed," Susan said. "Can we move on now? I'm getting depressed by all this talk, and I could use some action."

"Susan's right. We need to get going," Robert said, grabbing the nearest cart.

Clare followed his example, pausing to wipe her ax clean on the nearest patch of clean cloth she could find. The clotted black blood stank, and she wrinkled her nose. "Remind me to get something for the smell."

Mason grimaced. "You read my mind."

"Where to first?" Clare asked, looking around.

"We need weapons the most," Robert said. "There's no point in hoarding food or anything else if we can't defend it."

"That's true," Clare said. "Besides, I'll feel a lot better if I'm properly armed."

"I'm sure we all will," Mason said. "It'll give us an edge, at least. Zombies can't use guns."

"Then what are we waiting for?" Clare said, heading toward the aisles. Mason followed close on her heels, and it soon turned into a race. The left front wheel of her cart squeaked with every turn, and the right wheel was wonky. Still, she pushed as hard as she could, heading toward the weapons department.

"The last one there is a rotten egg," Mason cried, wheeling past her with a triumphant grin.

"We'll see about that," Clare replied, speeding up.

"Wait up, you two," Robert cried from the back. "There might be more infected around."

Clare doubted it. If there were any zombies left inside the shop, they'd have shown their faces by now. "Besides, they'd have to catch me first!"

A cross-section loomed ahead, and she glanced at the sign hanging above her head. Recognizing a possible shortcut, she took a sharp turn to the right. A space filled with tents and other camping gear blocked her way, but she didn't let that stop her. With a swift maneuver, she weaved through the objects in her path and crashed through a display of sleeping bags. They flew in every direction, and she exploded into the next aisle.

A quick look over her shoulder proved that she'd overtaken Mason. The way ahead was clear, and she jumped onto the cart with both feet. The momentum pushed her forward, and she wheeled into the weaponry section with a whoop of joy. "Yes, I did it!"

Mason showed up a second later, wearing a scowl. "No fair. You took a shortcut. You've been here before, haven't you?"

Clare shrugged. "Only once or twice, and so have you."

"Cheater," Mason mumbled.

"Loser," Clare taunted, not giving an inch of leeway.

"Am not."

Clare laughed. It felt good to be at her brother's side again. It had been too long since they'd talked, and she found she missed it. But now was not the time to reminisce, and she leaned over the counter to check behind it. "It's clear. Nothing is hiding over here."

Mason slid over the smooth bench and dropped down. A quick search revealed the keys, and he unlocked the display cases. A whistle of admiration sounded from behind as Robert appeared. Susan was right beside him, and the group gazed at the selection of weapons with eager curiosity.

Clare stared at the display, her hands itching. She was used to guns and had spent many a day on the firing range. To her, the weapons represented security and safety. They were an ace up her sleeve—something they would all sorely need in the coming days.

"What are you waiting for?" Mason said, quirking an eyebrow. "Help yourself."

"Don't mind if I do," Clare said, sliding over the counter with barely-suppressed haste.

A pair of Glock 17s with matching holsters and a belt went into her cart, along with a tactical shotgun boasting an extended magazine, plus a light hunting rifle. Ammunition and a couple of knives rounded out her selection.

"That'll do," Clare said with a big grin.

"What about now?" Mason asked. "We all need to be armed from this point onward. No more risks."

"Yes, I know," Clare said. She flashed a loaded pistol at him and looped the holster onto her belt along with a spare knife. "There. Happy?"

"It pays to be careful," Mason said, tossing her a haughty look. "We killed all the infected, but there might be more lurking around."

"That's why I've got you to watch my back, bro," Clare said, unrepentant.

Mason sighed. "Sometimes, I wonder if we're truly related."

"Wonder on your own time. We've got work to do," Robert intervened, eyeing the racks of weapons. "What about the rest of the guns? We should take as much as we can. Ammunition, as well."

"Got it," Mason said, loading his cart to the brim. He worked fast but chose carefully. They needed stopping power, but also reliability. Plus, the availability of bullets was a factor to consider going forward.

"What about food and clothes? Medicine? We need that stuff too," Clare protested.

"We do, but not as much as we need weapons. Without the means to defend ourselves, we're as good as dead," Robert said, stacking boxes of ammo onto the counter.

"That wasn't the plan," Clare said. "We're supposed to look for all sorts of supplies. Not just guns."

"I realize that, but the plan has changed," Robert said with a shrug. "With such a bounty before us, it would be dumb not to take as much as we could."

"He's right. Give it a few weeks, and this will all be a distant memory," Mike said, waving a hand at the full racks. "Everybody and his uncle will want weapons, and bullets will become a scarce commodity."

Clare thought it over. "Alright. Why don't you lot load up with guns while I grab some other stuff to tide us over?"

"I'd much rather we—" Robert began.

"Paisley's got nothing to wear. Not even a clean pair of socks," Clare said. "Just let me get a few things for her, at least."

Robert hesitated. "I forgot about Paisley, to be honest."

"Well, now I'm reminding you," Clare said. "Besides, we can easily come back for more guns tomorrow."

Mason nodded. "We can close the front doors and disable the sensors. That should keep the zombies out."

"I'm with Clare on this," Susan said. "That poor little girl has been through a lot. The least we can do is get her some clean clothes."

"Alright, but hurry, Clare. Five minutes tops," Robert said with a stern look.

"I'll meet you by the entrance," Clare said, wheeling her cart around.

"Be careful, and watch your back!" Mason called.

"I'll be fine," Clare replied, exasperated. But deep down, she appreciated his concern. She knew he had her back. He always had and always would.

193

As she headed toward the clothing section, her mind flew back to the night their parents died. She didn't remember much about the incident. It was all a blur filled with searing heat and smoke. She remembered yelling for help. The next moment, a firefighter had her in his grip and carried her to safety. She was lucky that night. So was Mason. The same wasn't true for their parents. She could still hear their screams when she closed her eyes.

It was the sound of them dying that drove her to drugs. The meds drowned out the noise and the guilt, numbing the pain until she could breathe again. It was the only time she could stand to be alive, and death became something to hope for until one fateful night.

That night she got her wish and overdosed. If it weren't for Mason, she'd be just another corpse decaying in the earth, food for the worms.

With a shudder, Clare forced her thoughts to the present. She checked the gun that rode on her hip and glanced at the ax in the cart. She couldn't afford to let her guard down. The infected could be anywhere, and she had to stay alert.

With her cart mostly empty, she tackled the racks and selected a couple of outfits for Paisley. She focused on the kind of stuff that would last: Jeans, boots, sweaters, cotton t-shirts, woolen socks, and sturdy jackets.

Next, she loaded up with clothes for herself and the other women at the station, guessing the sizes. She made sure to grab a wide selection of scarves, gloves, socks, and underwear as well.

It took longer than she'd planned, and five minutes sped past in the blink of an eye. Glancing at her watch, she grimaced. "Damn. I'd better head back."

Along the way, she snagged a few more things. Though her cart was almost full, she stuffed in a stack of towels, shampoo, conditioner, soap, toothpaste, and toothbrushes. While the items might not be essential to their survival, they would make living a whole lot easier. She also grabbed a stuffed bear from a display case and a couple of coloring books and crayons at the last minute.

It wasn't much, but Clare dearly wanted to see a smile on Paisley's face. Even if it was just for a second. *She's lost so much already, poor thing.*

"Clare! I was just about to look for you," Mason cried, breaking in on her thoughts. He flashed her an impatient look. "We've been waiting for ages."

"Ages? It's been a couple of minutes at the most," Clare replied.

"I was worried. I thought a zombie got you," Mason said.

"I can take care of myself," Clare said.

"Don't mind him," Susan said. "As you can see, the wait hasn't been wasted."

She waved a hand at their carts, and Clare eyed the contents with interest. Piled on top of the weapons was an assortment of snacks. All the junk food the shops sold around the tills, designed to lead people into temptation: Chocolate, chips, chewing gum, candy, lollipops, coke, pop tarts, and more.

"That stuff is bad for you, you know," Clare said with a chuckle.

"Who cares?" Susan said with a shrug. "If I'm going to die, I might as well go out on a sugar rush."

"Nobody is going to die," Robert said. "Not on my watch anyway. Now let's go."

They headed toward the firetruck where Sam and Amelia

waited with him leading the way. Their expressions were pale and anxious, but that soon turned to relief as the group approached.

"Robert," Amelia cried, waving at him through the window. He hurried over, and she scrambled out of the truck to embrace him. He wrapped her in his arms, lifting her clean off her feet while they kissed.

Clare watched with a touch of envy. It was heart-warming to see their devotion to each other, but it also reminded her that she was alone. Not that she needed anyone to be happy. It was a lesson learned long since. *You can't expect someone to love you if you can't love yourself.*

Shaking her head, she loaded her haul into the back of the truck, keeping an eye on her surroundings. The parking lot was still eerily empty, and she found it disturbing. The sooner they got back to the station, the better.

With a shiver of relief, Clare slid into her seat and shut the door. Sealed from the outside world, she could pretend the world was still ordinary and the apocalypse a figment of her imagination. For a short time, at least.

Chapter 27 - Robert

By the time they got back to the station, it was mid-afternoon. A chill breeze swirled through the trees, and piles of dry leaves painted the sidewalks in shades of brown, gold, and russet. The somber colors heralded the arrival of fall and reminded Robert of the cold season to come. *We need to prepare for winter.*

For the first time, he realized how much was at stake. Not only would they have to survive the zombies, but also hunger, thirst, the weather, and disease. Plus, they'd have to do it without the support of a functioning government.

Immediately, his thoughts flew to the future, and he began to list the things they'd need: Food, water, clothing, medicine, and fuel to name a few. But he pushed these thoughts aside once they reached the station and found it in a state of uproar.

The bay doors stood wide open, and the street swarmed with activity. Ruby watched the nearest road crossing dressed in full gear. She carried an ax and a whistle hung around her neck. When she spotted them, she waved them past with a broad smile.

Mason drew to a halt next to her and opened his window. "Hey, Ruby. What's going on here?"

"Clean up," Ruby replied, waving at Timothy and Benjamin.

197

They were dragging bodies across the tar and dumping them onto the back of a pickup truck. "We're getting rid of the dead, and you're just in time to help."

"Help?" Mason asked.

"Yeah, the faster we do this, the better," Ruby said, pointing at a couple of fresh corpses. "We've already had company today."

"We'll be right out," Mason said, driving the truck past her lone form toward the bay doors. Further up the street stood Ellen. She kept watch over the other crossing, her blonde ponytail fluttering in the wind.

Timothy and Benjamin didn't bother to greet. Their job was both tiring and sickening. The corpses they disposed of used to be people once. Real human beings with stories, lives, and families. Now they lay rotting in the sun, leaking blood, brains, and other unmentionable fluids.

Inside the garage, they found Theresa and Rick. They were putting up extra shelves and sorting through years of old equipment and other rubbish. Between the two of them, they created space for more supplies and got rid of any junk.

When she saw the fire truck, Theresa wiped her dirty hands with a cloth and moved closer. Her keen gaze scanned the inside of the cab, and she asked the dreaded question. "Briggs' family? Did you find them?"

"We found them," Robert replied, shaking his head.

Theresa's expression fell, but she perked up when she noticed Amelia. With a broad smile, she rushed forward and grabbed Amelia's hands. "I'm so happy to see you, my dear. You are a bright spot in an otherwise dismal day."

"Is it really that bad?" Amelia asked with a frown.

Theresa hesitated. "Perhaps, you should rest a bit first. It's a lot to take in, and you look tired."

"I'm fine," Amelia said. "A lot has happened since yesterday, and I've seen my fair share of death and suffering."

"You're right, of course. I did not mean to make light of your experiences," Theresa said.

"I would also like to know what's going on in the city, but maybe that can wait for later?" Robert interjected. "Timothy and Benjamin need help, and nightfall is just around the corner. We should be locked up tight before that."

"Agreed," Theresa said. "Amelia, dear. Please, make yourself comfortable in the kitchen while we wrap things up here."

"I can help," Amelia protested.

"So can I," Mike Evans added.

Theresa's gaze flitted from face to face. She missed nothing. Not Sam's pale complexion, the dark bags under Amelia's eyes, or the guns that rode on Robert, Mason, Clare, and Mike's hips.

"Do you think you could prepare dinner, Amelia? There are a lot of mouths to feed and they'll all be hungry come supper time," Theresa asked. "Perhaps this young man from Starbucks can help you. Bob, is it?"

"It's Sam, actually," he replied, ripping the name badge from his chest. "And I'd be happy to help. Anything that doesn't involve zombies."

"Then it's settled," Theresa said, waving them up the stairs.

Next, she turned to Mike and Clare. "Are you any good with those guns?"

"I'm a good shot, ma'am," Clare confirmed.

"I can second that," Mason said. "She's a lot better than me."

"I'm pretty good myself," Mike said. "I used to work security when I was a young man."

"Excellent. You can stand guard with Ruby and Ellen. Neither of them has a gun, and it's dangerous work. Keep those things away from our home."

"Yes, ma'am," they replied, hurrying off to their new posts.

"Mason. I don't want to tax you too hard with your head injury. You can take the hose and spray that gunk off the truck. Be sure to get it all and the floor too," Theresa said.

"I'm on it," Mason agreed, visibly relieved at the easy job.

Robert watched it all with suppressed amusement, impressed with Theresa's management skills. She knew Amelia and Sam were worn out and in need of a sense of normalcy. Cooking food would give them that, and it would serve the group.

Clare and Mike were good choices for guard duty. Both were competent shots and alert. Neither scared easy. As for Mason and Rick, they got easy jobs but they were injured. With that thought in mind, Robert turned to Theresa. "How's Rick's hand doing?"

"So far, so good. There are no signs of infection, and he hasn't turned. That's why I decided to let him out early. If he's not a zombie by now, it's not going to happen."

"Are you sure?" Robert asked.

"The CDC released some information about the disease," Theresa said. "Andrea picked it up online."

"What did they say?" Robert asked, curious.

"The disease is carried over via saliva. One bite is all it takes," Theresa said.

"What about blood? Scratches?"

"Unless it's a direct transfusion, it's unlikely. The virus is mostly concentrated in the saliva," Theresa said.

"So we don't need all these precautions?" Robert asked,

waving a hand at Mason hosing the blood and bits of flesh off the truck.

"Maybe not, but this disease isn't the only thing that can kill us. Rotting flesh and blood can cause all sorts of health hazards. For that reason, we'll continue to clean and disinfect anything that comes into contact with those things."

"What about the bodies?" Robert asked, nodding at Timothy and Benjamin. They'd loaded the last corpse onto the back of the pickup and were ready to drive off. "Where are they taking them?"

"There's an abandoned lot not far from here and nothing in the vicinity besides a couple of deserted buildings. I told them to dump the bodies there and burn them," Theresa said. "I warned them to be careful and make sure the fire doesn't spread."

"Good thinking," Robert said with a brisk nod.

"It will do until we can find a more permanent solution," Theresa said. She sighed and shook her head. "There's still so much we need to figure out."

"I know," Robert said. "We have a lot of work ahead of us."

"I'm almost too afraid to ask, but what happened to Brigg's family? And where did you get the guns?"

Robert told her the story, leaving nothing out. By the time he was done, Timothy and Benjamin were back from their trip, and Theresa pulled everyone to the relative safety of the bay.

"Good job, guys. Let's finish up, and we can all take a well-deserved break," Theresa said.

Timothy, Benjamin, and Mason hosed off the truck, followed by the pickup. After washing the floor, they cleaned and disinfected the remaining gear and axes. Rick cleared a few more shelves, and a box of trash went into the metal dumpster outside. Finally, they stored the guns and ammo in the locker room while Clare doled out clothes and toiletries to all who needed them.

As dusk crept over the city, Robert stared out into the gloom. "George and his team are still out there."

"I know," Theresa said. "They're not answering our calls or the radio."

"What do we do?"

"There's nothing we can do. Not at night anyway," Theresa said. She waved at Ruby and Ellen. "Close up, ladies."

"Yes, ma'am," they replied, shutting the first bay door.

"Can't we wait a little longer?" Robert asked.

"I'll station guards throughout the night. If they show up, we'll open for them. If not…" Theresa shook her head.

"If not, they're on their own," Robert said with grim finality.

"I'm afraid so."

As the second bay door slid shut with a clang, Robert sent out a silent thought. "George, if you're out there, stay safe, buddy. Stay safe."

Chapter 28 - George

Charged with rescuing the captain's wife and locating Lieutenant White's family, George, Elijah, and Bobbi headed out. Once they reached their first destination, the captain's home, they proceeded with their plan.

The idea was simple. Get in, grab the old lady, and get out. But the broken front door warned them all wasn't well. The house was in shambles, the furniture out of whack, and the living room carpet was soaked in blood. They never found a body. At least, nothing but a bloody shoe and a hank of gray hair attached to a piece of scalp. A grizzly find.

Their second stop ended in failure as well. The White's home was empty, and their driveway was vacant. A quick canvas of the nearby streets delivered nothing besides the usual destruction. That's when they found it. Or rather, them.

The car stood in the middle of the road, and at first, it looked abandoned. With caution, George exited the truck and jogged toward the vehicle, followed closely by Elijah. They held their axes in their hands, ready for action, while Bobbi covered them from the truck. She was the only one with a gun. Neither George nor Elijah were great shots and preferred hand weapons.

The car's windows were dark and grimy, an unusual sight.

It was only when he drew closer that he realized the truth. The windows weren't dirty. They were covered in blood. His heart sank into his boots, and he froze to the spot. He really didn't want to see what was inside the car and backed up a step. "This is bad."

"Whatever happened in there wasn't pretty," Elijah agreed.

"I don't think I want to know," George said.

"We have to make sure," Elijah said.

"Do we? It's pretty obvious they're dead."

"Come on," Elijah said, nudging him forward.

"Fine," George said, forcing himself to move. As he got closer, his eyes took in the smeared handprints and splashes of blackened blood. It covered the interior like a cloak, but a single clear spot drew his attention.

With bated breath, he looked through the opening. The first thing he saw was a teddy bear lying on the seat. The second thing he saw was a hand, a tiny one, clutching the bear. Hope blossomed in his chest until… "It's just a hand."

"What?" Elijah asked.

"It's just a hand. There's no arm," George replied. Bile rose up his throat, burning like acid.

Suddenly, a face smashed into the window, and a cacophony of snarls and growls filled the air. George fell back with a cry of horror, his heart jumping into his throat. His gaze fixed upon the small figure silhouetted against the bloody glass—a little girl.

Two more figures joined the child, and all hell broke loose within the car. The vehicle rocked on its axis as the occupants fought to escape its confines. Their fists and heads butted against the windows, and they clawed at the glass.

George stared at the little girl with awful fascination.

"Tammy. I'm so sorry."

"You knew the girl?" Elijah asked, helping him to his feet.

George nodded, his mouth dry. He'd seen her once or twice when her mom stopped at the station to greet her husband, Lieutenant White. She'd been a cute little thing in a sundress and pigtails. Now, she was a monster. A tiny, flesh-eating monster.

Trapped inside the car with her was the rest of her family. Her mom, Lindsey, and her older brother, Thomas. He remembered them too. They were just a normal, happy family like any other. All dead now.

"We're too late," George said, his heart heavy with regret.

"I'm sorry, man. Let's go. There's nothing we can do for them now," Elijah said, coaxing him to his feet.

"We should've come for them sooner," George said, resisting Elijah's pull.

"Don't do that to yourself," Elijah said, tugging on his arm. "It's not your fault."

"Isn't it?" George asked.

Suddenly, the truck's horn blared, and they whipped around in alarm. Bobbi waved at them through the half-open window. "Get inside! We've got company!"

George's eyes widened when he spotted the infected that appeared from every direction. They spilled into the open street like cockroaches, emerging from alleys, side streets, and looted shops. They were drawn by the noise and movement of fresh prey and eagerly closed in for the kill.

"There's too many of them to fight," George said, summing up the situation in an instant. "Run!"

He broke into a sprint with Elijah hot on his heels. Their boots pummeled the tar, their movements cumbersome with all the gear they wore. The distance between them and the truck closed but not quickly enough.

A knot of zombies rushed into the open space between them, cutting off their escape. George swore below his breath. They were surrounded and would have to fight their way through. With one swift move, he pulled the ax from his belt and gripped it with both hands.

George charged the nearest infected with his weapon raised above his head. He slammed the blade down onto the crown of its head and looked away when blood spewed from the wound. The zombie collapsed at his feet, and he jumped over it in one smooth leap. Seconds later, he reached the truck and slammed into its smooth metal side.

Bobbi was frantic and urged him onward with lots of yelling and screaming. "Hurry up, damn it. Do you want to get eaten?"

"Of course not," George replied, yanking open the door. He jumped into the cab and scooted over to make space.

Elijah dived in next and slammed the door shut. "Go, go, go!"

Bobbi cranked the truck into gear, and they lurched forward into the gathering crowd of zombies. A sickening crunch sounded when one of them fell beneath the wheels, and a spray of blood washed across the hood.

"Close that window," Bobbi yelled, throwing Elijah an angry look.

"I'm trying," he shouted back, hampered by the ax he carried and the thick gloves he wore.

"Well, try harder, damn it," Bobbi cried, pushing through the crowd. "Whose bright idea was it to leave it open in the first place?"

"Just shut up and drive," Elijah said.

More thumps and bumps sounded as Bobbi pushed through the crowd of bodies. Within seconds the entire front of the truck was covered in muck. The smell of decay invaded their nostrils, and George gagged. "Oh, shit. That's nasty."

"You're telling me," Bobbi said, pulling her shirt up over her nose. "Close the damned window!"

Elijah tossed aside his ax and yanked his glove off. With his bare hand, he closed the window with a couple of furious turns. It sealed them inside the cabin, trapping them with the smell.

"Now, who's bright idea was that?" Elijah said, tossing Bobbi a nasty look. But he shut his mouth when a corpse exploded across the side, covering the glass pane in clotted blood.

"You can thank me later," Bobbi said, steering them away from the hellish neighborhood.

"Thanks," Elijah grumbled as the ride smoothed out.

A couple of minutes later, they were in the clear, and Bobbi threw them a questioning look. "What happened?"

George stared at her, unable to form the words. "I... I can't... ."

"Just drive, Bobbi," Elijah said. "The Whites are gone."

"The kids too?" she asked, shaking her head. "Those poor people."

George closed his eyes and looked away. He didn't want to think about it. Didn't want to think about anything. *That hand. It was so small.*

Tears pricked his eyelids, and he shifted in his seat. Would he ever be able to forget that moment? He didn't think so. It was etched in his brain and burned into his retinas. I'll never be able to sleep again.

"George?" Bobbi said. When he didn't answer straight away,

she raised her voice. "George!"

"What?" He frowned at her, still caught up in the past.

"What do we do now? Do we head back to the station?" she asked.

"I don't know," George said. At that moment, he didn't care what they did. What did it matter when weighed against the tragic loss he'd just witnessed?

"Well, think about it," Bobbi insisted.

"Why should I? Can't you decide? Or Elijah?"

"I would if I could, but I'm not in charge here, and neither is Elijah," Bobbi said. "You are."

"Not anymore," George said, folding his arms.

"Snap out of it, will you?" Bobbi said, her voice sharp. "I'm driving blind here, and you'll kill us all if you don't make a decision."

George realized she was right. He could mourn Tammy and the rest of her family later, but Elijah and Bobbi were his responsibility, and so were the people back at the station. At that moment, he spotted a familiar sight, and inspiration struck. "Stop right there."

"What for?" Bobbi asked, slowing down.

"That's a pharmacy, and we're going to grab as much medicine as we can. We'll need it in the months to come."

"A pharmacy?" Bobbi said. "Are you sure?"

"Uh-huh. I've stopped there a few times in the past. I live three blocks from here," George explained.

"Fascinating," Bobbi said in a dry tone of voice, but she pulled over nonetheless.

Parked in front of the pharmacy, they studied the interior. The door was open a crack, and the lighting was dim, but it appeared deserted. After a thorough look around, they got out of the truck.

George took the lead and pushed open the door. It creaked as it swung wide, and he waited for something to jump out at him. When nothing happened, he nodded at Elijah. "It looks empty, but be careful."

"Got it," Elijah said.

"Watch our backs, Bobbi," he added, nodding at her gun.

"Will do," Bobbi said. She took up a position by the doorway, only a few feet away from the truck.

After a last look around, George ducked inside the shop. A couple of lights shone overhead, and glass crunched underfoot. A few of the shelves lay on the ground, their contents scattered. It was apparent the place had been looted, which was a shame. Still, he hoped they'd find enough to make their stop worthwhile.

It didn't take long to sweep the small space. Family-owned, the pharmacy had a homely atmosphere, far from the commercial varieties in the city center. Now he wondered what had happened to the family, and he hoped they were okay.

His foot bumped against a couple of baskets, and he handed one to Elijah. "Take as much as you can. Painkillers, cough syrup, anti-inflammatories, bandages, the works. I'll hit the back counter for the heavy stuff."

"I'm on it," Elijah said, taking the basket.

George moved toward the back, picking his way through the debris. Thankfully, there was no blood. No blood and no zombies. He spotted a shelf filled with protein bars and tucked a few into his pocket for later. He had a weakness for chocolate, especially the kind with nuts.

When he reached the main counter, he paused. "How are

you doing, Elijah?"

"I'm good," Elijah answered.

Reassured, George ducked behind the counter and filled his basket with as much as he could find. Despite being looted, the pharmacy had plenty left. There was a locked cupboard as well, tucked away in a corner. It probably contained the heavy stuff, but it was locked, and he had no time to waste.

Abandoning the locked cupboard, he opened the freezer. It contained a bunch of vials, and he debated whether he should take them or not. *I need a cooler for that, or the stuff will perish.*

Finally, he decided against it. They could always come back another day. Still, he wanted to grab at least one more basket and jogged to the front. "Bobbi. Can you hold this? I want to go back for another basket. There's still a lot left."

She eyed the basket. "How much are we talking about?"

"A lot, and it's the good stuff," George said.

"Then we should take as much as we can," Bobbi said. "In a few months, places like this will be stripped bare."

"What about keeping watch?" George asked.

Bobbi took a quick look outside. "It's deserted. There's not a zombie in sight. If we hurry, it won't take more than a few minutes."

George hesitated. "Are you sure?"

"We'd be fools to leave without this medicine. Remember, there are no more doctors, no more nurses, hospitals, or clinics. We only have ourselves and what we can scavenge," Bobbi said, her expression grim.

"Alright, but we'd better move fast," George said despite his misgivings.

Bobbi took his basket as well as Elijah's and ran to the truck. She dumped the contents inside and ran back. Baskets in hand, she pushed past George and made her way to the main counter. "Coming? We don't have all day."

"I'm coming," George said, rolling his eyes. He scooped up two more baskets and followed her, picking up items as he went.

Together, he and Bobbi cleaned out the back while Elijah swept the front. Once they each had a full load, they dumped the supplies into the fire truck and returned for a second round.

"Come on," Bobbi urged them when they lagged. "We're almost done."

"Alright," George agreed, but with every second that passed, he grew more nervous. He kept glancing at the truck. It was mere feet from the door, yet, it might as well have been miles. There was no back door, no escape route. *If the infected show up, we're trapped.*

The tip of his boot bumped against a box of pills, and he bent down to retrieve it. Suddenly, he heard a loud yell. Jerking upright, he spotted Elijah grappling with an infected.

They stumbled back and forth, bumping into shelves and toppling displays. Metal clattered against metal, and glass shattered on the floor. George winced at the awful racket, knowing it would draw more zombies, but that was the least of his worries.

The infected had a death grip on Elijah's helmet, exposing the lower half of his face, and its teeth were dangerously close to his jugular. It snapped at his flesh, inching closer and closer with every second that passed.

"George, Bobbi! Help me!" Elijah cried.

"Hold on!" George yelled, jumping across the counter. His boots hit the floor with a thud, and he ran toward the struggling duo.

He reached Elijah within seconds and grabbed the infected's collar. With a yank, he threw the zombie to the side. Suddenly, Bobbi was there, her pistol in her hand. A single bullet punched into the zombie's skull, spraying its brains across the floor.

The shot echoed through the shop, and George's ears rang with the force of the blast. He pressed both hands to his head to block out the sound, but there was no time to waste. Hands tugged at his arms, and he looked into Elijah's wide eyes.

"Come on. We have to block the door," Elijah cried.

"What?" George asked, still dazed.

"They're coming!" Elijah yelled, pointing at the front.

George turned to look, and his stomach dropped to the floor. Zombies streamed from every direction, pushing and shoving in their eagerness to get to the shop. They'd reach the entrance within moments, and there was no time to lose.

George jumped to his feet and sprinted toward the mob of infected. He smashed into the front runner, ramming it with his shoulder. The zombie flew backward, taking a bunch of its kind down to the ground. Bobbi snapped off several shots, most of them going wild, but a few found their target.

A small gap opened in the crowd, and George took full advantage of it. Grabbing the doorjamb with both hands, he slammed it shut. With his back pressed to the glass, he waved at Elijah and Bobbi. "Help me block the door."

Together, they barricaded the entrance with shelves, chairs, and anything else they could get their hands on. Once they'd finished, they stepped back to survey their handiwork.

"I think it will hold," Elijah said.

"It had better hold. There are too many of those things out

there to fight, and I only have four bullets left," Bobbi said, checking her magazine.

"What do we do now?" Elijah asked. "There's no way out. We can't kill them all, and the radio is inside the truck."

George shook his head. "We wait. Maybe if we lie low, they'll lose interest and move on."

"But that could take hours. Or days," Elijah protested. "Ruby is going to be so pissed at me."

"At least you'll be alive," Bobbi said.

"Not if she kills me first," Elijah said.

"Do you have a better idea?" George pointed out. "Robert and the others will come looking for us if we don't show up at the station."

"Hopefully," Bobbi said.

"At least we won't starve," George said, producing a couple of protein bars from his pocket. "There's running water in the kitchen and a bathroom in the back."

"You can have the water," Elijah said, walking toward a fridge filled with cool drinks, energy drinks, and fruit juices. "I'll have a coke. Want one?"

"I suppose we might as well make the best of it," George said, taking the proffered can from Elijah. The coke fizzed when he popped it open, a sound that was music to his ears. The cold liquid bubbled down his throat, and he groaned with pleasure. "Ooh, I've missed that."

"You and me both," Elijah agreed with a broad grin. "The end of the world sucks."

Bobbi snorted. "It's only been a couple of days. Try a few months from now."

George grimaced. "I don't even want to think about it."

"Well, stop playing around and help me cover the windows.

213

The zombies won't leave as long as they can see us," Bobbi said with a shake of the head.

One shelf contained a selection of stationery, and she grabbed a roll of sticky tape. A box filled with gift wrapping provided the material she needed to cover the glass, and she got to work. "Come on, you two. The quicker we get this done, the better."

George jumped in with a roll of Christmas wrapping followed by Elijah, and it wasn't long before the outside world was blocked from view. With a smile of satisfaction, he surveyed their handiwork. "That should do the trick."

"Only if we keep quiet," Bobbi said.

"My mouth is sealed," George said, zipping his lips shut.

"We can sleep in the back and take turns to stand watch," Bobbi ordered.

"Sounds good to me," George said, heading toward the small office in the back. With any luck, he'd find a sofa to put up his feet.

"Hold on," Bobbi said. "While we're stuck here, we might as well gather up the rest of the supplies and stack them by the door."

"Now?" George asked.

"Yes, now. We don't know what's going to happen. Someone might show up at any time, and we have to be ready to go," Bobbi said. "And when I say everything, I mean it. Protein powders, bars, cold drinks, water, medicine, toiletries, and even the baby stuff. We don't know what we might need in the future or how much, so take it all."

"Fine," George said, grabbing a basket. He couldn't refute her logic. She was right, as usual, but one thing was for sure. It was going to be a long night.

Chapter 29 - Andrea

Andrea squinted at the notebook in front of her. The lines were all squiggly and blurred, a clear sign that she was done working. She closed the book and capped the pen, placing both to the side.

She leaned back in her chair with a sigh and tilted her head from side to side. It had been a long day, most of it spent hunched over the desk, and the muscles in her back were tight. At least, it wasn't in vain. She'd made a lot of headway. Despite the lack of communication, there was still life left in the city. "But that's enough for now, right, Sebastian?"

Sebastian gazed at her from his spot on the couch, blinking lazily. He appeared calm, but the twitch in his tail betrayed his annoyance at being cooped up all day.

Andrea shot him a sympathetic smile. "Don't worry, kitten. It's only for a few days. I'll let you out as soon as you're used to your new home."

Her choice of words caused her to pause. *Is this really our new home? Or is it just another stop in a long line of temporary shelters?*

While not a fan of horror, she'd watched enough zombie movies to know that life would never be the same again. Unless the government could pull a rabbit out of the hat, life as she'd known it was over.

The thought caused a pang of sorrow to shoot through her heart. Already Andrea missed her house and everything in it. It wasn't much: A two-bedroom cottage on the edge of town. But it was cozy, and it belonged to her. It was her reward for a lifetime's worth of hard work, and now, she longed for its homey comforts: The smell of roses and lavender drifting from the garden on a cool summer breeze. The crackling warmth of the flames in the fireplace on a cold, dreary night. A good book from her study to pass a mellow afternoon. *I wish I could turn back the clock. I'd never have left the house if I'd known what would happen. There's enough food in my pantry to last us for weeks. I could've locked the gates and the doors and kept quiet. No one would've ever known we were there.*

With a shake of her head, she pushed the thought aside. There was no point in looking back, and her common sense told her she'd never have lasted long on her own. Her wish was simply that. Wishful thinking.

A touch against her leg caused her to look down. It was Sebastian. He'd sensed her distress and wanted to comfort her the only way he knew how. He gazed up at her with his grass-green eyes and meowed plaintively, his bushy tail curling around her ankle.

"Oh, Sebastian. At least I still have you," Andrea said, bending down. She picked him up and nuzzled his cheek, his long whiskers pricking her skin. He curled up on her lap, purring with contentment while she stroked his luxurious fur. The rhythmic vibrations soothed her, and she forgot her troubles after a while. It didn't matter where they ended up, after all. As long as she had him, she was happy.

A knock on the door interrupted her thoughts, and Andrea

called out, "Who is it?"

The door opened a crack, and Theresa's head popped around the corner. "Sorry to bother, but I thought you might like some tea."

"Thank you. I'd like that," Andrea said.

Theresa shut the door with a soft click and walked across the room with the teacup and saucer. She placed the items on the desk and took a seat opposite Andrea.

"How did it go today?" Theresa asked. "Did you make any progress?"

"I did," Andrea answered with a nod. She was about to reach for the notebook, but Theresa stopped her.

"Drink your tea, dear. As much as I'd like to hear about your findings, it might be better if you shared them with everyone over dinner," Theresa said.

"Alright," Andrea said, picking up the cup. She took a sip and raised her eyebrows. "This is an excellent tea."

"It's from my personal stash," Theresa confided. "Earl Grey. I've never been fond of coffee. I have a low tolerance for caffeine."

"I can appreciate that," Andrea said, taking another sip.

"How is Sebastian settling in?" Theresa asked, eyeing the cat on Andrea's lap.

"He's okay. Restless and a little bored, but he'll be fine," Andrea said.

"I suppose it will take a while for him to get used to the place," Theresa replied. "But I hope he likes it here."

"I hope so too."

"I'm sending Robert on a supply run tomorrow, and I'll make sure he gets whatever Sebastian needs. Food, litter, and anything else you can think of. Just make a list," Theresa said, waving at the notebook.

"That would be wonderful," Andrea said, her feelings toward Theresa warming by the second. "But how does Robert feel about it? He's not exactly thrilled by our presence."

"He'll get used to it," Theresa replied, her tone sharp. "You are one of us now. Sebastian too, and we look after our own."

"That is an admirable sentiment," Andrea said with a half-smile.

"Is something bothering you?" Theresa asked.

"No. I just can't help but wonder how long that ideal will last once the gloves come off," Andrea replied.

"You're thinking ahead, I see." Theresa tapped her fingers on the desk. "Good. I need straight thinkers around here. When the real hardships of the apocalypse set in, relationships will be tested."

"Exactly, and even this tight-knit community might buckle under the strain," Andrea said.

"That's why we need to make sure that doesn't happen," Theresa said. "We can, and we will weather this storm."

"Well, I'll help in any way that I can." Andrea finished her tea and placed the cup back on the saucer. "I can start by sharing some good news around the table tonight."

"Lord knows. We could all use some good news," Theresa said.

"Did something happen today?" Andrea asked.

"George and his team haven't returned. They're still out there somewhere," Theresa said with a worried look.

"And Robert's team?"

"They're safe, and they managed to rescue Amelia and a couple of others from her office."

"Amelia?"

"Robert's wife," Theresa explained. "Unfortunately, it was too late for Lieutenant Brigg's family."

"I'm sorry to hear that," Andrea said, and she meant it. Any loss was detrimental to the group, and they had to keep morale high.

"On the bright side, they stopped at a camping shop on the way back and retrieved a truckload of weapons and ammunition," Theresa said. "While I'm not exactly crazy about guns, we need them."

"As long as we're careful," Andrea said.

"Agreed, but that's not all. Clare was kind enough to grab some clothes and toiletries. She had to guess at the sizes, but there should be something to fit you."

"That was nice of her."

"It'll do for now. Hopefully, we can get more supplies in the days to come," Theresa said, standing up. She reached for the empty cup and saucer. "Let me take that to the kitchen for you."

"I'll join you," Andrea said, gently nudging Sebastian off her lap. "Dinner must be almost ready."

"You're probably right. Let's join the rest in the kitchen," Theresa agreed.

Together, they left the office. As Andrea closed the door, she waved at Sebastian. "I'll be right back, kitten."

"Has he eaten yet?" Theresa asked as they walked down the hall.

"Yes, I fed him an hour ago," Andrea confirmed. "Or else he'd be a very grumpy cat right now!"

Theresa laughed. "I can only imagine."

The kitchen was a hive of activity. People jostled for space, and the air hummed with conversation. Susan and Timothy,

219

both wearing aprons, placed the finishing touches on the food while Ruby passed around plates, and Mason distributed the knives and forks. Robert took two jugs of cold water from the fridge and filled a round of glasses.

"Have a seat, everyone," Susan said, yelling to be heard above the din. She spotted Andrea and Theresa and smiled. "There you are. I was just about to call you. Dinner is almost ready."

"It smells delicious, my dear," Theresa said with a smile.

"Thank you, Susan," Andrea added, taking the nearest empty chair. She found herself sitting between Ruby and Benjamin, neither of whom she knew very well. Or not at all, if she was being honest.

A strange woman waved at her from across the table. "Hi. Andrea, is it? I'm Amelia. Robert's wife."

"Nice to meet you," Andrea said, operating on autopilot.

"And this is Sam and Mike," Amelia added. "They were with me when Robert rescued us."

Andrea nodded at the strangers and forced herself to engage in small talk. It was not a situation she felt comfortable with, being an introvert, but she persisted. The sooner she made a few friends, the better.

Still, it was a relief when Susan and Timothy interrupted, negating the need to chat. They placed dinner in the middle of the table and took their seats. The food looked and smelled delicious, and her stomach cramped with anticipation. She hadn't eaten since breakfast and couldn't wait to dig in. Neither could anyone else, but they waited until everyone sat down.

Clare and Paisley were the last to enter, and Andrea studied the child from the corner of her eye. She was glad to see the girl had regained some color in her cheeks, though she ducked her head and tried to back out when faced with a room full of adults. *Poor thing. She's lost everything, and now she's being raised by a bunch of strangers. It's the stuff of nightmares.*

"Come on, sweetie. It's okay," Clare said, coaxing Paisley toward a chair. "Aren't you hungry?"

Paisley nodded, chewing on her thumb.

"I promise we won't bite," Robert said with a benign look.

"And you look so pretty in your new pajamas," Theresa cried, waving the girl closer.

The rest of the group chimed in, making a big fuss of Paisley's outfit. The friendly faces allowed the child to relax, and she chose to sit between Theresa and Clare, her two favorite people.

"Dig in, everyone," Susan said, waving a hand at the food.

"Yes, help yourselves," Theresa added. "We can talk business afterward."

"Sounds good to me," Robert said, reaching for a platter piled high with fried steaks. He passed it around, and everyone dished up except for Ruby.

"I'm a vegetarian," Ruby said in answer to Andrea's curious look.

"You are? So am I."

"It's nice to know I'm not the only one," Ruby said, offering her a bread roll.

"Thanks," Andrea said, taking the roll.

"There's lentil and vegetable stew," Susan said, pointing at a bowl in the middle of the table. "No meat or meat by-products. Promise."

"You made that? For us?" Andrea asked, surprised.

"Theresa told me you don't eat meat, and that's one of Ruby's favorite dishes," Susan said.

"She's right," Ruby said, spooning a generous portion onto her plate. "I could eat this all day, every day."

Andrea took a bite, relieved to find that it was delicious. The stew was both hearty, filling, and nutritious, precisely what she needed after a long day's work. She rounded it off with a portion of garden salad and settled down to her meal while studying the people around the room.

The firefighters talked, laughed, and joked with each other like they were a family, and she supposed, in a way, they were. With the life-and-death situations they faced almost daily, mutual trust was a necessity.

Even Robert seemed happier now that he had Amelia by his side. A fact that put Andrea more at ease, as well. She knew that Robert's opinion carried weight with the group, and she needed them on her side. Now that he had his wife back, Robert might look at her with kinder eyes.

In any case, she was determined to prove that she could carry her weight. And she would do exactly that as soon as dinner was over and Paisley had gone to bed. Theresa was right. They could weather the storm, but only if they had help. Outside help.

Chapter 30 - Robert

Robert finished the last of his steak and turned his attention to the salad and bread rolls. The food was simple but well-prepared. Even the lentil stew smelled delicious, though the very fibers of his being rebelled against the thought of never eating meat again. *No, thank you. I'm not a rabbit.*

It didn't take long for him to polish his plate, and he pushed it aside with a groan of satisfaction. He wasn't the only one. All around the table, appreciation reigned for the chefs of the evening. "I have to hand it to you, Susan and Timothy. That was an excellent meal."

"Why, thank you," Susan said, returning his smile. "I'm glad you think so."

"Oh, I do. Where did you learn to cook like that?" he asked.

"My father owned a restaurant, and I grew up in the kitchen hanging onto his apron strings," Susan said.

"And you, Timothy?"

Timothy shrugged, his copper curls glinting in the light. "I picked up a few things from my mom. She loves to cook, bake, and preserve. She even had a stall at the farmer's market every Saturday. People used to come from miles away to buy her goods."

"Have you heard from them recently?" Theresa asked,

placing her knife and fork delicately to the side. She dabbed at her mouth with a napkin and took a sip of water from her glass.

"Yes, ma'am. I got a text message saying they're safe and hunkering down until this thing passes."

"Thing?" Theresa repeated with a smile.

Timothy's cheeks reddened. "I'm not rightly sure what to call it, ma'am."

"The apocalypse," Robert said. "That's what you call it."

"I also heard from my son, Noah, today. I sent him an email on the office computer, and he replied," Susan said with a look of intense relief.

"Is he okay?" Robert asked, concerned. He'd never met Susan's son, but he could only imagine how anxious she must feel.

"They're safe and docking off the coast of France. So far, they've managed to keep the infection from coming on board, and they have enough supplies to last them a couple of months," Susan said with a shaky smile. "With any luck, they can ride out the worst of it."

"You must be relieved," Robert said.

"Yes, but I'm still worried. I can't help it. I'm a mom," Susan replied with a tiny shrug.

"Does this mean I can contact my family?" Ellen asked, leaning forward. "And Rick can try phoning his brother again?"

"I don't see why not," Theresa said. "If messages are getting through, the lines can't be completely down."

"No, they're not. There are gaps. Small moments of opportunity when the lines aren't jam-packed with signals," Andrea said, jumping into the conversation.

"Oh? That's interesting," Robert said, his brow furrowed. "Is the government still in charge? Are they operational and working on the problem?"

"That I can't say," Andrea said, shaking her head. "The people I contacted today know as much we do, which isn't a lot."

"People? You got hold of other people?" Robert asked, excitement blossoming in his chest. "Who? Where?"

"We can get to that in a moment, Robert," Theresa said. "First, let's clear the dishes and get certain people to bed." She threw a meaningful look at Paisley, and Robert got the hint.

"Of course. Sorry for jumping in like that," he said. He took his plate and reached for Amelia's. "Let me help with the clean-up."

"Thank you, dear," Amelia said, flashing him a brilliant smile.

He reached out and squeezed her hand, content that she was safe and back by his side again. It was all that mattered. She meant the world to him, and he couldn't imagine going through life, or the apocalypse, without her.

"I'll be back in a moment. Don't start without me," Clare said, interrupting his thoughts.

She guided a sleepy-looking Paisley away from the table, and Robert waved at the girl. "Sleep tight, little one. Don't let the bedbugs bite."

"Good night," Paisley replied with a yawn.

She shuffled off in her new pajamas and slippers, and his heart went out to her. He realized how much they needed her to be okay because if she could recover, they all could. To the people inside the station, she represented hope: hope and the possibility of a future.

Once Clare and Paisley were gone, the rest jumped in to help with the chores. Within minutes, they'd packed away the leftovers, washed and dried the dishes, and made coffee and tea for everyone.

Once they'd all settled down with a drink of their choice, including Clare, Theresa cleared her throat. "Is everyone here?" A rumble of assent rose around the table. "What about Paisley?"

"She's asleep," Clare said with a grin. "It didn't take much. She was out the moment her head hit the pillow."

Theresa chuckled. "Well, I kept her busy dusting shelves and counting stock today. I'm not at all surprised she's tired."

"You made her do chores the whole day?" Amelia said. "What about playtime? Schooling?"

"We don't have any toys, and we're not equipped to teach kids here," Theresa said. "It's one of the many things on my list. In the meantime, keeping her busy will take her mind off her situation. It's the best I can do for now."

"You're right, of course. I didn't think of that," Amelia said.

"What about Elijah?" Ruby asked. "He's out there somewhere, dead or alive."

"They're our first priority. If they're not back by tomorrow morning, we'll look for them, I promise," Theresa said.

"What if they show up during the night?" Ruby asked.

"We'll post guards around the clock. Who wants the first shift?" Theresa asked.

"I do," Ellen said, raising her hand. "I won't be able to sleep much anyway."

"I'll take the second shift," Rick said.

"I'll help," Mike Evans offered.

"Thanks, Mike. We appreciate that," Robert said. He didn't expect much of Sam, however. The boy had been struck by the loss of Jane and didn't have anything to say or volunteer.

He'll come around eventually.

Several more members volunteered. Finally, the roster was filled, and plans were put in place if George and his team should arrive during the night.

"We'll get them back, Ruby. They're still alive; I know it," Theresa said.

"Thanks. I appreciate it, but if he shows up without a damn good story, I'm ripping him a new one," Ruby said with a grim look.

"Poor Elijah," Benjamin muttered.

Ruby threw him a sharp look. "That's between us."

Benjamin shrugged and kept his mouth shut, unwilling to take it further. Not even to save his friend's ass.

"With that settled, we should discuss our plans for the coming days," Theresa said, quickly changing the subject. "Any thoughts?"

"You mean besides rescuing George and the rest if they don't show up tonight?" Robert asked.

"Besides that," Theresa said, inclining her head. "We have to put a strategy in place, and while I've got plenty of ideas, I'm also open to your input."

"We need supplies and lots of it," Robert said.

"Yes, we do," Theresa agreed. "But getting those supplies won't be easy with those things out there."

"We can start with our homes," Ruby suggested. "It's familiar territory, and we can all contribute something. I've got lots of extra clothes and bedding at my house."

"I've got a garage full of equipment we can use," Benjamin said.

"That's not a bad idea," Theresa said. "It would be safer than hitting the shops and malls."

"Let's not forget the outdoor center we visited today," Robert said. "We killed the only infected inside and blocked the entrance. The place is a literal warehouse filled with all sorts of stuff. Weapons, clothes, tools, gear, food, water, and more."

"I can attest to that," Clare said, chiming in. "Plus, they've got toys, stationery, and books for Paisley."

"I hope they've got books for us, too," Amelia said. "Anything to relieve boredom."

"You raise a good point," Theresa said. "With our daily lives disrupted, it's important that we keep our spirits high. Books, movies, music, and board games would help achieve that goal."

"What about pet supplies?" Andrea asked, leaning forward. "Do they have any? Sebastian needs food and litter."

"I'm not sure," Clare said, chewing on her bottom lip.

"Robert?" Theresa asked, raising an eyebrow.

She clearly expected some gesture from him, and he heaved an inward sigh. "I'm sure they have a section dedicated to pets. If not, I'll make a point of finding what you need."

"Thank you," Andrea replied with a look of surprise. "I appreciate that."

"It's nothing," Robert said, surprised to find he meant it. Now that he had Amelia, his earlier frustration with Andrea had vanished. It wasn't her fault she loved her cat. It wasn't something he understood, never having had any pets, but each to their own.

"What happens when the fresh stuff runs out?" Amelia asked. "Things like milk, cheese, cream, fruit, and vegetables?"

"We should gather what we can and store it," Timothy said. "My mom taught me how to preserve and can, and we can freeze a lot of it."

"Presuming we have the storage facilities," Theresa said.

"That means adding freezers to the list of stuff to get," Robert mused.

"And beds," Theresa said. "What happens if we find more survivors?"

"We need more space," Robert said.

"And where would we get that?" Theresa asked, waving a hand around. "We're already bursting at the seams."

"I don't know," Robert admitted.

"What about the buildings on either side of us? We can clear them out, fortify them, and make them part of the station," Elijah said. "I'm in construction, and it can be done if we have the equipment and material."

"It's too dangerous," Robert protested. "We can't be in the open for long with those things out there."

"We can block the roads leading to the station," Ruby suggested.

"With what?" Robert asked.

"Cars. There are lots of them just standing around," Ruby said. "We can barricade the roads and station armed guards on the roof."

"That's an excellent idea," Robert said, inclining his head.

What about water, fuel, and electricity?" Benjamin asked. All heads turned toward him. "Think about it. The power is bound to go out at some point. When that happens, the water goes, and the fuel pumps too."

"He's got a point," Clare said, looking glum.

Mason shook his head, talking for the first time. "What about the fuel station around the corner? We can include it in our territory and install a generator to run the pumps if they don't have one. That gives us a few months' supplies, at least."

"And we already have solar panels and a generator installed

229

here at the station," Theresa said. "It's not enough to run the entire building, however, so we'll need more."

"We can install tanks on the roof and fill them up while we still have running water," Elijah said. "Plus, we could set up a rain catchment system."

"Mm. None of these measures will be enough in the long term, but it's a start," Theresa said. "Assuming we can get our hands on everything we need."

"We can grow our own fruit, vegetables, and herbs, too," Timothy said.

"Where would we do that?" Robert asked.

"On the roof. We'll need potting soil, seeds, containers, and gardening equipment, but I can get it going in no time," Timothy said with a bright smile.

"Wow. The list keeps getting longer and longer," Clare said with a glum look.

She wasn't the only one. The prevailing mood in the room had gone from hopeful to hopeless in less than ten minutes.

"Talk about doing the impossible," Robert said, slumping in his chair.

"We can do it," Amelia said, looking around. "It won't be easy, and it'll be hard work, but I know we can do this. Look what we've accomplished already."

"Accomplished?" Clare asked.

"Look around you. We're safe. We have food, water, and weapons," Amelia said. "Thanks to Andrea, we know more people are out there."

Robert's heart warmed in his chest. *Trust Amelia to be the voice of hope in the crowd. She never quits, and she never gives up.* "You're right, sweetheart. We can do this, and we will." He looked at all the faces around the table and smiled. "Now, who's up for more coffee?"

Chapter 31 - Ellen

With their immediate plans for the future made, the conversation turned to the other survivors out in the city. That was where Andrea came in.

"Tell us what you learned today," Theresa said, smiling at Andrea.

Ellen settled back in her chair, cradling a fresh cup of coffee between her palms. She gave Andrea her full attention, curious to know what the woman had discovered. Still, she couldn't help but be aware of Rick's presence next to her. Every so often, his knee brushed against hers, and her heart leaped into her throat. It was incredibly distracting.

Andrea cleared her throat and waited for silence before she began to speak. "I was able to contact a small group of survivors this morning. They've taken refuge at a nearby office block. There are three cops, a couple of reservists, and a handful of civilians."

"That is good news indeed," Theresa said.

Murmurs rose around the table, and some of the doom and gloom in the atmosphere dissipated.

"But do go on. Don't let us interrupt," Theresa said with a wave.

"Their leader, Officer Frank Hearn, told me there are more

people holed up at a nearby school. Mostly teachers, children, parents, and a handful of other refugees," Andrea said. "He told them to hunker down for the moment."

"Anyone else? Emergency services? Paramedics? The Mayor?" Theresa asked.

Andrea shook her head. "Nobody has heard from the government here in town, and the hospital has gone dark. No surprise, considering the infection must've hit them the hardest."

"That's it?" Ellen asked, a knot in her throat.

"I can't get through to anyone else, including the emergency services, and the Internet is a mess of conflicting reports, stories, and rumors," Andrea said. "I'm still trying to make sense of it. When I have something concrete, I'll share it with you guys."

"That's depressing," Ellen said, her mood going south.

"There is one more thing," Andrea said. "Officer Hearn suspects more people have taken refuge at the local library and the town hall," Andrea added.

"The town hall?" Theresa asked. "Weren't they planning a fundraiser there this week?"

"Uh-huh, and they were collecting food and second-hand clothes," Susan said with a nod. "I bet it's a gold mine for supplies."

"If that's true, survivors will be able to live there for quite a while," Theresa said.

"A logical step," Andrea agreed.

"We should try to meet with this Officer Hearn," Robert said. "Perhaps if we work together, we can take back the city."

"With just a handful of people?" Ellen asked, frowning. "Three officers, two reservists, and us?"

"We have to start somewhere," Robert said with a shrug. "Besides, there has to be more of us out there."

"I suppose so," Ellen conceded, hoping it was true.

"It's a plan, and as Robert says, we have to start somewhere," Theresa said. "Perhaps you can set up a meeting with this Frank Hearn, Andrea?"

"I'll do that first thing tomorrow," Andrea agreed.

"Try to learn more about the infection and find out what's going on in the rest of the country," Theresa said. "We need more information."

"I think we can all agree on that," Ellen said, looking at Rick. He nodded. "Knowledge is power."

"Speaking of knowledge. It would be best if you looked up articles and guides on survival, too, Andrea," Amelia said. "You've got a printer, right?"

"Right," Andrea said.

"Print out anything useful. First-aid, food storage, prepping, making candles, soap, hydroponi—"

"Hydro what?" Robert asked.

"Hydroponics," Amelia said, rolling her eyes. "I'll explain later."

"It's a fine idea and a good use of my time," Andrea answered. "It will fill the hours between communications. Most of the time, the lines are either dead or busy. Even the Internet lags."

"I wonder how long it will last," Ellen murmured, her thoughts flying ahead to a future with no technology. A time when all of humanity's recent advancements would be rendered useless by a wave of the undead.

"Let's not think about it now," Theresa said. "It's time for bed, in any case."

"Hear, hear," Robert said, pushing back his chair. "I could

use a good night's sleep."

"Me too," Amelia said, stifling a yawn.

The couple left the room to find their bed, and the rest followed suit. Ellen got up as well and turned to Rick. "I'll see you when it's your turn to stand guard."

"I'll be there," he replied with a crooked smile, and her stomach filled with butterflies.

Walking on air, she made her way to her station. There, she leaned against the windowsill and gazed out into the darkness. Silence fell as everyone went to bed, and the lights dimmed until only the kitchen light shone.

Ellen didn't mind. The darkness was her friend, and it was a beautiful night. The moon shone against the cobalt sky, cloaked in a tapestry of stars. Still, the knowledge that the city now belonged to the living dead was unsettling, and a shiver ran up her spine.

In the road below, nothing stirred but a cool breeze: that and the occasional rat scurrying among the rubbish on the sidewalks. The street lamps cast pools of yellow lights at intervals, and she searched them for signs of the infected. There was none.

Wherever they were, it wasn't at the station. They were probably out in the streets looking for prey. Not for the first time, Ellen wondered what they were up against. How did the zombies come to be? Was it bio-terrorism? War? An accident. Or was it Mother Nature herself, raining down destruction on the plague that besieged her? For they were a plague. Of that, she was sure.

Ellen had seen enough in her young life to know that kindness didn't come naturally to human beings. They were driven to death and destruction, their ceaseless hunger for more causing them to devour the earth and all its riches.

Now it was all gone. Half of humanity was dead, dying, or hiding, while the rest had become mindless cannibals. *What will become of us?*

She had no answer to that question. Just like she didn't know what had happened to her family back in South Africa. She'd tried to phone them numerous times with no luck, and worry for her loved ones gnawed at her subconscious.

Ellen chewed on her thumbnail, worrying at it until the flesh tore and bled. Pain pulsed through the abused digit, and she swore beneath her breath. "Damn it."

"Chewing your nails again?" a deep voice asked from behind.

Ellen jumped, her heart banging in her chest. "Rick? Is that you?"

Rick stepped forward into the soft glow of the candle that lit the room. "It's me."

Ellen managed a shaky laugh. "You shouldn't scare me like that."

"Pfft. You don't scare that easily," Rick said with a crooked smile.

"What are you doing here?" Ellen asked, leaning back against the wall. "Shouldn't you be sleeping?"

"Sleeping? When it's the end of the world?" Rick laughed. "I'd rather be here with you, standing guard."

"Really?" Ellen asked, her heart skipping a beat.

"Really."

"Well, you're not missing much. It's pretty quiet down there," Ellen said, indicating the street below.

Rick nodded. "I wonder where the zombies are. I'd expect them to be crawling all over the place."

"Me too."

"Maybe they're not as active at night," Rick mused.

"Maybe, but we don't know much about them, do we?" Ellen added.

"No, and that's a mistake," Rick said. "We need to know what we're up against."

"What happens when we run out of food and water? Electricity?" Ellen said, thinking ahead once more.

"Isn't that what we're working to prevent?" Rick asked. "You heard Andrea. There are other groups out there. Survivors like us. Together, we can take the city back from the dead."

"I sure hope so," Ellen said. "Because if we can't, we're doomed."

"Don't worry," Rick said, wrapping an arm around her shoulders. "I won't let anything happen to you."

"I'm just worried about my family. I haven't heard anything from them since this all began."

"I know, and it's terrible. I worry about my brother and his family too. I sent them a message telling them to come here if they can or to hole up if they can't," Rick said. "I hope they get it."

"I hope so, too," Ellen said. She leaned into Rick's side, drawing comfort from his strength.

"Your family will be okay," Rick said. "From what you've told me, your dad's pretty tough, and they should be safe out on the farm."

Ellen sighed. "I suppose so."

"Have faith."

"Faith? That's a lot to ask for in times like these," Ellen whispered.

"I know, but we have to keep trying. You heard what Andrea said. Messages are going through. Just not the way they used to."

Ellen nodded. "I keep hoping my phone will ping. It's maddening."

Rick chuckled. "Like waiting for your crush to call back after a date."

"Exactly," Ellen agreed, reminded of her secret feelings. For a time, silence reigned, and she thought of all the things she longed to say to Rick. Finally, she couldn't take it anymore and scraped together her courage. "Rick, I want to—"

"There's something I've been meaning to—" Rick said simultaneously.

Ellen chuckled. "What were you saying?"

"Ladies first," Rick prompted.

But the moment was lost. Her bravery fled, and Ellen shook her head. "Nothing much. Just that I'm tired. It's been a long day."

"Go to bed," Rick urged. "I'll finish your watch and mine."

Ellen hesitated. "Are you sure?"

"Get some rest. Tomorrow will be another long day," Rick said, shooing her away.

"Alright, I'll do that. See you in the morning," Ellen said, disappointed.

"See you," Rick replied with a crooked smile, the same one that sent her heart tumbling into a void.

Ellen wanted to kick herself as she made her way to her bed. *I had the perfect opportunity, and I blew it. Idiot!*

But tomorrow was another day, and she was determined to open her heart to Rick, come what may. It was the end of the world, after all. What did she have to lose?

Chapter 32 - George

George woke up at the crack of dawn. It was impossible to sleep further anyway. The chair was both uncomfortable and too small for his lean body. He extricated himself from its arms with a groan and rubbed his aching back. Bobbi was still fast asleep on the double couch, her usually grumpy expression serene.

He tiptoed not to wake her and made his way to the bathroom. With a flick of a switch, the single light bulb overhead flickered to life. He emptied his full bladder, washed his hands and face, and brushed his teeth with a toothbrush and paste he'd found on one of the shelves earlier. A spray of deodorant finished off his morning ritual, and he walked to the front of the shop.

Elijah stirred when he heard George approach and spoke in a low whisper. "You're up early."

"Couldn't sleep on that infernal chair any longer," George said grimly.

"I know what you mean," Elijah said. "My back still hurts from earlier."

"I see the zombies are still out there," George said, tilting his head toward the windows. Though the infected no longer banged on the glass, they were still there, the shuffling of their feet loud in the early morning air.

"Yup, they're still there. I don't know what we're going to do," Elijah whispered with a dejected look.

"Pray for a miracle," George said with a grunt. He chose an energy drink from the fridge and downed it in one gulp. Swallowing a burp, he waved at Elijah. "Go on. Take a break. I'll keep watch."

"Thanks," Elijah said. "I'll make coffee and see if I can scrounge up something to eat."

"There's still bread left in the kitchen, butter in the fridge, and soup packets in the cupboard," George said. "We finished all the cereal last night."

"Soup and bread it is," Elijah said.

"Sounds good," George said, settling down in a nearby chair.

He stared at the shopfront and the mob of infected that blocked their escape. The fire truck was only a few feet away, but they'd never make it. The zombies were too strong, too fast, and too many. *Damn. What are we going to do?*

The minutes ticked by while he waited, twiddling his thumbs. His impatience grew, and he shifted restlessly from side to side. The muted sound of voices came from the kitchen, and the clink of spoons in cups. *Bobbi must be up.*

He was soon proven right when Elijah and Bobbi joined him. Elijah handed him a cup of soup and two slices of buttered bread. "Eat up. After this, it's protein bars and shakes until we either run out or get out."

"I can't wait," George grumbled, dipping his bread into the soup. The food was meager but hot and tasty, better than a shake any time of the day. The thought of spending days cooped up inside the pharmacy and surviving on liquids, and bars was enough to make him sick. "Maybe we should make a run for it."

"Are you crazy?" Bobbi asked in a fierce whisper.

"We can't sit here forever," George argued.

"Don't be a dumb ass," Bobbi replied.

"We'll die," Elijah added.

"It's worth a shot," George said.

"No, it's not," Bobbi said, shaking her head.

"Oh, come on. Don't be a coward," George said, his tone rising.

"Keep your voice down, or I'll shoot you," Bobbi said, her eyes glowing.

George snorted. "You wouldn't d—"

"Shut up. Both of you," Elijah said, looking toward the exit.

"Don't tell me what to do," Bobbi said, rounding on him.

"Listen," he insisted. "There's someone outside."

Silence fell as all three strained to listen.

George jumped from his chair when he heard the sound of an engine rumbling in the distance. "It's them. They've come for us."

"Who?" Bobbi asked.

"Our friends," George said, running toward the door. "Robert or Mason. Someone. They've come looking for us."

"Then we'd best be ready to move fast," Bobbi said, indicating the baskets of supplies they'd gathered.

Seconds later, gunshots rang out, and the zombies at the door peeled away like paint on a rusty gate. As soon as the exit cleared, George grabbed a chair wedged into the barricade blocking the door. He tossed it aside and grabbed the next, aided by Elijah and Bobbi. Soon, they'd cleared the barrier and stared at each other.

241

"What now?" Elijah asked. "Do you think it's safe?"

"Beats me," Bobbi said.

"I'll take a look," George offered.

"I'll back you," Bobbi said, removing her gun from her belt. "I only have four bullets left, so if there are more infected than that, you're doomed."

"Good to know." George dared a quick peek outside. The bright light nearly blinded him, but all the infected were down, shot to ribbons. The metallic smell of blood hung in the air, and he covered his mouth with his shirt.

"Is it clear?" Bobbi asked.

"It looks like it," George said, his eyes watering from the smell. "The zombies are dead."

"Who shot them?" Bobbi quizzed.

"Is it Robert? Mason?" Elijah added.

"I'm not sure," George said, squinting into the sun.

A police car was parked on the curb, and three people with guns approached the pharmacy: two men and a woman, all in uniform. The leader, an older man with a stern expression, stopped a few feet away. "Anyone in there?"

"Over here," George answered with a wave. He stepped outside and shaded his eyes against the sun. "Are you the police? I mean, like… the real police."

"Yes, we're the real police. What's left of it anyway. I'm Officer Frank Hearn," the leader said, "and this is Officer Sarah Campbell and Officer Leo Torres."

"Nice to meet you. I'm George; this is Elijah and Bobbi Todd. We're with the fire station down on eighty-nine."

"Thanks for saving us," Elijah added.

"We saw your firetruck and thought we could lend a hand," Officer Hearn replied.

"Well, you came at the right time. We were properly stuck in there," George said.

"Yes, we appreciate it," Elijah said.

"Glad we could help," Frank Hearn said with a brisk nod.

"Not to be a buzzkill, but we'd best get going," Bobbi said, pushing past George. "Our friends at the station will be worried."

"We've been missing since last night," George explained.

"No problem. I understand. We'll stand guard while you get your things," Frank said, watching as Bobbi lugged two baskets to the truck.

"Do you want some?" George offered, waving at the supplies. "We packed up the entire shop, and there's plenty to go around."

"No, thanks. We're set for now. Besides, you have a lot more people by all accounts," Frank said, waving a hand.

"How do you know that?" Bobbi asked with a suspicious frown.

"We made contact with your station yesterday. I spoke to a lady named Andrea," Frank said.

"Oh, right. The cat lady," Bobbi said.

"The what?" Frank asked with a puzzled look.

"Never mind her," George said, grabbing a couple of baskets. "She's just joking."

"Which is unusual for her," Elijah said with a smothered grin.

"Stop yapping and move your asses," Bobbi snapped.

"Yes, ma'am," they chorused.

Together, the three of them loaded the supplies into the truck. Finally, they were ready to go, and George turned toward Officer Hearn. "Thanks again for your help, and er…

you're welcome to join us at the station."

"Thanks, but we've got a place of our own, and we're set for the mo—"

"Sir," Officer Sarah Campbell interrupted. "We've got a problem. The school is under attack."

"The school? How bad is it?" Officer Hearn asked, growing pale.

"It's bad, Sir," Sarah said, stricken. "Half of it's on fire."

"On fire? We'd better get over there right away," Frank yelled, waving her and Torres toward the waiting car.

"We'll be right behind you," George said, running toward the driver's side. "Right, guys?"

"Err, right," Elijah said.

"Ah, hell," Bobbi swore. "That was not the plan."

"We're talking about children here, and I am a firefighter," George protested. He jumped behind the wheel and twisted the key in the ignition, his heart bouncing inside his chest like a jackrabbit.

Bobbi and Elijah tossed in the last few baskets of supplies, sending pill bottles rolling across the floor. The moment they were in the truck, George floored the gas and raced after the squad car with its flashing lights. "Are you guys up for this?"

"Do we have a choice?" Bobbie said with a pointed look.

"I guess not," George said with a rueful shrug.

"It's too late now, anyway," Elijah said. "We said we'd help, and it sounds like they need it."

"Fine. I'll radio the station for help," Bobbi said, giving up the fight.

"Good thinking," George said, grateful they'd chosen his side. While the world might have changed overnight, he wasn't about to let the zombies eat a bunch of kids. *Let's do this!*

Chapter 33 - Clare

Shrill screams blasted through the night, and Clare jerked awake with a start. Terror coursed through her veins, and her pulse shot through the roof. For a moment, she didn't know where she was, the environment around her strange and threatening. "What the hell?"

She jumped up, looking for the source of the noise. The cries emanated from the bed beside her, and she almost passed out with relief. *Thank God. It's just Paisley. Not some zombie trying to chew my face off.*

Clare tossed her blanket aside and hurried to the girl's bedside. Paisley tossed and turned, caught in the throes of a nightmare. Clare gave her shoulder a light shake. "Hey, sweetie. Wake up. You're having a bad dream."

Paisley's eyes fluttered open, and she sobbed, "Mommy! Mommy, where are you?"

Clare melted at the words and pulled the child into her arms. "It's okay, sweetie. It's okay."

"I want my mommy," Paisley insisted, tears running down her cheeks.

"I know, sweetie, and I'm sorry, but your mommy is gone," Clare whispered, rocking the girl back and forth.

"No, no, no," Paisley cried, shaking her head.

"It'll be alright. I promise," Clare said.

Night lights around the dorm room flickered to life, and curious faces popped up over the dividers that separated the beds. "Is she okay? What's wrong?"

The voice belonged to Theresa, and Clare nodded. "She had a bad dream."

"Poor thing," Amelia murmured.

"She'll be fine," Clare said. "Won't you, sweetie? You'll be alright because you're a big girl now."

"I... I am?" Paisley asked between sobs.

"Of course, you are," Clare said with complete confidence.

"O... okay."

"How about a cup of warm milk?" Theresa asked. "That'll make you feel better, I'm sure."

"How does that sound, sweetie?" Clare said, wiping the tears from Paisley's face.

"With ci...ci... cinnamon and sugar?" Paisley asked with a hiccup.

"Sure thing, sweetheart," Theresa conceded. "With cinnamon and sugar."

She pulled her robe around her body and hurried toward the kitchen while Clare stayed behind with Paisley. After a while, the child calmed down, and Clare tucked her back into bed. Once Theresa returned with the warm milk, it didn't take much for the little girl to nod off again. Soon, she was fast asleep.

Clare stood up and stretched her arms above her head. "I need a hot shower."

"It's barely four in the morning," Theresa protested.

"I won't be able to sleep further anyway, and I volunteered to stand watch at five. I might as well get an early start."

"Up to you, dear, but I'm off to bed again," Theresa said, stifling a yawn.

"I'll keep an eye on Paisley," Amelia said.

"We all will," Theresa added. "We're her family now, and family looks out for one another."

Clare thought about that while she showered, the hot water jetting onto her skin. It drowned out all other sounds, wrapping her in a cocoon of self-absorption. One that allowed her thoughts to wander free.

After her parents died, it was just her and Mason. Brother and sister. It had been hard at first, and she mourned her father and mother with every fiber of her being. Now, she was used to it and wore her loneliness like a shield. The only time she let her guard down was with Mason. He alone could scale the walls around her heart.

But all of that was about to change. The world was in flames, the dead hunted the living, and she was trapped with a bunch of strangers. Okay, maybe trapped was a strong word. She was stuck, rather. Still, Clare didn't know how she felt about that, especially about the part where they were all supposed to be one big happy family.

"We'll see about that," she muttered as she toweled herself off and pulled on clean clothes. The outfit was practical and straightforward: A pair of cargo pants in khaki green, a black t-shirt, and sneakers. A light jacket kept the chill at bay, and she twisted her hair into a tight knot at the nape of her neck. She didn't bother with all her jewelry, wearing only a few rings and ear studs. She didn't want to give the zombies something to grab onto.

Ready to face the day, Clare fetched a water bottle from the kitchen. It was too early to eat, and she didn't want to bother making coffee. Mike, one of the newcomers, stood guard at one of the windows overlooking the street, and she walked over. "Hey, Mike. You can go to bed now. I'll take over."

"Bed? Now?" he said with a snort.

Clare shrugged. "A shower then?"

"That sounds better," Mike said, flashing her a smile. "I'll even bring you a cup of coffee afterward."

"Toss in a couple of donuts, and it's a deal," Clare said.

"I'll see what I can do," he said.

"Thanks," Clare said, turning to the street below. It was cold and lonely, the road deserted.

"It's quiet down there," Mike said, his voice low. "Too quiet. It gives me the creeps."

"No zombies?"

"I saw one or two, I think. It's hard to tell in the dark."

"Yeah, I bet," she murmured. "No sign of George or his team?"

"Nope. Nothing."

"I hope they're still alive."

"So do I. We need every hand on deck, or we won't make it," Mike said.

"I know," Clare said with a hint of regret. It seemed she was well and truly stuck at the station. *No more lone-wolf shit for me.*

"Can I ask you a few questions?"

"That depends on the questions."

"I'm new here, and I don't know these people from a bar of soap," Mike said.

"They're good folks," Clare said. "Theresa is like a mother to everyone. Strict but fair. Other than her, Robert and Susan are the oldest. They're strong and dependable."

"I gathered that much. The Captain?"

"He's gone. The zombies got him and Lieutenants White and Briggs. Their families, too, I hear."

"That's unfortunate."

"Mason, my brother, has been here a couple of years. He, George, and Timothy are the newest, but they're good guys. So are Rick and Ellen."

"What about Ruby, Elijah, and Benjamin?"

"Ruby's been here awhile. Elijah's her husband, and Benjamin's a friend of theirs, I think," Clare said. "I don't really know him, Sam, or that Andrea woman."

"I don't know much about Sam either, and I've yet to meet Elijah and Bobbi," Mike said, scratching his head. "

"I guess we'll find out what kind of people they are soon enough," Clare said, her mood darkening. She didn't like unknown quantities.

"Thanks for the info. I'll be back with that coffee," Mike said, picking up on her mood.

"Sure thing," she said, watching him leave.

He seemed nice enough. Maybe a bit soft after years of working in an office, but he'd shape up soon enough. He had to, or he'd become zombie bait.

With a shudder, Clare tucked her hands into her pockets for warmth. It was sobering to realize what their lives boiled down to now that it was the end of the world. Either you had what it took to survive. Or you didn't. *The question is: Which one am I?*

Chapter 34 - Robert

Robert dropped into the nearest chair with a yawn that threatened to swallow the kitchen and everyone in it. Amelia placed a cup of steaming hot coffee in front of him, and he groaned with pleasure as he took the first sip. "Oh, yeah. That sure hits the spot."

"I'm surprised you're awake," Amelia said teasingly. "You slept like a log."

"Uh-huh," Benjamin piped up. "You kept me up all night with your snoring."

"I don't snore," Robert protested but winced when the entire room laughed. "Okay, fine. Maybe I snore a little."

"A little?" Benjamin exclaimed. "Dude, you're something else. You're on another level, I'm telling you."

"Yes, I don't know how Amelia handles it night after night," Ruby said with a chuckle.

"With difficulty, I'm sure," Mason said.

"You get used to it," Amelia said, squeezing Robert's hand.

"Now that's real love for you," Benjamin said, shaking his head.

"Shut up," Robert said, but he didn't mean it. He felt good. Too good to get angry over a bit of teasing.

"So, what's on the itinerary today?" Benjamin asked.

"We find and rescue George, Elijah, and Bobbi first," Robert said. "Everything else comes after that."

"Exactly. I want my husband back," Ruby said, her eyes glittering.

"Don't worry, Ruby. Elijah will be fine," Amelia said with a soft smile.

"He'd better be fine, or I'll kill him myself," Ruby said with a low growl.

"As soon as everyone is awake, I'll tell them we're off to look for them," Robert said.

"I'm going with you," Ruby said.

"So am I," Benjamin added.

"What about me?" Amelia asked.

"You stay right here, my love. We haven't fitted you with any gear yet, and you can't use a gun," Robert said with a shake of his head.

"Fair point," Amelia conceded.

"The same goes for the rest of the newcomers," Robert said.

"Forget it," a freshly showered Mike said, entering the kitchen. "I'm not sitting here like a wimp while you risk your lives out there."

"You're not equipped for it," Robert said.

"That's my problem," Mike insisted.

"Let's talk about it over breakfast," Amelia suggested. Always the mediator, she quickly diffused brewing tension. "Where do you keep the bacon and eggs?"

"I'll show you," Mason offered.

While they cooked breakfast, Robert prepared a fresh pot of coffee and brewed a smaller pot of tea for Theresa. One by one, the rest of the station drifted into the kitchen: Susan, Timothy, Theresa, Ellen, Rick, and Clare. All except for Andrea, who chose to stay in the office.

"Sebastian is feeling a little cranky," she explained, pouring herself a cup of tea.

"Poor baby," Theresa commiserated. "I'll bring you a plate of food."

"Thank you," Andrea said, hurrying back to the office.

After a quick meal, everyone settled down to discuss the day's events. The argument began when Robert broached the subject of newcomers going on runs.

"I'd like to help, but I don't know how much use I'll be out there," Sam admitted.

"Me too," Amelia said.

"We don't expect you to try," Theresa said. "Not until you've been trained."

"I can use a gun and want to help," Mike said.

"So do I," Benjamin added. "Everyone else is pulling weight, and I've helped fight off the infected. Why can't we help now?"

"Until we can get all of you fitted with some sort of protective clothing and weapons suited to your capabilities, you can't go anywhere," Robert insisted. "That includes Elijah and Bobbi. They shouldn't have gone with George in the first place."

"Are you saying it's their fault they're not back yet?" Ruby asked, her expression guarded. "That they did something wrong?"

"No, that's not what I'm saying, but they should stay put in the future," Robert said, folding his arms across his chest.

"That's ridiculous," Mike said.

"Agreed. We're all in this together," Ruby said.

"Maybe, but we shouldn't take unnecessary risks," Amelia said, raising a hand for silence. "We can't afford to lose anyone at this point."

"We can't afford to do nothing either," Mike said.

"Alright. That's enough," Theresa said. "You all raise valid points."

"What do you suggest?" Robert asked.

"Those willing and able to fight the infected should be allowed to do so," Theresa said. "But I'll only issue guns to those who know how to use them. The last thing we need is for an accident to occur. All firearms will remain in lock-up when not out on runs. Got it?"

A rumble of accent rose around the table.

"As for those who cannot fight like Sam, Andrea, and Amelia, there is lots for them to do here at the station. All of the work does not lie outside of these walls. Plenty of it is right here," Theresa added. "Not only that but the station should not be left undefended."

"That's true," Robert said. "I didn't think of that."

"Excellent point, Theresa," Amelia said.

Suddenly, Andrea stormed into the kitchen. "Drop everything, guys. We have an emergency. The school is under attack, and it's on fire!"

"School? What school?" Robert asked, momentarily stumped.

"Bobbi just radioed asking for backup," Andrea said.

"Bobbi? What's she doing at a school?" Robert asked.

"Long story short: George, Elijah, and Bobbi are alive and on their way to a school with Officer Hearn. They're asking for help."

"And they shall have it," Theresa said, rising from her chair. "Robert, grab your gear and get to the truck. Andrea, find out which school it is and give him directions."

"Will do," Andrea said, rushing back to the office.

"Who's going with me?" Robert asked.

"I am," Clare said.

"Me too," Mason said.

"I'm coming as well," Mike said, his mouth set in a stubborn line.

"Count Benjamin and me in, as well," Ruby said.

"I'll follow with Ellen and Rick," Theresa said. "Someone needs to stay behind to protect the rest. Susan? Timothy?"

"We'll stay, right Timothy?" Susan said.

"Do I have to?" he asked with a crestfallen look.

"There are people here who can't fend for themselves like Paisley. You wouldn't want something to happen to them?" Susan asked.

"Okay, I'll stay," he answered.

"You'll get your chance, Timothy. The rest of you, meet me in the bay. I'll open the weapons locker," Theresa said.

A mad scramble ensued as everyone rushed to grab their gear. Robert, Mason, Ruby, Ellen, and Rick pulled on their uniforms, while Benjamin, Mike, Clare, and Theresa had to make do without them. However, it was an emergency, and there was no time to waste.

Once they were all assembled, Theresa handed Susan the keys to the guns. "It's all yours now."

"You can count on me," Susan said. "I'll keep everyone under this roof safe."

"Me too, ma'am," Timothy said, bobbing his head.

The bay doors slid open, and Theresa reversed out in the double-cab truck that acted as a support vehicle with Ellen and Rick. The rest piled into the firetruck while Robert said goodbye to Amelia.

"I'll be right back, sweetheart. I promise."

"Be careful," she whispered, pressing a kiss to his lips. "I love you."

"I love you too," he replied before jumping behind the wheel.

With a roar of the engine, he reversed out of the bay. The doors clanged shut, and he drove off feeling reassured. Whatever he faced at the school, it would be with the knowledge that his wife was safe.

Following Andrea's instructions, the truck picked up speed as he raced toward their destination. It wasn't hard to spot. A pillar of dark smoke billowed into the sky like a beacon of doom.

The familiar thrill of answering a call flooded his veins, and he smothered a grin. In the back of his mind, he heard the captain yell, "Gear up and get ready. This is a working fire, and we're the cavalry."

For a single moment, it was as if nothing had changed. Yet, everything had changed. A mob of zombies faced them at the school, crowding the street and parking lot. The creatures snarled, their attack on the school interrupted as vehicles raced in from all sides: The police, the firemen, and Theresa's truck.

Robert screeched to a halt and looked at his teammates. "Are you geared up and ready to go?"

"Ready!" they answered with grim expressions.

"Let's do this!" he cried, grabbing the radio. "Theresa, are you there? Over."

"Go ahead, Robert. Over," she replied.

"Can you cover us from your vehicle while we clear a path to the school? Over," he asked.

"Will do. Out," Theresa said.

255

"Mason, Ruby. You two grab the hose. The rest of you, follow me."

"Yes, Sir!" they yelled, tumbling out of the cab.

As Robert's boots hit the ground, he pulled out his gun and growled at the crowd of infected. "Come on, you ugly fuckers. Who's first?"

Chapter 35 - Mason

Mason ran toward the compartment where the hose was stored and yanked it open. He grabbed the roll and pulled it out. Ruby was close on his heels, and together they shouldered the burden.

"Where's the fire hydrant?" Ruby cried.

"I don't know," Mason said, searching the field. However, it was impossible to see anything through the press of infected, and he gave up with a helpless shrug. "Robert, we need to get closer."

"I'm on it," Robert replied, waving to Mike, Benjamin, and Clare.

Together, they raised their guns and aimed. A volley of shots slammed into the crowd, and a couple of zombies dropped, but it didn't have quite the effect they'd hoped. Most of the bullets went wild, while others did little or no damage at all. The infected kept advancing with only a handful going down to headshots. Hitting a moving target the size of a bowling ball wasn't as easy as it looked on TV. None of the firefighters were experienced shooters except Clare, and even she was used to stationary targets.

Watching the scene unfold, Mason fought against a wave of despair. "Shit. This isn't working.."

"Should we help them?" Ruby asked, her voice strained.

Before Mason could answer, a second barrage of gunfire sounded, drowning him out. Theresa, Ellen, and Rick had joined the fight, blasting off a withering wall of fire from another angle.

More bullets whizzed through the air as the police officers joined in, and a slew of infected hit the ground. Faced with a battery of gunfire from three directions, the undead fell by the dozens, and Mason whooped with joy. "This is it!"

But his satisfaction was short-lived. First one, then another, and another gun clicked on empty. An awful silence descended over the scene. Yells sounded as Theresa, Robert, and the rest rushed to reload, overlaid by the growls of the infected.

"Reload! Reload!"

"Hurry up, damn it!"

"Shit! This stupid thing—"

One by one, the combatants slammed magazines into their guns and let off a fresh volley of shots. Everyone except Robert and his teammates. They were too close to the mob and in danger of being overrun.

A zombie latched onto Robert, its teeth sinking into his arm. It gnawed at the thick material of his suit like a dog with a bone. He tried to shake it off, but the infected wrapped both arms around him in a bear hug.

Clare bashed it on the head with her pistol butt, and it rounded on her with a vicious snarl. Abandoning Robert, it tackled her to the ground, and they rolled across the tar in a tangle of limbs.

"Clare!" Mason cried, his blood turning to ice.

He dropped the hose and sprinted to her aid, yanking his ax from his belt. Within seconds, he reached her and slammed the blade into the zombie's skull. It stiffened, its eyes rolling into the back of its head before it slumped across Clare.

Pinned to the ground, she struggled to get free. "Get it off! Get it off!"

Mason grabbed her arm and hauled her to her feet. "Are you okay?"

"I'm fine," she yelled, fumbling at her belt for a magazine. She reloaded and snapped off a couple of shots while Mason hacked at anything within reach. Robert and Benjamin had their axes out too and stormed a cluster of infected. Blood misted the air as their blades cut a swathe of destruction through the undead.

Seconds later, George and Elijah joined the fray, screaming like banshees. They fought like madmen, and the tar grew slick with a vile mixture of blood, offal, bile, and brains.

"Stand together. Hold your ground," Robert commanded, waving everyone closer.

The firefighters closed ranks, forming a tight circle. With Theresa's group and the police officers providing backup, they faced the horde.

"Come on, guys. We can do this!" Mason yelled.

He lashed out at a zombie, catching it with a glancing blow on the shoulder. Its clawed hands grabbed hold of his sleeve, desperate to reach the warm flesh underneath.

Mason kneed it in the groin, but the infected didn't even blink. It felt no pain and attacked with renewed vigor. Gray fingers latched onto Mason's helmet and yanked him toward its open mouth. All he could see was a gaping maw filled with twin rows of gnashing teeth. Pieces of flesh were stuck between the incisors, and its fetid breath smelled like a rotting carcass left out in the sun.

259

"Holy shit!" Mason yelled, gagging on a flood of bile.

His eyes watered as he fought against the zombie's pull. It snapped at his face, grinning like a shark.

Click, click, click.

Click, click.

Click.

Panic rushed through his veins. The zombie was a lot stronger than he'd ever have thought possible. Bit by bit, it dragged him closer.

Suddenly, the thing let go and collapsed to the ground, half of its head blown away. Clare flashed him a grin over the smoking barrel of her gun. "Watch yourself, bro!"

"Thanks, Sis," he acknowledged with a nod.

Another infected rushed him, but this time he was ready and split its skull in half with an overhand blow. Pulling the weapon free, he tackled another and another until he could hardly lift his arms.

Clare kept firing, and heads exploded around her like overripe melons. Clotted black blood covered their clothes and skin in a miasma of filth.

"Keep it up," Mason cried, kicking the legs out from underneath an infected. It collapsed, and he ended its undead life with a chop of the ax.

"Just a few more," Clare yelled. She ejected an empty magazine and reloaded it in one smooth move. With quick precision, she dropped two more zombies.

Little by little, the crowd of infected thinned until the path to the school was clear. Seeing an opportunity, Mason ran toward Ruby and grabbed the hose. "Let's go."

They stormed toward the entrance and found the fire hydrant, with the rest providing cover. They plugged it in and got the water flowing while Robert and his team cleared away the last of the infected.

Mason studied the school and wondered if they were too late. Smoke billowed from the broken windows, and searing heat radiated outward in waves. Half of the school was on fire, and the structure groaned underneath the strain.

"Concentrate on the entrance," Robert ordered. "We need to get inside."

"We're on it," Mason said, nodding at Ruby.

Water jetted into the blaze while everyone waited with bated breath. It was a tense moment, and Mason prayed it would be enough. Fire was an unpredictable beast, dangerous at its best and lethal at its worst.

Gradually, the heat dissipated, and the flames receded. They had it under control for the moment, but Mason knew it wouldn't last. They advanced on the school until the entrance was clear, and he waved at Robert. "Hurry!"

Robert nodded and waved at Ruby. "I'll take the lead. Two minutes. In and out. Got it?"

"Got it," Ruby replied.

"What about us?" Mike asked, waving at himself, Benjamin, and Clare.

"You're not firefighters," Robert said.

"But we can help," Mike protested.

Robert hesitated. "It's too dangerous."

"We're going whether you like it or not, and we're wasting time," Mike said.

"Fine," Robert said with a growl. "Clare, help Mason with the hose. Our lives might depend on it. Mike and Benjamin, stick close to me."

"Alright," Mike said.

Benjamin nodded.

With Robert and Ruby in the lead, they headed toward the entrance. One by one, they ducked into the opening, disappearing into the dense smoke.

Mason chewed on his bottom lip while he waited. This was the worst part. The waiting. Not knowing whether all of your friends would make it out alive.

Still, he had a job to do, and he focused his efforts on keeping the flames at bay. It was a losing battle. Whenever the fire seemed to die down, it returned with renewed force in a different spot, and Mason realized it would rage out of control without more help. Help they didn't have.

The structure groaned, its wooden beams expanding and contracting with the fierce heat. Glass exploded outward up and down its length, and part of the roof collapsed inward with a thundering crash. A wave of searing ash and sparks washed across the assembled onlookers, and Mason knew their time was up. *Come on, come on, Robert. Hurry the hell up!*

As he was about to give up all hope, Robert and his team emerged from the entrance, herding a stream of people through the doors. They ranged in shape and size. From the young to the old. Parents, teachers, administration staff, and children.

They were coated in soot, barely able to breathe, and frantic. The kids screamed, and the adults cried with relief at being rescued. Some suffered from burns, painful and debilitating. They were a pitiful knot of shivering humanity, and Mason's heart went out to them. They were lucky to be alive.

Not for the first time, he thanked the stars that he'd chosen to become a fireman. In the beginning, it was a knee-jerk reaction to his parents' death in a freak fire, but now he was grateful. Saving people and fighting fires was his life. It gave him direction and a sense of purpose which was more than most individuals had. Even better, it gave him a family.

The station was his home, and its people were his people. They would never abandon him, betray him, or leave him behind. For the first time in a long time, he had someone other than Clare who cared about him, and that made life so much sweeter. He only hoped Clare could find that sense of belonging too, but he knew she wasn't ready.

Restless and rebellious, she was still looking for her place in the world. Strangely enough, he thought that the apocalypse might give her that. So far, she was handling it like a pro, and she seemed a lot more confident in her abilities. *Just give it time. She'll find what she's looking for—one day.*

Chapter 36 - Theresa

Theresa took swift charge of the survivors and turned to Frank for assistance. "Officer Hearn."

"Yes, ma'am," he said, turning to face her with a sharp nod of acknowledgment.

"Can you and your colleagues set up a safe perimeter while we deal with the wounded and arrange transport for the survivors?"

"Transport?" he asked. "Where will they go?"

"We'll take them in," Theresa said.

"Do you have enough room?" he asked, eyeing the knot of parents, teachers, and children with a doubtful frown.

"We'll make do," Theresa said.

"Are you sure?" Frank Hearn asked. "I would take them, but the office block we commandeered is not exactly comfortable."

"We'll simply have to fit them in, won't we?" Theresa said. "As for your home, we need to talk."

"Talk?"

"Yes, I believe we should work together. We plan to expand the station to either side, giving us more room for people and supplies. We also want to grow food on the rooftops, cordon off the entire block, and claim the nearby clinic and fuel station," Theresa added.

"That's a tall order, ma'am," Frank said with a whistle.

"Exactly. Which is why we have to work together. With your help, we can do it," Theresa said.

"I see," Frank said, his eyes calculating. "As you said, we need to talk."

"In the meantime, we have to take care of these people," Theresa said, waving a hand at the school.

"Of course. Officers Campbell, Torres, and I will set up a perimeter, but you need to hurry. More infected will be drawn by the noise, and we don't have a ton of firepower."

"I'll send a couple of extra hands to help you out," Theresa said, hurrying toward the firefighters.

They were gathered to the side, examining each other for wounds and potential infection. With her heart in her throat, she asked the dreaded question. "Are any of you hurt? Have you been bitten?"

"No, we're all good," Robert said, looking around. "I think."

"You think?" Theresa said with a raised eyebrow.

Robert chuckled. "I know."

"It's just a few bumps and bruises. Nothing serious," Ellen said. "We'll be right as rain in no time, I promise."

"Thank goodness for that," Theresa said, relaxing a little.

"What do we do now? More zombies will come, and these people can't look after themselves. They're helpless," Robert said, waving at the survivors."

"I know. We'll have to take them in," Theresa said. "Robert, I want you, Mason, Elijah, Ruby, and George to round up the survivors and load them into the fire trucks. Treat only those who are badly wounded. The rest will have to wait until we get to the station."

"I'll take care of it," Robert acknowledged.

265

"Rick, you and Ellen can gather up the equipment and hoses. Officer Hearn and his fellow officers will give us as much time as they can."

"What about me?" Bobbi asked.

"And me?" Clare added.

"You two can give Officer Hearn and his fellows a hand. You're good shots and can buy us more time," Theresa instructed.

"Yes, ma'am," Clare acknowledged. Together, she and Bobbi jogged toward the squad car with their guns at the ready and formed a rough perimeter around the scene.

"Benjamin, come with me. We can take care of any stragglers," Theresa said.

"You mean, kill them?" Benjamin asked.

"It has to be done. If we leave them, they might harm other people," Theresa said. "Besides, would you want to live like that?"

"No, I wouldn't," Benjamin admitted, pulling out his gun.

Theresa picked her way through the corpses littering the road, pausing to examine each body. A woman with blonde hair rasped at her. One hand was missing while the other scrabbled at the tar. An ax blade had sheared off part of her scalp, and both her legs were broken, but she was still alive.

Theresa gazed at her with a mixture of horror and pity. She looked like a soccer mom dressed in a pink jersey and slacks. Raising the gun, she put a bullet between the woman's eyes. The shot was loud, and she wanted nothing more than to run away, but more infected waited for mercy. Or deliverance from their miserable existence. While they might be monsters now, they used to be people. Ordinary human beings with hopes, dreams, and families. All gone now.

With that thought in mind, Theresa continued the grizzly task until nothing moved anymore. Sighing with relief, she reloaded her pistol and tucked it behind her belt. It did no good to walk around with a half-plenty gun.

"Are we done?" Benjamin asked, his face pale.

"We're done," she said. "Thank you, my boy."

He nodded and stumbled away, making a beeline for Ruby. She welcomed him with open arms, and together they coaxed the last few survivors into the trucks.

Robert completed a quick inspection of the vehicles ensuring everything was in place, and nobody would be left behind. Meanwhile, Bobbi and Clare fought side by side with the officers to keep more of the undead at bay.

A quick glance showed Theresa that they were fighting a losing battle. Infected poured in from every direction, a testament to how far gone the city was. The dead outnumbered the living by the hundreds, the thousands, and the tens of thousands. *We need to get out of here.*

"Robert, it's time to go," Theresa said, urging him on.

"We're ready," he replied. "What about Officer Hearn and his people?"

"I'll ask them to escort us back to the station," Theresa said. She reached for the radio at her belt. "I'll also warn Susan and Timothy that we're coming back with a load of people, some of them injured."

"Good idea," Robert said.

"Bobbi, Clare, and I can drive ahead to give them a hand," Theresa said.

"We'll be right behind you," Robert said. He turned back toward his teammates and shouted, "Let's pack it up, folks. Get a move on."

Theresa hurried toward Officer Hearn. "We're ready to go. Will you escort us?"

"Sure thing," Frank replied, snapping off a few more shots. "Let's get out of here."

Theresa called Bobbi and Clare. "You're riding with me."

"It's about time," Bobbi said. "It's getting hairy out here."

They piled into Theresa's vehicle and raced away from the scene, followed by the two fire trucks and the squad car. Theresa radioed Susan with a warning. "We're coming in hot and heavy with several survivors, some of them wounded. We need food, water, beds, and first aid. Over."

"We'll be waiting," Susan acknowledged. "Are some of the survivors infected? Over."

"It's possible. They'll have to be examined. Over."

"I'll get the decontamination bay ready. Over," Susan said.

"See you in a few minutes. Out," Theresa said.

"We're taking all of them?" Bobbi asked with a look of disbelief.

"We took you in, didn't we?" Theresa replied with a pointed look.

"Alright," Bobbi conceded with a shrug. "Thank goodness we raided that pharmacy."

"Pharmacy?" Theresa asked.

"Well, we weren't gone all night on a joy ride. We were stuck inside a pharmacy. Officer Hearn and his fellow officers rescued us," Bobbi said.

"That explains a lot," Theresa said.

"We stripped the place of everything it had. Meds, first-aid kits, protein bars, shakes, toiletries, baby stuff, you name it."

"That will go a long way toward helping out," Theresa said with no small measure of relief.

Even so, she was worried. The station was not equipped for so many people. Still, they had no choice. They couldn't turn anyone away. Not when there were so few of them left. *This is where we make our stand. It's either everyone for themselves, or we stand together and fight. I say we fight.*

Chapter 37 - Rick

Rick watched from the sidelines as Ellen tended to the wounded crammed into the back of the fire truck. A young boy suffered from burns to his left arm and hand, and tears streamed down his cheeks.

"It hurts," he whimpered, lips quivering.

"I know, and I'm sorry," Ellen whispered, her eyes a liquid blue. She peeled back the singed material of the boy's sleeve. Luckily, the cloth came away without trouble, but the skin below was an angry crimson hue, and wet blisters covered the surface.

"Is he going to be alright? How bad is it?" the boy's mother asked.

"He's lucky these aren't third-degree burns," Ellen said after a brief examination. "With the proper treatment, he should heal without any complications."

"Thank you so much," the woman said with marked relief. "Can you give him something for the pain?"

"Yes, of course," Ellen said, handing the boy some painkillers. "Take these. They will help, and Rick will give you some water."

"Here," Rick leaned over and gave the boy bottled water.

"Th… thank you," the boy said with a slight hiccup.

"You're very brave," Rick said with a kind smile.

The boy returned his smile and wiped away his tears, trying hard to look courageous in front of the firefighters.

Ellen moved on to the next person, and Rick helped as much as possible. However, his bandaged hand hampered his efforts, and the wild ride didn't help either. He swore when the truck swerved around a corner, and he bumped his amputated fingers against the metal side.

"Are you hurt too?" the boy with the burns asked.

"Yup," Rick answered. "I lost two fingers to a zombie."

"Really?" the boy asked, eyes wide with ghoulish wonder.

"Really."

"And it worked? You didn't turn into one of those monsters?" the mother asked, recoiling despite herself.

"I'm here, aren't I?" Rick said. "It's been more than two days now."

"Wow," she muttered, clearly at a loss for words.

Ellen flashed him an amused smile and leaned over to whisper in his ear. "Careful now. They'll think you're the boogeyman."

Her warm breath sent a shiver down his spine, and he cleared his throat. "As long as you don't think that, it's okay."

"Never," she replied, bumping him with her shoulder.

He was saved from replying when the truck stopped in front of the station. The other firetruck was behind them, followed by the squad car and Theresa.

The bay doors rolled open, policed by an armed Susan and Timothy. Susan waved them inside and directed them to an available spot. When all the vehicles were inside, the doors shut with a bang. Susan and Timothy inspected the trucks and area before giving the all-clear. "You can get out now, folks. Please, follow us."

Ordered chaos ensued as everyone scrambled to obey. With remarkable calm, Susan and Timothy directed the wounded to an area equipped with stools, mattresses, and medical supplies while the rest were herded to the decontamination booth.

Andrea operated the booth and examined everyone for possible infection, assisted by Benjamin. As qualified EMTs, Robert, Ruby, and Theresa treated the injured.

Afterward, Amelia guided everyone upstairs to the kitchen, where a rough meal of water, cold drinks, chips, cookies, and peanuts awaited. It wasn't much, but more than Rick would've thought possible in such a short period. Even Officer Hearn looked impressed and press-ganged George into a quick tour of the station.

Theresa and Ellen organized extra beds. Luckily, they possessed extra blankets and mattresses, which now came in handy. The supplies George and his party had scored earlier were packed away with the weapons, ammunition, fire axes, and gear. A quick clean-up of the bay removed any contaminated material, the trucks were hosed down, and the building was secured.

It took the entire afternoon to get everyone squared away, and Rick was relieved when it was all over. The wounded, the kids, and their caretakers occupied one dorm room: Fed, bathed, and treated. The rest convened in the kitchen with coffee and tea, called together by Theresa and Officer Hearn.

Rick found a spot next to Ellen and squeezed her hand. Her expression was strained, and a niggle of worry made him ask, "Are you alright?"

"I'm okay. Just tired," she said. "It's been a long day."

"It has," he agreed.

"I wonder what we're going to do now?"

"Let's hear what Theresa has to say. She always has a plan."

"That's true," Ellen said, leaning against him.

Theresa occupied a spot at the head of the table and raised a hand for silence. "Thank you all for being so patient. I know it's been a long, tiring day, and you've suffered a terrible ordeal, but I'd like to welcome you to our station. As you can see, we're operational."

"Does this mean the government is still in charge?" one man asked.

"No, it does not," Theresa said. "So far, we are all survivors of this terrible plague and all in the dark regarding national and international affairs."

A low murmur broke out.

"But, we are working hard to find more information and to locate possible resources and other survivors. Together, I believe we can take back our city and defeat the infected that desecrate our streets."

"Do you think so?" a woman asked with desperate hope.

"I do. All I ask is for your continued cooperation and assistance. We cannot do this alone. Neither we firefighters nor the police. We need your help."

"Are we supposed to stay here then? It's too small. There's not enough space," another woman protested.

"We're working on that," Theresa said reassuringly. "Again, I ask for your patience. In the days to come, we'll all have to contribute whatever knowledge and skills we possess. Can I count on you?"

After a couple of seconds, a round of nods and yesses answered her question.

Theresa smiled, her eyes shining. "Thank you, and I bid you welcome to our home. Dinner is at seven. In the meantime, feel free to use the books, games, and puzzles in the rec room."

Slowly, the crowd dispersed. Andrea returned to the office and her job as a liaison with the outside world. Susan, Timothy, and Amelia cooked dinner. Theresa made further arrangements for the survivors, and Clare volunteered for the first watch. The rest were free to do as they liked, and Rick found himself alone with Ellen.

An awkward silence fell between them, filled with everything they didn't say. Ellen ducked her head, avoiding his gaze, and he wracked his brain for something to say. He wasn't used to feeling this way. Usually, their relationship was relaxed and free. Now, he felt like a teen boy faced with his crush.

Suddenly, Ellen's phone beeped as a message came through, and she checked the screen. Before his eyes, her face transformed as pure joy flooded her features. "Rick, you won't believe this."

"What is it?"

"It's my dad! He says they're on the farm. They've formed a coalition with the neighboring farms to keep everyone safe."

Overcome, Ellen jumped into his arms with a happy squeal and wrapped her arms around him. Rick returned the embrace, his face buried in her hair. He inhaled her warm, familiar scent, and his heart contracted inside his chest.

Before he could stop himself, he blurted out the words he'd been longing to say. "I love you, Ellen. I always have, and I always will. I don't know why it took me this long to admit it."

Ellen jerked away and stared at him with wide eyes. Her mouth worked, and he feared he'd misjudged for a moment. Then she smiled, and he sagged with relief.

"I love you too, Rick. So much it hurts sometimes," she said.

Rick pulled her close and pressed his lips to hers, unwilling to waste another second. "You're mine, Ellen Engelbrecht. Now and forever."

Epilogue - Robert

That evening, Robert stood on the roof of the station. Amelia stood next to him, nestled inside the crook of his arm. Above their heads, a carpet of stars sparkled in the sky, undisturbed by airplanes or helicopters.

Together, they gazed over the city, a desolate landscape filled with broken dreams, death, and destruction. In the distance, fires still burned. One of them was the school, and he hoped the blaze didn't spread. *At least there's no wind tonight.*

The deserted streets were empty, devoid of the usual hustle and bustle. No cars drove past, no hooters honked, no party-goers stumbled from packed bars and nightclubs, and no bums loitered in dark corners.

Without the bright lights and noisy traffic, it felt strange. Like an alien city from another dimension populated by monsters risen from the depths of hell or cooked up in a petri dish in some fancy lab by scientists playing God. Who knew where the infection came from? Would they ever learn the truth? Robert didn't think so.

"What do we do now?" Amelia asked with a touch of hope-lessness. "It's gone. Everything we worked for, everything we achieved. Just gone."

Robert gave it serious thought. There were no easy answers,

276

but he had to give her something to hold on to. Something to keep her going when all else seemed lost. "Now we build a new future. A new world for all of us."

"Do you think we can do it?" she asked with a shiver.

He nodded and pulled her closer to his side. "I do. I believe we can do anything we set our minds to. And do you know who taught me that?"

"Who?"

"You did."

"Do you mean that?"

"With all of my heart."

She nodded and turned back to the city they called home. "Then let's do it. Let's rebuild. But this time, we do it even better than before."

Robert smiled. "With you by my side, I can do anything."

The End.

Turn the page for a sneak preview of the next book in the series, End of Watch. Continue the adventure now!

Do you want more?

So we've reached the end of Trial by Fire, and I really hope you enjoyed reading the book as much as I enjoyed writing it. If you did, please consider leaving a review. It would be much appreciated. But that's not all. The sequel, End of Watch, is now available on Amazon. Read further for a sneak peek and continue the adventure!

End of Watch - Heroes of the Apocalypse, Book 2:
   https://www.amazon.com/dp/B09NRXG28Y

Prologue I - Frank

Officer Frank Hearn stared at the pile of paperwork on his desk with growing pessimism. His watch told him his shift was only half-over, and he still had several hours to go. A throbbing headache had taken up residence inside his skull, and the arthritis in his left elbow was acting up. Flexing the joint, he slumped back in his seat and ran both hands through his hair. "I'm getting too old for this shit."

"You? Old? Not a chance in hell, Sarge," a cheerful voice quipped from the doorway.

Frank looked up and forced a half-smile. "What can I do for you, Sarah?"

"It's not what you can do for me, Sarge, but what I can do

for you," Sarah said, producing a cup of coffee with a flourish. She plopped the polystyrene cup down before him, spilling hot liquid all over his notes. "Black, no sugar. Just the way you like it."

"Sarah, that wasn't necces—" Frank began, reaching for a pile of crumpled paper napkins. He mopped up the mess, smearing ink all over the place.

"But that's not all. I also got your favorite," she said, not giving him a chance to speak. Reaching into her pocket, she pulled out a brown paper bag and handed it to him with a grin. "Two jam donuts sprinkled with sugar and fresh from the corner shop."

Frank eyed the squashed packet but didn't open it. It looked like someone had driven over it with their car. "That was... very nice of you, Sarah. Now, what do you want?"

Sarah shrugged. "Nothing."

"Nothing?" Frank said with more than a hint of disbelief. "I find that very hard to believe."

After twenty-odd years on the beat, he'd learned that nothing was for free. Not even from the eternally optimistic and annoyingly bright Sarah Campbell. On probation, she carried an air of innocence that bordered on naivety. It couldn't last. Not in the career field she'd chosen, but he wasn't about to tell her that. Reality would set in soon enough without him hurrying it along.

"Come on, Sarah. Spit it out," he said, reaching for the coffee. He eyed the cup with a dubious look, wondering if it tasted as bad as it looked.

"Go ahead, Sarge. It's the good stuff," Sarah said, egging him on.

"Thanks," he grumbled, taking a tiny sip. To his surprise,

the brew was hot and fresh.

"See? I'm not a complete idiot. I get things right on occasion," Sarah said, bouncing from one foot to the other.

"Don't sell yourself short, Sarah. You're excellent at stirring up trouble."

"Am I?"

"And you still haven't told me what you want."

"Well, there is one little thing," Sarah hedged.

"I knew it," Frank said.

"Can I have the day off tomorrow?" Sarah asked. "I know it's short notice, but my sister's getting married, and she's having a meltdown because her dress doesn't fit, and I promised her I'd help her find a new one, and the only time she can get off—"

"Alright, that's enough," Frank said, holding up one hand to stop the deluge of words. "Not another peep."

Sarah swallowed her next sentence with an audible gasp and shut her lips. Her cheeks grew red until it looked like she'd explode, and Frank suppressed an eye roll. *Lord, have mercy on me. I can't. I just can't.* "Yes, you can have the day off, but you'd better not make a habit of it, or you're out the door. Got it?"

"Thank you, thank you, thank you!" Sarah cried. "You won't regret this, I promise."

"I already am," Frank said, waving her away.

She skipped toward the door. "You're the best, Sarge."

"Whatever," Frank mumbled, taking another sip of coffee. The stuff was good—no doubt about it, but the donuts were a total loss. He dumped the packet into the rubbish bin and reached for a stack of papers. "Might as well get this done."

For the next hour, he lost himself in the joys of administrative work. A pile of police reports and a list of recent incidents waited for his attention. He perused the list looking for trends while the radio operated in the background.

Frank paid it no heed. He only used it to keep track of the officers on shift, but it had been a quiet shift with only the usual petty crimes in progress. That changed when a sudden rash of assaults, looting, and homicides came through on the air.

"Four two one. There is a disturbance on the corner of Park Avenue and Melville street. Please respond."

"Dispatch. This is four two one. We are en route."

"Four three six. There are reports of looting in the city center near Town Hall."

"Dispatch. This is four three six. We're on our way."

"Four five nine. An assault has been reported at seventy-eight Tanner street. Please respond."

"Dispatch. this is four five nine. ETA three minutes."

"Four seven five. There was a call about a homicide at a local residence."

Static.

"Four seven five. Please respond."

Static.

"Four seven five. This is Dispatch. Please respond."

Still nothing.

Frank stared at the radio, perturbed. Patrol car four seven one was operated by Officer Leo Torres and his partner Randal Sikes, and it was unlike either of them not to respond.

"Four seven five." The dispatcher's voice rose in pitch. "Please respond."

"Dispatch. This is four seven five," came the response at last. "Officer down. I repeat, officer down."

Frank froze in his chair. The voice belonged to Leo Torres, and he listened with care as the situation unfolded.

"What is your location, four seven five?" Dispatch asked.

"178 Central street," Torres said.

"All units in the vicinity, please respond," Dispatch said.

"Four two one, en route."

"Hurry! All hell just broke loose out here. People are killing people, biting them. Shit, they're eating each other. Randall, wait for m—"

Static.

"Four seven five. What is your situation?" the dispatcher asked.

More static.

Frank frowned. "What did he mean they were eating each other? That's impossible."

Either way, he needed to find out what was going on. These were his officers, his shift, and his responsibility. He'd be damned if he let anything happen to them.

Grabbing his keys, phone, and wallet, he stood up, but a shrill scream sent ice running through his veins. To his surprise, the sound didn't stop or lessen in volume. Instead, it grew louder in pitch until he thought his eardrums would burst. The muffled pops of gunshots followed soon after, and his heart skipped a beat. Something strange was going on. Something dangerous. Not prepared to waste more time, he ran to the door and yanked it open.

After the relative peace of his office, the sheer noise assaulted his senses like a battering ram. The hallway was crowded with fellow police officers flooding the narrow passage. They were all headed in the same direction: The front desk and reception.

Only a few seconds had passed, but the screams grew in number, punctuated by gunfire and the sound of breaking glass. It sounded like a war zone, and Frank ran through all the possible scenarios in his head: A bomb, terrorists, random shooters, or a terrible accident.

Suddenly, a terrific crash shook the building, and several people fell to their knees. Shock was written on every face, quickly followed by panic. A car horn blared, the noise bouncing off the walls until it melded with the chaos and formed a symphony of terror.

Darting into the passage, Frank elbowed his way through the crowd. "Out of the way. Move it, please!"

Two secretaries huddled inside the doorway of an office, and he waved them back. "Kate, Donna, get inside and lock that door."

"Yes, Sergeant," Kate replied, slamming the door shut.

Frank continued his dash to the front of the station and reached the reception within seconds. There he paused to get his bearings, shocked by the sight that met his eyes.

An officer was down on the ground, wrestling with two men. They were civilians, by the looks of it, but there was nothing civilized about their behavior. Growling, they snapped at the fallen officer's face with their bare teeth.

Another policeman was backed into a corner, his eyes wide. His gun clicked on empty as a trio of similarly crazed-looking people closed around him. The nearest pounced on him and tore into his cheek, peeling away a hunk of flesh. Blood fountained from the wound and sprayed across the attacker and victim, bathing them in the crimson fluid.

"Help me!" the officer screamed, his voice raw with agony.

"Hold on," Frank yelled.

He yanked his gun free from its holster and ran toward the struggling duo. A stray elbow hit him in the stomach, and he almost went down. Struggling to keep his balance, he cried, "Hold on!"

Too late.

The infected sank its teeth into the officer's throat.

Blood pumped from the wound, spurting from the severed artery.

Frank locked eyes with his colleague, and he saw the moment it was over. The moment when the man's eyes glazed over in death.

"No!" Frank cried, even though he knew it was too late.

With desperate hope, he kept going, even though it was an impossible task. The press of bodies grew worse, and he got hit from all sides. A crazed woman spotted him and pounced with a vicious growl. Her nails raked across his cheek, and he reacted without thinking. His fist connected with her jaw, and she crashed into a knot of fellow crazies. They went down in a tangle of limbs, and a space opened in the crowd.

Frank looked for the officer he was trying to save, but the man was gone. Lost. Whirling around, he sought some form of absolution. Someone to help, to save. Instead, all he saw was death and destruction.

A woman with crushed legs slithered toward him like a serpent, leaving a trail of blood and slime on the floor. Her bloodshot eyes fixed on him, and her lips peeled back from her teeth in a predatory grin. Dragging herself toward him with her arms, she moved surprisingly fast.

Frank pointed his gun at her face, eyes narrowed. "Stop, or I'll shoot!"

The woman ignored him and kept coming.

"Stop. This is your last warning!" he repeated.

No reaction. Not a flicker of intelligence showed in her dead gaze. There was nothing left of the person she used to be: nothing but a soulless husk driven by the need to feed.

"Please, stop," Frank said, taking a step back. He didn't want to shoot her. Hurt her. Kill her. It went against everything he stood for in life. Everything he believed in.

The woman lunged forward and latched onto his leg. Her fingers dug into the calf muscle, and she went in for the kill. Gnashing teeth closed on his shin, but he jerked away in time. Instead of meat, she got a mouth full of pant material.

"Let go of me," Frank yelled, shaking his leg.

Refusing to budge, the woman hung on like a leach.

Desperate, Frank pointed his gun at her head. "I said let go, damn it!"

He fired a shot next to her ear, hoping it would scare her away. Instead, she ignored him and kept coming.

Frank gaped at her, unable to believe what was happening. His ears rang with the blast, and he couldn't hear anything. He'd pulled the trigger right next to her temple, close enough to burst an eardrum, but she kept coming.

Unstoppable.

Invincible.

Impossible.

Suddenly, the woman's head exploded into a thousand fragments, and she slumped to the ground. Her hands grew slack, and he pulled free from her grip. All life faded from her gaze until she was an empty shell. A monster no more.

Frank backed away from the corpse with an air of bewilderment. Time lost all meaning, and everything around him turned into a blur. Caught in a haze, he stood there, staring like an idiot. *What the hell is happening? This is crazy! Just crazy!*

Suddenly, Officer Sarah Campbell grabbed him by the elbow, the same one riddled with arthritis. Pain seared through his nerve endings, acting as a shock to the system. It cleared the fog from his brain, and he shook himself awake.

"Are you okay?" he asked, turning to Sarah.

"I'm fine, Sarge," she replied. Her eyes were wide, and her cheeks flushed, but she appeared unharmed and remarkably calm considering the situation. Pointing at the dead woman, she said, "You have to shoot them in the head. It's the only way to stop them."

"What?"

"They're zombies, Sarge. You have to destroy the brain," she said.

"That's ridiculous," he scoffed.

"Look around you, Sarge. It's the apocalypse," Sarah insisted.

Frank shook his head, but his keen eyes quickly took in the situation. A car had smashed through the front window, and shattered glass covered the floor. The horn blared nonstop, caused by the figure slumped over the wheel. The passenger door stood wide open, and a trail of gore led to the woman by his feet. She'd either died in the crash or caused it. *Probably the latter.*

People milled about in fear and confusion, a mixture of police officers, admin staff, and civilians. Many appeared to be driven mad by an unknown agent. Was it a type of nerve gas or a bio-weapon? A virus or a bacterial infection? Something cooked up in a lab by scientists who liked to play God? Or was it natural? A weapon deployed from the bosom of Mother Nature herself? The biggest killer of them all.

Whatever it was, it drove people insane and turned them

into ruthless cannibals. They stalked the station, hunting their prey. They pounced without mercy when they found it, unfazed by blows or shots. The screams of their victims cut through the noise like a razor blade, and blood coated the walls. The station had become a slaughterhouse.

A couple of infected sprinted toward them, one wearing a torn business suit and the other a uniform. Frank raised his gun but froze when he recognized the officer. His blood ran cold, and he fought against the nightmare vision that raced toward him. *No. Not him. Not Steve.*

"Steve, please," Frank pleaded.

But Steve was gone.

Frank's finger tightened on the trigger, but he couldn't bring himself to shoot. Instead, his brain flashed back to a recent memory. A night spent watching football in the home of his friend and fellow Sergeant, Steve Kingsley. His wife, Lydia, cheered with them, tossing popcorn all over the couch each time her team scored a try. Their kids, two boys, played in the background—an ordinary family on an ordinary day.

Not anymore.

"Steve, please. I'm begging you. Stop," Frank tried again, unwilling to believe the undeniable truth. "Please."

Steve never slowed, faltered, or wavered from his relentless objective. To kill, maim, and feed.

"Shoot them," Sarah cried, appearing at his side. "They're not human anymore."

"I can't," Frank said, shaking his head. "That's Steve. Steve!"

"Not anymore," Sarah said, snapping off a couple of shots. Both bullets missed. "Damn it!" She aimed again, her expression determined. "He's not your friend anymore, Sarge. He's dead!"

Her third bullet hit Steve's chest, and blood exploded from his shattered sternum. A fourth bullet punched through his shoulder, and a fifth cut a groove in his scalp. Broken and bloody, he snarled but kept coming.

"That's impossible," Frank said, horrified. "He should be dead."

"I told you, Sarge. He's not human anymore. He's a zombie," Sarah yelled.

"There's no such thing."

"Yes, there is!"

Sarah's sixth shot found its mark, and Steve crashed to the ground. He took the infected man in the suit with him, their bodies entangled in a mess of limbs.

Frank backed away, shaking his head. *Steve's dead. A zombie. I can't believe it.*

But the evidence lay before him, and he knew he needed to snap out of his funk. For Sarah's sake, if not his own.

"What now, Sarge?" Sarah asked as more undead headed their way. They needed to do something fast or be next on the menu.

"Follow me," Frank cried, running toward the front desk.

He vaulted over the top and crashed to the floor on the other side. Sarah landed next to him in a shower of debris. Paperclips, pens, notebooks, staplers, files, and a couple of phones rained down upon them. The area behind the desk was empty, and the wooden counter was attached to the wall. It provided a barrier between them and the infected, and they were safe for the moment. Sheltered.

Taking stock, Frank returned to old habits. "Officer Campbell, report."

"Yes, Sir," Sarah said with a brisk nod. "After leaving your office, I went on patrol with Officer Hines and…."

"And?" Frank prompted.

"It's the same everywhere, Sir."

"What do you mean, the same?" he said, stunned.

"It's like this everywhere," she said. "One minute, everything was fine, and then we started getting reports about shootings, beatings, break-ins, accidents, and murders. We tried to contain the situation, Sir, but the more we tried, the worse it got. It was like… like…." Her hands flapped in the air as she sought the perfect analogy.

Frank nodded, his expression grim. "Like a wildfire burning out of control."

"Exactly!"

"Where's Officer Hines?"

"He…" Sarah bit her lip. "He's dead."

"Infected?"

"Not anymore. I took care of it."

"You killed him?"

"I had no choice, Sarge. He was going to kill me."

Frank nodded, thinking of Steve. *At least she had the guts to do it. You didn't.* "Are they really dead, though? Zombies?"

"I saw a man running around with his guts hanging down to his knees, Sarge. I saw… I saw a woman kill her son. She tore right through his jugular without blinking an eye." Sarah shuddered, and a single tear ran down her cheek. "She ate her own child; if that's not proof enough of zombies, I don't know what is."

Frank swallowed, sickened to the core of his being. "I can't believe this is happening."

"Well, Sarge. It's happening whether we like it or not," Sarah said.

"When did you become so tough?" Frank asked, eyeing her with surprise.

"I've always been like this, Sarge," she said, flashing a grin. "You just didn't see it before."

"I've been a fool," Frank said.

"You said it. Not me," Sarah said, checking her magazine. "I only have three bullets left. Not enough to get us very far."

"We're not going anywhere," Frank said.

"But, we must get out of here," Sarah protested.

"No, we have to clear the station and save as many people as possible," Frank said.

"We can't. The place is overrun, Sarge. There's too many of them and only two of us." Sarah peeked over the edge of the desk. "As it is, I don't know if we'll make it out."

Frank looked over the counter, dismayed to find she was right. The front entrance was open and infected poured into the building. They jammed the opening in their haste to get inside, snapping at each other with angry snarls.

Even more crawled through the smashed window, not caring when they cut themselves to ribbons on the jagged pieces of glass. Bodies littered the floor. Dead. Others stirred with the first signs of reanimation. They spasmed, flopping around in the same pools of blood that brought about their end.

Survivors, desperate to escape the surge of undead, stampeded in the opposite direction. They headed deeper into the building, flooding its hallways and offices by the dozen. The infected followed, drawn by their screams of fear and horror. "They're making a mistake. They'll be trapped inside with nowhere to go."

"They can get onto the roof," Sarah said.

"Then what? They'll be stuck," Frank said.

"There's the fire escape and the back exit through the kitchens," Sarah said.

"Yes, but how many of them will make it without our help?" Frank asked, wincing at the screams of the dead and dying.

"It's not up to us, Sarge. We can't help them. We can't stop this," Sarah said.

"These are our people. Our friends. Our colleagues," Frank said, staring at the fleeing backs of the people he'd known for years. All doomed.

"I know that Sarge, but what about the people outside? My family? Steve's family?" Sarah said. "The whole city is under siege, and we're of no use to anyone if we're dead or infected."

"This is an infection, then? Did you hear something?" Frank asked, eager for information.

"I heard a bit on the radio. It's a virus, and it's transmitted through saliva."

"Saliva?"

"Bites," Sarah explained. "If you're bitten, you turn into one of them."

"Scratches?" he said, pointing at the deep cuts left on his face by the woman who'd attacked him.

"Not that I know of," Sarah said.

Frank slumped against the desk. "That's comforting."

"Besides, you'd know soon enough if you were sick."

"What do you mean?"

"It works fast. Even faster if you die during the attack," Sarah said. "Officer Hines… I thought he was dead, and he was. But it only took a few minutes before he wasn't dead anymore."

"I'm sorry."

"That's why we have to get out of here before it's too late,"

Sarah added in a fierce whisper. "My family needs me."

"I know," Frank said with grim finality. As much as he wanted to save everyone, it wasn't possible. *Live to fight another day.*

"What's the plan?" Sarah said with a sigh of relief.

Frank pointed at the crashed car. "If we can get inside that vehicle, we can drive out of this nightmare."

"You reckon?" Sarah said, her voice thick with doubt.

"It looks intact. No smoke, no water, or oil on the floor. The driver just smashed through the window."

"The tires are flat. Slashed by the glass," Sarah said.

"Well, we don't have to get far," Frank said. "Just away from here."

"True," Sarah conceded with a shrug.

"I'll get rid of the driver. You jump into the passenger side and close the door," Frank said. "Got it?"

"I do, but…." Sarah flashed him a look.

"But what?"

"There are so many of them. We'll never make it."

"We don't have a choice," Frank said.

"Just let me think about it for a second," Sarah pleaded, her eyes squeezed shut.

"We don't have time for that. The infected will spot us any moment now," Frank said with a shake of his head.

"Wait. Maybe this will help," Sarah said, holding up a stack of notebooks and a roll of tape.

"Help with what?"

"You'll see," Sarah said, wrapping a notebook around his forearm and taping it in place. Once finished, she repeated the procedure on the other side and followed up with his shins. "There you go. Protective gear."

Frank flexed his limbs, impressed. "Good idea."

"I'm next," she said, waving her arms in front of his face.

"Come on, he said with a grunt.

Afterward, Frank looked at Sarah. "Are you ready for this?"

"No, are you?" she asked, her gun gripped in both hands.

"Not even a bit," Frank admitted.

"On three?" Sarah asked.

"On three," Frank said with a brisk nod. "One, two, three, go!"

End of preview. Get the book here:

End of Watch - Heroes of the Apocalypse, Book 2:
https://www.amazon.com/dp/B09NRXG28Y

Your FREE EBook is waiting!

If you'd like to learn more about my books, upcoming projects, new releases, cover reveals, and promotions, simply join my mailing list. Plus, you'll get an exclusive ebook absolutely FREE just for subscribing!

Yes, please. Sign me up!
   https://www.subscribepage.com/i0d7r8

About the Author

AUTHOR OF THE APOCALYPSE

South African writer and coffee addict, Baileigh Higgins, lives in the Free State with hubby and best friend Brendan and loves nothing more than lazing on the couch with pizza and a bad horror movie. Her unhealthy obsession with the end of the world has led to numerous books on the subject and a secret bunker only she knows the location of.

Visit her website at www.baileighhiggins.com for more information on her upcoming projects, new releases, and giveaways. Sign up for her Newsletter and get your Free Ebook, Tales from the Apocalypse, today.

SURVIVAL IS JUST THE BEGINNING

WEBSITE: https://www.baileighhiggins.com

Printed in Great Britain
by Amazon